Running with Angels

Running with Angels

by
Kenneth W. Brooks

An Imprint of Haven Hall Publishing

© 2001 by Kenneth W. Brooks

ISBN 0-97202-500-6

All rights reserved. No part of this publication may be reproduced or transmitted in any form or by any means without written permission of the publisher.

Scripture quotations are from the Holy Bible, New International Version (NIV), © 1973, 1974, 1984 by the International Bible Society.

Printed in the United States of America

Published by Haven Hall Publishing, PO Box 11385, Murfreesboro, TN 37129

Dedication

This book is dedicated to my lovely wife, Linda whose faith inspired and launched my efforts beyond the limitations of my well constructed logical barriers.

And in loving memory to my friend, Bob Johnson; a man whose life exemplified Matthew 19:18b, "And love your neighbor as yourself."

Contents

Preface	11
Introduction	13
Mandy, Oh, Mandy	16
Babu, a Friend Indeed	23
No Time for Lunch	27
Face to Face	36
Last Whipping	50
War in the Front Yard	55
Trouble with a Capital T	62
Don't Like Your Looks	66
When the Bus Failed to Stop	78
No More Letters	85
Humes High	95
Memphis State	130
Graduation and Beyond	155
The Whirlwind	170
New Light	189
Round One	203
Round Two	216
Round Three	227
Round Four	241
Round Five	251
Victory Round	261
CFC	266
Full Circle	276
Further Reading	283

Preface

Having a story to write and having the ability to write it are not the same. Success comes to those who discover their natural talents, choose their careers accordingly, and pursue it with a passion. Writing is not my talent or my passion. With this understood, why am I attempting to write this book? Because buried within these pages and hidden from the casual observer lies a story with a message that transcends belief. If just out of hands reach, a little beyond understanding, and on the far side of human knowledge, how easily we disbelieve. With youth life can appear cruel and unfair, but we must live with a thread of hope, allowing both life and hope to mature. What is it about Mark's life that will draw the reader into a free fall toward the conclusion of his story? Considering that he is consumed by confusion, loneliness, and pain, what could uproot Mark from the past and plant him within sight of paradise?

As a reader, look beyond the shortcomings of this writer's style; find the story and allow the message to become real in your life. I feel compelled to record Mark's journey so that others can be afforded the same opportunity to be called. Be cautioned — this is written

Preface

not only to expose you to life changing events but also to influence your life. This book will take you on a roller coaster ride from darkness to light, from despair to hope, from knowledge to wisdom, from grief to joy, and from death to life.

Buckle up! Read on. This may change your life.

Introduction

From the time I saw my dad pull into the drive behind the wheel of a navy blue Ford sedan, I dreamt of owning my own vehicle. No used six-cylinder sedan for my first car, no sir. Mine would be a brand spanking new red sports car with eight cylinders awaiting my every command.

Our first car was supposed to be black. Dad had talked for two weeks about this shiny black Ford. But, black it was not. As plain as my eyes could see, this car was navy blue.

As Dad proudly stepped out of the car, my mother pulled me to the side and whispered, "Don't say anything to your father about the car's color."

I said nothing. I accepted the fact that the car would always be referred to as black. In fact, we described it as our black Ford from that first day until it was later repossessed.

Only after my father's death did Mother reveal the motivation for her strange request by explaining, "The horrors of war inflicted many scars on your father, scars that went much deeper than his physical wounds. After the war, your father could no longer see color, only black and white."

Introduction

Now, here I sat behind the wheel in my faded Levi's, khaki shirt, and well-worn Asics running shoes, guiding my car down the Interstate. Red it was not; sports car it was not, but it did have eight cylinders. Maybe it was a little worn, but it was my own car that served me well. The dream of the red sports car had become only a distant childhood memory after the days at the orphanage.

The snow fell more deliberately. I reluctantly turned on the windshield wipers. With so little snow sticking to the pavement, traffic continued to flow beyond the speed limit as the Interstate wound through the landscape. As the car leaned into a curve, my body involuntarily tensed, my senses quickened in anticipation, but nothing happened. Put me on the highway, put some distance behind me, then expect the unexpected. This I knew and understood; therefore I stayed prepared.

I'd been driving for ten hours. I'd left Murfreesboro, Tennessee at 5:00 a.m., and still had two more hours of driving to reach Flushing, a small town on the outskirts of Flint in central Michigan. The snow had started as I crossed the state line an hour ago.

As the Interstate wove through the rustic farmland, I marveled at how the snow turned the aging houses and barns into postcard-worthy scenes. For me to associate snow with beauty was ironic. If anyone had asked three months earlier for my perspective on those soft, white crystalline flakes, I would've said, "Wet, cold, and slippery."

To say I had a chip on my shoulder would be an understatement. My life was far from perfect, but I always found a way to cope. I had a good job at General Motors Institute of Engineering Technology in Flint as a technical specialist maintaining their administrative software system. I had two close friends—Babu, who also worked at GMI, and Carl in Arkansas.

Every day was a struggle, but I faced each obstacle with relentless determination. The word *fear* was not even part of my vocabulary. This is not saying I was one tough guy, but I had an iron will and tremendous mental discipline. I tackled everything with reckless abandon, from my job to my running—but then I met this girl.

Yes, I met this girl. And what did Babu have to say?

"Oh, another girl, huh?"

But when Mandy Gayle Martin strolled into the GMI library, she got my undivided attention and began the first steps toward restoring my hope for salvation.

Chapter One

Mandy, Oh, Mandy

I always marveled at how Babu assumed my mental ability was on the same level as his own. In other words, since I was his closest friend, if Babu was a genius, then I must be a genius, too.

So when he came into my office with that look on his face that I could never quite figure out, I knew I was in trouble. I tried unsuccessfully to see the title on the sheaf of papers in his hand, then said, "What's with all the paperwork?"

Babu's penetrating black eyes dropped to his right hand. "Oh, just a technical paper."

"Did you write it?"

"Yeah," he said. "I was hoping you would proofread and correct my English before I submit it for publication."

"What's the title of this paper?"

With lightning speed, Babu thrust the ten typewritten pages into my hand, spun around, and was out the door before I could open my mouth. My eyes roamed the type on each page as I attempted to measure the content.

Finally, I focused on the six words at the top of the first page: *Programming Artificial Intelligence into Computer Systems.*

Well, was this the blind leading the blind, or what? Babu being only three years removed from India and I having struggled through college English—how could I say no?

For this reason I was at the GMI library on a Tuesday evening. I had left GMI at four o'clock, gone to the U of M recreation center in downtown Flint to run ten miles on their one-tenth-mile indoor track, showered, and returned to the library. With a stack of reference books and much determination, I was beginning to grasp the concept of Babu's paper.

Just as I was gaining confidence, I noticed a girl carrying two large books, headed in my direction. I was in one of the study rooms attached to the library. She walked past two other rooms and sat down at a small table directly across from me. As I watched her enter the room, I felt something important was happening, but little did I know.

If one has ever watched a gentle breeze move tall grass across a field, this is how she crossed the room and settled into the chair. In all my life, I had never seen anyone so lovely. Her long, silky black hair framed her face and contrasted with her milky white skin. She wore no makeup, allowing her natural beauty to radiate from her face.

I gasped. So taken by the moment, I'd forgotten to breathe.

She caught me staring. Instead of seeming offended, she gave me a gentle smile.

Mandy, Oh, Mandy

I attempted to regain my composure and return to the paper. Forget it. My thought processes had been short-circuited. I looked down at my hands; both palms were wet from perspiration. Sweat? Not me. It took two to three miles of running to produce a few beads of moisture across my brow.

There was only one thing I could do.

With sweaty palms and a lack of courage that stopped just short of fear, I blurted, "Hi, my name is Mark Matthews. I work here in the computer center. Are you a new student? I don't think I've seen you before."

To her credit she did not jump and bolt for the door, but instead replied, "Well, yes and no. Yes, I am new, but no, I'm not a student. I've been using the library to do some research. My name is Mandy Martin."

Was this beautiful angel actually carrying on a conversation with a mere mortal such as I? With slightly more confidence I continued. "It's unusual for me to be here after four o'clock. That's probably why I haven't seen you."

"Well, I've seen you jogging all over Flushing," she quickly replied.

I straightened up in my chair. "Actually, I don't jog," I said. "I'm a runner. Joggers run at a comfortable pace, don't keep up with their time, and just attempt to stay fit. Runners time their pace, push out of their comfort zone, and train with a purpose."

Mandy thought for a brief moment, then said with a faint smile, "Oh, I see. If the person looks like he is enjoying running, he is a jogger. If he looks serious and in pain, like you, he is a runner."

Hey, this girl is not only attractive, I thought, she has wit and a sharp tongue. I was ready to move on to another subject. Eyeing the two books in her arms, I replied, "What's that you're reading? It looks like Greek."

"It's Hebrew," Mandy said. "This is a Hebrew Bible. The other book contains root meanings for Hebrew words and phrases from the scriptures. I spent a year studying in Jerusalem while in college. I graduated six months ago, but the study habits are still with me.

"There's no other book like the Bible. It contains unlimited knowledge and wisdom presented at the correct level and depth for the reader, so each individual receives the proper amount for the moment. That's why you may read the same verse at a later time and receive new meaning and truth."

She stopped short and bit her lip, then added sheepishly, "I guess you can tell this is one of my favorite topics."

Boy, I was not prepared for this discussion. I sat for a moment staring at her incredible beauty before I somehow managed to mutter, "Yes . . . but for some of us, it's a difficult topic and, in many ways, a mystery."

"Oh, I'm sorry. I guess I assume everyone is a Christian and loves the Bible."

I squirmed in my chair, briefly thought about my past, and replied, "I didn't say I'm not a Christian. This is a tough area for me. To be perfectly truthful, at times I'm not sure just what I believe."

This beautiful girl had found the weak point in my armor and exposed it in just a matter of minutes. What could I say to redeem myself before all was lost?

To my relief, Mandy said, "Well, let's change the subject for now and start over. My full name is Mandy Gayle Martin. I graduated from college this past June

19

Mandy, Oh, Mandy

with a degree in arts and sciences and a major in English literature. Then I entered a six-month missionary training program—three months of instruction, and three months working at a mission. Kim Fernandez, Janice Vandyke, and I completed the training together and were assigned to the Flint Inter-City Mission. We are sharing an apartment in Flushing, and also one of the mission's vans. Tonight I have the van by myself. I couldn't interest either of them in an evening at the library."

I leaned back in my seat, looked around the room, and began to relax. My hands had stopped sweating, my breathing was back to normal, and my head had stopped spinning. Who was this lovely girl, I wondered now, and why was she sitting across from me watching my every move?

I finally thought past the questions flooding my head and replied, "My middle name is Wayne. My mother wanted to name me Mark Luke Matthews, which would cover three of the four gospels. My father wanted to name me John Wayne Matthews, because he loved cowboy movies. As a compromise, I was named Mark Wayne Matthews.

"I graduated three years ago with a degree in engineering technology and a double major in math and computer science. After graduation I applied for a position in academic computing at GMI. They narrowed the choice to Babu and me. They re-interviewed, still couldn't decide, and finally hired both of us."

"Did you know Babu before that?" she asked.

"No," I answered, "I didn't meet Babu until the first day we reported for work. Go figure—a Southern boy fresh out of college, an Indian new in this country, and both hired for the same position. As odd as it may seem, we became instant friends. After working together for these past three years, we are now more like brothers."

"Is there more to his name?" Mandy asked. "It sounds like a nickname or abbreviation."

"His full name is Babusankah Ranganathan. Since that's such a mouthful, everyone calls him Babu. He's the reason I'm at the library tonight. He wrote this paper that he intends to submit for publication. I've been given the responsibility of proofreading and correcting the English. Since you are an English major, would you be interested in helping? I have an extra copy."

As her dark blue eyes skimmed the first page, she said, "This looks like Greek."

I chuckled. "No, it's just some heavy computer theory. Babu is a pretty bright guy. Well, actually, he's a genius—there's no doubt about it. I have the technical stuff figured out. I just need help with the flow of his English. Babu tends to get words out of place when he writes."

Glancing down at my watch, I realized it was after ten, which was late by my standards. Okay, here was my chance.

"It's getting late," I said. "Maybe we could meet again and go over the paper." I held my breath. Good grief—what was this girl doing to me?

To my amazement, Mandy replied, "I'd like that, but not before Saturday. We're going to work late the rest of the week. We don't have that many weeks left at the mission, and we want to wrap up some of our projects. I'll give you my number. Call, and we'll plan for Saturday."

Wow, was this incredible, or what? Trying to conceal my excitement, I said, "That will be great. It's after ten o'clock. Are you okay getting to your apartment alone?"

"I'll be fine," she replied, "but you can walk me to the van."

And as I walked her to the van, my feet hardly touched the ground.

Chapter Two

Babu, a Friend Indeed

Although I had wished a thousand times to meet the girl of my dreams, it had never happened. I was born for loneliness; this much I knew and understood. Now, right out of the blue, Mandy Gayle Martin appeared and . . . what? I wrestled with this *what* issue as I drove to my apartment. Love at first sight? Maybe in the movies, but not for a guy like me. Nothing comes easy, I reminded myself. For me, life is a constant uphill struggle. Yet . . . could this be the girl of my dreams? I could well imagine spending the rest of my life with her.

My head was spinning. I had to talk to someone or I would not be able to sleep. But by the time I parked and headed for the stairs, it was ten-thirty. Should I wait until morning to tell Babu about meeting Mandy, or should I wake him? There was no doubt Babu was asleep. During the week he rarely stayed up past ten o'clock. Neither of us could be considered night owls, even on weekends.

I made up my mind and knocked on his door. As I waited, I reflected on how we'd come to be in the same apartment complex, and how thankful I was that he was here.

Babu, a Friend Indeed

Babu and I had lived at the Kingston Manor apartments for three years. I had left Memphis, Tennessee early on a Friday morning, pulling all my possessions in a small trailer. I spent that first night in Flint at a motel. But, by the next afternoon I had signed a year's lease for a furnished single-bedroom apartment at Kingston Manor.

Babu was staying with a cousin in Chicago. He had been in the United States for only a month. On that same weekend he flew to Flint, checked into a motel, and took a cab to GMI. We met for the first time on Monday morning. Looking back, that first day was awkward to the point of being uncomfortable. He was quiet and reserved; I was not so quiet and not so reserved. We both felt a bit uneasy; both concerned about the fact that we had been hired for the same position, or so we thought.

In the afternoon, I overheard Babu say he was going to take a cab after work to look for an apartment to rent. I pondered this for a few minutes and decided it was not acceptable. "Babu," I said, "cabs can be expensive. Why don't you look at Kingston Manor? If you like the place, you can rent there too, and we will ride together until you buy a car."

He leased the last furnished one-bedroom, and we rode to work together for the first few months.

I laughed to myself as I thought about . . . the car. We finally found Babu a car. It was only three years old, had low mileage, and seemed in excellent condition. The owner was buying a new car and, instead of trading, was selling his old car himself.

As we were paying, Babu casually said, "I've never actually driven a car."

I did not actually say, "Are you kidding me?" But it was what I was thinking as I replied, "No problem; I'll teach you to drive." Now we had to get both cars back to our apartments with only one driver. Thankfully, the owner agreed to deliver.

We spent many, many weeks perfecting Babu's driving skills—but I'd think about that some other time. Right now, Babu was fumbling with the lock on the other side of the door. As the door opened, I said the first thing that popped into my head. "Were you sleeping?"

He gave me that *What a dumb question* look, rubbed his eyes, and said, "Now, what do you think?"

Excellent point, Babu, I thought as I entered his apartment. "I'm sorry I woke you," I said, "but something very important happened tonight."

Babu's eyes widened. "Are you okay?"

"Yeah," I replied, "I'm fine. But I met this girl at the library tonight."

I watched the expression on his face change from concern to annoyance as Babu considered that for a moment.

"Oh, I see, very important," he said. "You met another girl—as if you don't tell me that about every other month."

"This is different," I replied. "I've never met a girl like her before. Her name is Mandy Martin. She works with the Flint Inter-City Mission. You know, that building downtown, across from the Greyhound bus station. At first I thought she was training to be a nun, but I think she's just very religious. She seems so alive, confident, and in control; just talking to her makes you feel better."

I waited while Babu went into the kitchen, got a glass of water, and returned to the living room before I continued. "When a guy meets a girl for the first time,

Babu, a Friend Indeed

although he never admits it, there's some degree of lust going on in his mind. When a guy walks into the computer lab needing help, you hardly look up. For a pretty girl, you fall all over yourself trying to help her."

Babu squirmed a bit. "No, I assist because that is part of my responsibilities. But maybe I do a better job helping the ladies," he reluctantly admitted.

"The point I'm trying to make is that with Mandy, I never felt that way. Don't get me wrong—she's very attractive. But there is much more to her than her looks. She was so polite. When I stared, she only smiled. When she was talking about the Bible and saw I was struggling, she changed the subject. She's the first truly righteous woman I've met since my mother."

He didn't seem convinced. I continued. "You know how hard it's been for me to talk to you about my childhood. I do believe I could spill my guts to her. While I was with her, I felt the urge to tell her not only the truth but the whole truth, holding nothing back."

I now had his full attention. Babu's black eyes shone and his expression grew concerned. "You sound so serious," he said.

"Yes, dead serious—but it's getting late. I'll let you go back to bed. We can talk more tomorrow. Thanks for listening. You are a friend indeed."

Chapter Three

No Time for Lunch

Wednesday was one of those special days at work when problems overtook chance and spread out of control. They started in admissions, spread into student records, and finally spilled over into the business office. As fast as I resolved one, two more appeared. At times it seemed as if the wheels were coming off the administrative system.

There was no time for lunch. The very integrity of my system was in question, and I was not willing to let it fail.

Babu was sympathetic, but this was not his area. He could handle any threat to his system and not even break a sweat. I always managed to get the same results but worked twice as hard to stay in control. Babu was the expert for one system and I was the expert for the other. Each system ran on its own mainframe and was operated by its own computer language. We could help each other with the routine, but not with downright disaster.

Over three years earlier, when we completed that first day at work, we were both still puzzled about why two of us were hired for the same position. Only a few days later, we got the real lowdown.

No Time for Lunch

While we were being interviewed, the systems manager for the administrative computer gave two weeks' notice. He had decided to go back to teaching, a noble gesture on his part. A new administrative system was being installed. After a year of training and testing, the new system was ready to go into production. He got cold feet and bailed out.

Now there *were* two positions to fill. Both of us were qualified for the academic system, but neither had experience or training for the administrative system.

Without explanation, they assigned me to the new administrative system, written in Cobol. The Engineering Department considered Cobol a business language and did not even offer it as an elective. I had never seen a line of Cobol code. Night after night, I took home stacks of manuals.

Within a month the new system was released to production, and I was in control—or maybe, at times, out of control. There were days when everything worked well and days when everything went wrong. Today was the latter.

By 5:00 p.m. things seemed back to normal. One thing for sure, Babu was perturbed. Every time I skipped lunch, he became upset—not because I didn't eat, but because we did not play Ping-Pong.

For nearly three years we had played Ping-Pong at lunch. On weekends, when the weather allowed, we played tennis. Since neither wanted to beat the other, we only practiced. For competitive games we played as doubles partners for both Ping-Pong and tennis.

When we came to GMI, I had never played Ping-Pong, and Babu had never played tennis. Babu was a Ping-Pong gunslinger whose game was all offense. In constantly practicing against him, I developed a totally defensive game. I was left-handed, and Babu was right-handed. Teamed as doubles partners, we were hard to beat. The same was true for tennis, except I was all offense, and he was defense. At doubles for either tennis or Ping-Pong, we could hold our own against any of the faculty or students—well, except for my Chinese students.

Thinking back, I realize they were not really my students, but everyone in the computer center, including Babu, called them my Chinese students. They were the reason I had my own office, just like our computer center director, while everyone else had a small cubicle.

About six weeks before the beginning of our second semester at GMI, we received notification from the State Department that thirty Red Chinese students from mainland China would be attending GMI as part of a five year exchange program. Since I was in charge of the administrative system, all their personal data, including a billfold-size picture of each, was given to me.

There were fifteen boys and fifteen girls. All were eighteen and all spoke perfect English. They had sent one request before their arrival. Each wanted to be given an American first name to use while in our country. Naturally, I was assigned the task. Babu found it rather amusing, but I did not see the humor in it. For thirty days, I took a different picture on my daily run, and finished each run with a name.

Upon their arrival, the Chinese students swamped my cubicle and thanked me for their American names. After that, although each had an assigned faculty advisor, they came to me with all their problems, concerns, and issues. The traffic became so congested, I was given my own office. There I was, not many years their senior, acting

No Time for Lunch

like their dad. Although this interfered with my work and created many extra hours in the office, I grew to love helping them and watching them adjust to our ways.

Two, Paul and Grace, made a perfect score on GMI's three-hour calculus placement test. This had never happened in the eighty-year history of GMI. I was proud and Babu was impressed.

One thing was for sure; at Ping-Pong we were no match for any two of my Chinese students. They had no clue when it came to tennis, but they were the masters of Ping-Pong.

Each semester they sought my advice less frequently. Now they had pretty much left the nest, but I still had fond memories of fathering to each of them. And I still had my own office.

So after a long day with no lunch and no Ping-Pong practice, I left work at five o'clock and headed to the U of M track to run ten miles. The weather was bad. Actually, on any winter day in Michigan the weather often went from bad to worse. Whoever coined the phrase *Winter Wonderland* must have been born and raised in the North. Anyone from the South would know better. The South has three months of winter, three months of spring, three months of summer, and three months of fall. Here, winter lasts from mid-October to mid-April, followed by two months of spring, two months of summer, and two months of fall. What's wrong with this picture? Those born and raised in the North accept this as normal, but I know the seasons are out of balance. The wind, the ice, and the snow were bad enough, especially for a runner, but I missed the sun the most. When *Old Man Winter* arrived, the sun took extended vacations, sometimes for weeks at a time. These continuous overcast days could be downright depressing. Not this week, though; not after meeting Mandy Gayle Martin.

As I was completing the seventh mile of my run, a guy ran up behind me and, instead of passing, followed stride for stride. This was the third time he'd done this in the last two weeks. I'd already decided that, if he did this one more time, I'd see just how fast and hard he could run.

At the start of my tenth mile I increased the pace. He stayed right with me. The race was on. For the next four laps we ran as one. On the fifth lap I slowly pulled away. My goal was to lap him before I finished that tenth mile.

On the ninth lap, as I passed, he slowed to a walk. I'd won, but it was a hollow victory. I'd run too hard without enough oxygen at a pain level well beyond acceptable—all this to satisfy ego.

I still relished my triumph while I showered, but then I realized how much Mandy would have disapproved. I also realized I had skipped lunch and was close to starvation. I called Domino's in Flushing.

Ordering pizza after running on the track required only my name, since it occurred on such a regular basis. I'd say, "Mark Matthews."

They would reply, "One medium cheese pizza to go."

Why only cheese? The fact was, Babu did not believe in eating anything requiring the life of the donor. Out of respect to him when we ate together, I adjusted to his diet. Without Babu I would eat most meat, except beef. For long-distance training I found it too heavy and hard to digest. As for cheese pizza, I'd eaten so many over the last three years, I reached a point where I no longer liked toppings on pizza.

No Time for Lunch

By seven-thirty I had devoured the pizza and dialed Mandy's number. The idea of someone other than Mandy answering the phone never crossed my mind.

One of her roommates asked, "Who can I say is calling?"

"Mark Matthews," I replied weakly.

For a moment, I questioned whether she'd still want to talk to me, but the sound of her voice dispelled such thoughts. We discussed Babu's paper first, and then worked on our Saturday meeting.

We agreed to meet at the entrance to Auto World on Saturday morning at nine o'clock. Her roommates would drop her off, then pick her up that afternoon. Mandy preferred this arrangement since it could be considered a *meeting*, and not a *date*. I really didn't care what she called it. I was overjoyed at any opportunity to see her again.

With the details concerning our meeting covered, our conversation shifted to learning more about each other. At this point Mandy made a request. Would I mind if we limited our phone getting-to-know topics to her, Kim, Janice, and Babu? She would prefer talking about me face to face.

It sounded good to me. So, for the next two hours, I was barely able to squeeze in a few sentences. She started with the day she was born and wove a fascinating story of a remarkable, God-fearing family.

Her mother Mary and her father David were missionaries in Malaysia. They had been there for the past six years; before that they'd been in Indonesia, and before that, in the Philippines. Mandy was a well-traveled girl.

By nine-thirty I was wiped out. After a long day and a long phone conversation, I was ready for bed, but instead I headed downstairs to talk to Babu. I had to be sure he was not still upset by my no-time-for-lunch day. Besides, I wanted to give him an update on Mandy. The day had been so hectic, neither of us had brought up our conversation from the night before.

Babu had made a good point. I really did have a bad track record when it came to meeting the girl of my dreams. But he'd exaggerated the frequency. It happened maybe every six months, but not every other month—no way. At least failure did not deter my effort, although it did reinforce my belief that I was destined for loneliness.

As for Babu, I was bound and determined not to let him suffer the same fate. But, no matter how hard I tried, none of my matchmaking efforts on his behalf ever got off the ground. Without doubt, Babu was attracted to women—I'd watched the way the pretty ones wrapped him around their finger in the computer lab. So far, though, he'd dodged every woman I shoved his way, even the Indian professor's attractive daughter. Babu was very shy, but there was more to it than mere shyness. I just couldn't figure it out.

As I entered Babu's living room, I searched for the slightest sign of imperfection, but finally accepted that it was in perfect order, as usual. No matter the time, day or night, Babu's apartment was always spotless. During the years at the orphanage, I had learned to clean, re-clean, and clean again. My apartment stayed neat, but it could not hold a candle to this place. With this confirmed, I turned to Babu, who was patiently waiting for me to speak first, and said, "Sorry I skipped practicing at lunch today." I figured we'd better take care of the Ping-Pong first, before I brought up Mandy.

"It's okay," he replied. "I could tell you were having a rough day. I remembered that western movie's title you taught me: it was a *Bad Day at Black Rock* for you."

No Time for Lunch

Lately I was having more than my fair share of bad days. "You got that right. So many departments were having problems, they had to line up to get tickets."

This brought a big grin to Babu's face. "Did you ever get caught up? When I left at four o'clock, your office was still full of people."

Now that I had him smiling, I could move on to the real issue at hand. "Yes," I said, "but it took until five o'clock to get the last one out of there. That's not the reason I came down this late. I've been talking to Mandy—or maybe I should say listening—for the past two hours."

That smile quickly faded from Babu's face. "I knew that was coming. What is so different about her? I've never seen you so taken by someone before."

"Babu, you are just going to have to meet her," I replied. "Words can't do this girl justice. She was born with a Christian spoon in her mouth and—"

"Wait a minute," Babu interjected. "What does Christian spoon mean?"

"Oh, I guess that's a slang expression. Do you understand the meaning when I say a person is born with a silver spoon in his mouth?"

Still looking confused, Babu replied, "Christian spoon or silver spoon, neither makes sense."

"If you say a person was born with a silver spoon in his mouth, it means he was born into wealth without having to earn it," I explained.

"Okay, I understand," Babu replied, "but what about a Christian spoon?"

I was making progress. "I guess you could say I kind of extended the meaning into another area. From birth, she's been around religious people and religious training. This is not to be taken negatively. I see it as an advantage.

It's shaped her into a person who has her act together. She knows who she is, and she likes herself. I wish I could say the same about myself."

Babu reached out, laid his hand on my shoulder, and said, "I think I understand. I also think you have your hands full. I can already see her changing you, but maybe for the good."

"What do you mean?" I protested. "I'm the same. For the first time, I've met a girl who is real and truly cares about people."

Babu held up his hands. "Don't take me wrong. I just meant you've never been willing to lower your guard and let a girl get close. With Mandy, I see that guard dropping."

"You are dead right, as usual," I replied. "But once you meet her, you'll see why I'm okay this time."

The clock on Babu's mantle struck ten. "It's getting late," I said. "Thanks for listening. Good night, Babu."

As I headed out the door, Babu replied, "That's what friends are for. Good night, Mark."

Chapter Four

Face to Face

Without question, the natural laws of science do not apply while waiting for someone; time can actually slow down. In fact, the amount it slows down is directly proportional to how impatient one grows.

I'd arrived at the entrance to Auto World at eight-thirty Saturday morning.

Thursday and Friday had come and gone uneventfully, with one major exception. On Friday as Babu and I practiced Ping-Pong, something happened that had never happened before. I returned the ball short and high. As usual, Babu pounced forward and slammed it like a rifle shot. Without conscious control, I got the paddle on the ball at just the right angle. It zipped across the net, ricocheted off the table, and glanced harmlessly off Babu's chest.

He said, "Excellent shot."

I replied, "Don't be bringing that slow stuff at me."

We both broke out laughing.

Mandy and I talked on the phone for hours, both Thursday and Friday. A pattern was developing. I would leave work, go run on the track, grab a bite to eat, talk to Mandy, and then go downstairs to talk to Babu. The more we talked, the more I questioned why she would be interested in me. One thing was clear; this girl was special.

I told her how I'd met Babu and how we'd become such close friends. I told her all I knew about his family, which was little, since he was not the world's biggest talker. If you wanted to know something, you had to ask, because he was not going to volunteer. Babu also had made friends with several Indians who taught at GMI. One was from Nagpur, and they spent hours talking about their hometown. That was how I learned more about his country and their people.

Babu's family would not be considered wealthy by our standards, but in India they were part of the upper class. His father was a government official in Nagpur, a city in central India in the Maharashtra state. His mother was an accomplished musician. He had a younger sister who was still in high school. He also had a close friend whom he had known since grade school. His friend, his mother, and his sister each wrote him once a month. Sometimes Babu shared details from a letter, but most of the time he would not.

I often asked him why he didn't take a vacation and go home to visit his family.

He always said, "Maybe next year."

It was not a question of money. GMI paid us well. Neither of us was a big spender; we were both able to tuck more than half of what we earned into savings. So I was puzzled. Why didn't Babu want to go home?

Mandy agreed. Then she asked about his beliefs.

I could not answer. I knew he didn't believe in taking life, not even the life of a mosquito. I respected his diet but drew the line when it came to protecting myself from a biting mosquito.

37

Face to Face

Finally we went over Babu's paper, and she gave me the corrections over the phone. I carried the paper down to Babu and told him this was truly a team effort. He was pleased. He submitted the paper, which was accepted and later published in a technical journal.

As for Kim and Janice, to my amazement, Mandy learned more about their lives in only four months than I knew about Babu after three years.

Kim Fernandez's mother was a Native American and her father was Spanish. Although theirs was a non-tribal marriage, they lived on the Sandia Pueblo Reservation that borders the Sandia Mountain in central New Mexico. Sandia is one of nineteen pueblos. It covers approximately 23,000 acres east of the Rio Grande River near Albuquerque. The Sandia Pueblo own and operate the Sandia Casino and the Bien Mur Indian Center.

Kim's parents worked for the Sandia Casino until Kim was fifteen, when something tragic happened. Her parents quit the casino, went to work for the Bien Mur Indian Center, joined the Sandia Catholic Mission, and became involved in the mission's social services for the reservation.

As hard as Mandy tried, she could not get Kim to talk about the tragic event, but Mandy felt it had influenced Kim's decision to train for missionary work.

Mandy gave a detailed account on Janice that lasted for another hour. Janice had been born to Dutch parents in Holland, Michigan. Holland's Protestant Reform churches, close ties to the Netherlands, Dutch costumes, wooden shoes, and flowers give the small town an intriguing Old World flavor. Acres and acres of tulips bloom each spring, turning Holland's hillsides into a rainbow of colors.

These Old World traditions, values, and lifestyle shaped and defined Janice's life from childhood to college. Until her senior year at Hope, Janice had never ventured outside of Ottawa County. Holland was the center of her universe. She loved her parents, her church, her college, and her community.

During the summer of that senior year, Janice accompanied a group of classmates on a tour of the Netherlands. Something happened during the trip that caused Janice to put her nursing career on hold and enter the missionary training program. Like Kim, Janice would not discuss what happened during her tour of the Netherlands.

So, Mandy did not know why either of her roommates was doing on-the-job training at the Flint Inter-City Mission.

What about Mandy, I wondered. After hours of telephone conversations, I'd concluded that Mandy was training for missionary work because of her parents, but she didn't have any concrete plans for her immediate future.

Auto World did not open until nine o'clock. As people started to gather near the door, I checked my watch again; maybe it had stopped, or at least was losing time.

Auto World, an indoor entertainment complex with the automobile as its theme, had opened in downtown Flint two summers ago. Unfortunately, it had not caught on, and would likely shut down unless attendance increased. Babu and I had visited the complex the week it opened, but then it had been so crowded, we left after less than an hour. There was plenty of automobile history, from the Model T to cars of the future. The problem seemed to be the lack of entertainment attractive to kids.

Face to Face

I thought it would be an excellent place for Mandy and I to spend a casual day and talk face to face.

At exactly nine o'clock the mission van came around the corner. As if on cue, the sun briefly broke out from behind the clouds, and its rays moved up the stairs and bathed the entrance to Auto World in sunlight. Mandy stepped out of the van and started up the stairs. With this brilliant light source at her back, her long, flowing dress became transparent, revealing every perfect contour of her body.

As I soaked in this spectacular view, Mandy reached out, took my hand, and said, "So, have you been waiting very long?"

Shifting my focus from her figure to her face, I replied, "Only about thirty minutes, but it seemed much longer. I went to the track earlier this morning and ran twenty miles. By eight-thirty I'd showered, and since I was only two blocks away, I arrived early."

Mandy looked more perplexed than impressed. "Twenty miles—that's two hundred laps. Don't you get bored running circle after circle?"

Now, I'd never thought about it quite that way. After a brief moment of consideration, I replied, "Not really. If I couldn't think, I might be bored. But as long as my mind is free to roam, I'm not limited to the circles, as you put it."

"Well, stranger," Mandy said as we reached the ticket booth, "I feel like you know me well. So now it's your turn."

Boy, she did not waste time getting to the issue at hand. "I knew that was coming," I said as I paid for the tickets, but as we began our tour of Auto World, I didn't have a clue what to say. How do you begin discussing a past that's been kept privileged and private for years? I finally admitted, "Well, my past carries many painful memories. Some I've shared with Babu, but most I've kept bottled up inside."

I looked at her. "Your life is in balance. You're at peace with yourself. You can look forward or behind, and you see a lighted path in either direction. You have so much faith, like my mother, that you can even see beyond the light."

I looked away and shook my head. "Everywhere I look, I see darkness. I have little faith, little belief, little hope, no future. But I cope and endure. There is a war going on inside my head. By sheer will, I stay in control. I refuse to give in and let the pain destroy me. I don't understand why you're interested in talking to me, but I'm thankful for it. I feel compelled to open my heart and soul to you, but you may not like what you see." I offered a weak smile. "So where do I begin?"

Mandy reached out, took my hand, and said, "How about when you were born?"

I considered this, but starting at my birth wouldn't take into account how my mother and father met, the war, or their marriage—and all of these events ultimately influenced my life. No, I needed to go back even further.

We sat down in an area containing cars from the early fifties. There, right across the aisle, was a navy blue Ford sedan that was identical to my parents' first car. At that moment, it seemed like my life's history was somehow linked to the American automobile. As I thought back to our navy blue Ford sedan, it brought back fond memories of my mom and dad. Now more at ease, more prepared for this journey into the past, I said, "No, I'll begin with my mother."

* * *

Face to Face

Her maiden name was Hazel Phillips. She'd been born when my grandmother was in her late forties; she was an only child. Both of her parents passed away while she was still in her teens. When I entered the picture, she had no living relatives.

While doing volunteer work at a military hospital, she met a man who had been wounded in the war and was suffering from shock. His half-brother was his only living relative. I always thought this common circumstance—this lack of family—drew them to each other. After three months in the hospital, he was declared well, they were married, and my mother became Hazel Matthews.

Her new husband, Hermit Matthews, had worked at Firestone Tire and Rubber Company in Memphis, Tennessee before joining the army. He returned to work at Firestone as a tire builder.

Two years later, I was born. They wanted a big, healthy, bouncing boy, but even though I was big—over ten pounds—I wasn't so healthy. The news was bad on all fronts. The difficult birth left my mother unable to have more children. And their newborn baby had an opening in his heart.

The doctors assured my parents that the opening would likely close without requiring surgery, but after five days in intensive care my condition had not improved. The doctors met with my parents and said, "Your son is getting weaker by the day. Surgery is now our only option; unless we operate, he's not going to make it."

My mother asked about the danger of a heart operation on a baby. They said I had a 50 percent chance of making it through the surgery. She said, "No, that's not good enough."

Nothing the doctors said would change her mind. That night, when my father left for work, she carried her Bible into their bedroom and placed it on the foot of their bed. She got down on her knees and began reading and praying. Dawn found her still on her knees at the foot of the bed, praying. As daylight entered the bedroom window and crept across the room to the foot of the bed, she closed the Bible, placed it on the dresser, and waited for my father.

As soon as the doctors saw her, they said, "We have great news—sometime during the night, the opening closed."

Three days later, I was released to go home.

* * *

Mandy's eyes were wide. "Wow, your mother had great faith, just like my parents." She considered for a moment, then added, "In fact, I've been blessed with many relatives with tremendous faith. Years before I was born, my grandparents—Gary and Brenda—founded a church in Murfreesboro, Tennessee. They started in their living room, but quickly outgrew their small house. They moved to a motel, then to a tent on property they'd purchased for a church. After much effort and prayer, Christ Followers Church opened its doors. My dad's older brother, Adam, is now pastor of CFC, but Gary and Brenda are very much a part of the church."

If her uncle is the pastor, what about Gary, I wondered. "Does your grandfather work full-time for the church?" I asked.

"Heavens, no," she replied. "Granddad has a woodshop next to their home. He's a master cabinetmaker. In fact, my grandmother says that she's not sure what Gary loves more—Our Lord or wood. I know she's only

Face to Face

kidding. Granddad does love his wood, but it does not compare to his love for the Lord."

She shifted forward, once more bestowing her full attention on me. "Let's get back to your mother. It sounds like she also loved the Lord and put all her trust and faith in Him."

"Yes," I replied. "Her faith sustained her through much sickness and a difficult marriage. As hopeless as her marriage appeared, she never gave up. She stayed with my father when most would have called it quits. Instead of focusing on his shortcomings and failures, she focused on his strengths and loved him for who he wanted to be and not for who he was. She always told me my father was a very intelligent man trapped in an uneducated body."

"Tell me more about your father. I want to better understand him."

I though back to my father, back to stories I'd heard about my father as a small boy. I drew a deep breath, and began his story.

* * *

When my father was eleven, my grandfather died from gangrene. An apprentice switchman at the railroad yard where my grandfather worked dropped a railcar on the wrong track, and my grandfather's leg was crushed between two railcars.

On one of my father's visits to the hospital, my grandfather said, "Son, if they don't remove this leg, I am going to die."

The doctors continued to attempt to save the leg, but gangrene set in, and sure enough, my grandfather died. In the hard times that followed, my grandmother struggled to raise my father and his half-brother Calvin on the small railroad pension.

Calvin was my grandmother's child from a previous marriage that lasted only six months. The man had left her while she was pregnant with Calvin. At the time of my grandfather's death, Calvin was fifteen and only in the ninth grade, but he was already a starting linebacker for the varsity football team; therefore he stayed in school. My father quit school, even though he was in the fifth grade.

An Italian truck farmer living next door gave my father his first job. He was paid a token amount but received all the fresh produce the family could eat. My father worked the rest of his life and never returned to school.

Calvin was chosen all-state for football during his senior year. He received a full four-year football scholarship but was kicked off the team during his second year for excessive drinking. After he lost his scholarship, my grandmother died. Around that time, my father started drinking and, as hard as he tried, was never able to overcome the bottle.

It's difficult, looking back, to distinguish between what I actually remember and the things my mother impressed upon me. I do remember she and I rarely missed a Sunday morning service at the Baptist church around the corner. We normally walked, but every so often my father went with us. Some of my fondest memories are of those occasions, when he sang some of his favorite old religious songs as he drove us to church and then to dinner. Those were the times when I felt the most secure and part of a family. Unfortunately, those times only happened about once every six months.

It required very little to send him on a drinking spree—an unpaid bill, my mother getting sick, something happening at work. Just life itself was more than he could manage. My mother spent many an hour, and later many a letter, attempting to curb my anger and replace it with compassion and understanding toward my father. In some ways she did give me enough understanding to allow me to love my father despite the suffering, but it doesn't remove the anger or allow for true forgiveness.

He couldn't deal with stress. He'd overturn the dinner table over a glass of milk spilled by a seven-year-old boy. Then my mother would cry herself to sleep while my father went to buy a bottle. My mother explained that this behavior was a result of the war and was not his fault.

He never talked about the war, and my mother wouldn't answer my questions. He'd make a quick exit if a movie or television showed a war scene. After his death I discovered the box of medals and ribbons he received during the war—the Purple Heart, the Bronze Star, numerous campaign ribbons. This time, when I questioned my mother, she relented and told me how he was wounded and that he'd nearly died from shock.

The enemy overran the foxhole he was sharing with his friend from boot camp during heavy front line combat. His friend took a direct hit right below his helmet that blew his brains all over my father. At that same instant my father was hit. Severely wounded, he lay in the foxhole for hours before the medics found him, in shock and near death from loss of blood. He recovered physically, but he was never able to deal with the memories of the war. After hearing this, I had a better understanding of my father.

He was not a big man—about my height, five feet, eight inches, but a lot stockier. His arms were out of proportion to the rest of his body. They looked like they belonged on Popeye.

He had problems dealing with life itself, but he feared no man.

In a factory like Firestone, if you changed shifts or tire lines, it was understood that you would ask permission of the workers to come to their line. My father forgot this courtesy and didn't ask permission when he moved from the second to the third shift. On his first night, eight builders cornered him in the break area.

"Oh buddy," one said as he took off his belt, "you didn't ask permission to build on our line. We're going to have to give you a little whipping."

My father said, "You're right. Sorry I forgot, but you're not going to whip me."

"Now that you've gotten smart," the builder replied, "we're going to give you a big whipping."

"You may whip me, I will grant that, but whoever holds my arms is going to the hospital tonight," my father said calmly.

His total lack of fear paralyzed them. Not one man would step forward.

This was one of the characteristics I respected in my father. He was brave, honest, and hardworking. Even when he drank, he maintained his values. He never drove if he'd been drinking. Many times he walked home or slept in the car after a night of drinking. He was also a very proud man. He would not ask for or accept help from anyone.

* * *

I paused. "Is this too much detail?" I asked Mandy, hoping I wasn't overwhelming her. "I just wanted you to have a good understanding of my mother and father."

"No, I want to understand," she said. Her brows drew down in concern. "You asked me why I'm interested in Mark Matthews. I'll tell you. Remember I told you I'd

Face to Face

seen you running in Flushing? What I didn't say was that I made Janice circle the block so I could see you again, or how, when I saw you in the library study room, I felt compelled to meet you."

"Why?" I blurted.

"That's what I'm trying to tell you. I saw pain in your eyes. Yes, I know you are the professional runner, and all runners run with pain. They may run with pain, but it doesn't scratch the surface compared to what I saw in your eyes. It riveted me. I couldn't even sleep that night. Where could so much pain come from? How could anyone live, carrying pain like that? You didn't fool me with that running pain story. When you aren't running, it's still there. I see it right now."

So this was why Mandy wanted me to wait until we were face to face. This girl is downright amazing, I thought. Good thing I'm not trying to hide anything from her; it would not do a bit of good. She can see right through you, I warned myself as I watched her pull a lock of her beautiful black hair around to the side of her face and roll it between her thumb and fingers. She did this whenever she got excited. At least I was observant enough to notice that little habit.

"I wasn't trying to fool you," I protested. "How was I to know you can look through someone like that? No one else, not even Babu, ever saw it. He sees only what I allow. After I finish, you will better understand the reasons why. But for now, since you brought this up, I'll admit that what you see is real." I paused and looked down at my hands, then slowly unclenched them. I shook my head. "I don't understand how you see it, but I admit it's real. It is so real!" I punctuated that by dropping my fist onto my leg, then I drew a deep breath. "It's the reason I train and race so hard. The pain from running too hard temporarily numbs the real pain. It helps me cope even when it's hopeless."

"With God anything is possible," Mandy murmured.

"I respect your strong faith and beliefs," I said. "In fact, I envy them. But if there really is a God, He declared war against me a long time ago, and I don't see either of us signaling for a truce."

"Don't say that," Mandy exclaimed. She tugged frantically on a lock of her hair.

Wow, our conversation had gotten pretty deep. Maybe we should back off a little and catch our breath before continuing, I thought. What in the world was I doing here anyway, baring my soul to this girl? But that question was easy to answer. I wanted to; in fact, I wanted this wonderful girl to understand everything about me, both good and bad. I wanted someone who cared to know and understand me. Here that someone was, and I was not going to miss the opportunity.

I looked deep into her beautiful dark blue eyes and returned with an understanding that everything was going to be okay. "I'm sorry," I said. "At times I'm so confused, I don't know what I believe."

We rose and continued walking. As we rounded a corner, the aroma of home cooking filled the air. Sure enough, the food court lay straight ahead.

"It's lunchtime," I announced, "and I'm starving."

"You're always starving," she replied. "Okay, let's get something to eat."

Chapter Five

Last Whipping

Before the fork reached my mouth, Mandy said, "Do you mind if I bless the food?"

"Oh sure, go ahead," I said while trying to inconspicuously place the fork back on my plate.

As Mandy prayed, my mind wandered back to my parents' dining room with the round wooden table, the four mismatched chairs, and the pleasant aroma of home cooking drifting from the kitchen and spreading throughout the house. Before each and every meal, my father would nod at my mother and say, "Hazel."

This was the signal for her to say, "Our gracious Father, bless this that thou provide, watch over and protect our family, in Christ's precious name—Amen."

Hearing Mandy say, "Amen," brought me back from my childhood and I realized that I had not heard one word of her prayer. Being close to starvation, I consumed everything in sight as Mandy talked and picked at her plate.

Before I could swallow the last bite, Mandy said, "You may continue."

"Continue? Sure, no problem," I replied. "Just give me a second to get my bearings."

As I wiped my mouth with the napkin, I mentally searched back for where I'd left off. Found it! I laid down my napkin. "My memory of events before the second grade is probably based more on what my mother told me and not what I actually retained," I warned Mandy. "I guess the first significant event that etched details in my mind was my last whipping."

* * *

I had just started the second grade. It was a weekend, and my father was drinking. To this day, I can't remember just what I did to make him so angry. He rarely gave me whippings, and had never whipped me when he was drinking.

Usually, when I did something that really upset my father, he took off his belt and hit me with it three or four times. Driven by his anger combined with the strength in his arms, the belt bruised if it hit clothing, but it drew blood if it hit skin. When I was even younger, the first blow made me wet myself. Later I learned to grit my teeth, and I was okay. I also learned to jump to the floor and curl into a ball to protect my bare arms and legs.

So, he was angry. As he took off his belt, I jumped to the floor, curled in a ball, gritted my teeth, and waited for the first blow. Instead I heard a loud slap.

"Hermit, you're not going to whip our son when you're drunk," I heard my mother shout.

I looked up to see the perfect outline of my mother's hand on the side of his face. The imprint was so detailed that I probably could have seen the fingerprints, if I'd been closer. My father had dropped the belt, made a fist, and was drawing back his arm. He had never hit my mother before. In fact, I don't remember them ever fighting. This was the first and only blow I ever saw pass

Last Whipping

between them. It was the first and only time I ever heard my mother yell at my father. Even when they disagreed, Mother never raised her voice.

I jumped to my feet and grabbed his arm. "Dad, don't hurt Mom! Don't hurt Mom! You can whip me!"

My father reached across with his other arm and pulled me up against his chest. He held me so tightly, I could barely breathe. Finally he gently lowered me to the floor. I looked up and saw tears flowing from his eyes. He turned and went back into the bedroom. That's the only time I ever saw my father cry.

He never whipped me again. Nothing I did upset him. I could even spill my milk at the dinner table, and he was okay . . .

* * *

As I finished the sentence, I watched huge tears puddle in the corner of Mandy's eyes until the pull of gravity sent them trickling down to splash on the table. I stopped and said, "Mandy, don't start crying. I won't be able to continue if you cry."

"I'm sorry; I'm okay. It's not just you; I feel so much compassion for your father, too. He was never allowed to be a little boy. No wonder he struggled with life."

"You're right," I said. "He never experienced being a boy. I remember the time I was playing ball with some boys in a field next to our house. We were taking turns throwing the ball up and hitting it to each other. When it was my turn to bat, my father came outside to watch. We called him over and asked him to bat. He was reluctant, but we insisted.

"I had to show him how to hold the bat and throw up the ball to swing. He tried over and over but kept missing the ball. Finally he hit the ball solid. It went the length of the field and kept going and going." I paused and chuckled at the memory. "I'd never seen a ball hit that far! To this day, I've not seen anyone, not even in a major league game, hit the ball so far.

"We searched the woods beyond the field but never found it. My father went to the store and bought us a new baseball. He felt bad over losing the ball, but we kept marveling over how far the ball traveled. That made him feel better, so he admitted he had never swung a baseball bat before."

I felt my smile fading. "I learned there were a lot of things he never did as a boy. He never played football or basketball. He never went swimming or hunting or fishing. Things we take for granted were never part of his childhood. All he knew was work and more work while his half-brother Calvin went to school and excelled in sports."

"What happened to Calvin after he lost his football scholarship?" Mandy asked.

"I was heading in that direction," I replied. "But first, let's take advantage of this array of automobiles and look around."

A sign over an entrance adjacent to the food court announced *America's Sports Cars*. I glimpsed Thunderbirds and Corvettes, and as we entered, I realized the room held every model year, starting in the 1950s and running through the present. This room was full of what dreams are made of. All were drop-dead beautiful. But right in the center, a baby blue and white 1958 Thunderbird slowly revolved on a pedestal. The sight nearly, but not quite, compared to Mandy entering the library study room. In fact, it reminded me of Mandy: elegant, tasteful, classy, stylish, graceful, dignified. All these could describe either.

Last Whipping

As I soaked in the splendor of this lovely machine, I realized that Mandy looked a wee bit impatient. I ignored her. Surely, as we toured this building, I could look and talk at the same time.

Chapter Six

War in the Front Yard

Upon spying an area titled, *America's First Auto*, I cried, "Forward! Look at all these Tin Lizzies."

"What is a Tin Lizzie and why are they all black?" Mandy asked with considerably less enthusiasm.

"Ford Model Ts," I said. "Henry Ford set into motion a change in our nation's way of life with his mass production of the Model T utilizing the assembly line. By mass producing the Model T so inexpensively, he brought the cost of owning an American automobile within reach of the average citizen."

"I knew that!" Mandy replied, "but why are they all black?"

"Oh, sorry." I took a moment to admire the multitude of models filling the room. There were Model T roadsters, coupes, runabouts, town cars, and touring cars. "There are two reasons," I said. "Producing one color was faster and cheaper; therefore basic black became the color of choice."

War in the Front Yard

"Well, that makes sense," Mandy said. "It's obvious you're very fond of these old black cars, and I can appreciate that. But can we try to keep them from becoming too much of a distraction? I'm eager to find out more about Calvin."

"Sure, no problem," I said. Okay, so these fine old cars were a bit of a distraction, but they were not the real reason I was dragging my feet concerning Calvin. The topic of Calvin was not for the faint of heart. I hoped Mandy was up to it.

* * *

Calvin heard that the Bears were having a tryout camp in Chicago. He and a couple of his football buddies headed to the windy city with lofty aspirations of making the team.

In each scrimmage, Calvin made outstanding defense plays, one after the other. After the tryouts, the Bears selected one player to look at further—Calvin. For two weeks he was put through a multitude of conditioning, speed, strength, and agility tests.

I'll never forget how proud my father was when we received the call telling us Calvin had made the Chicago Bears' taxi squad. Calvin was on the same team as his football hero, Dick Butkus. We were certain Calvin would move up from the taxi squad and play linebacker for the Chicago Bears alongside the great Dick Butkus.

I told Calvin, "I am going to be a linebacker in the NFL, too."

It never happened for Calvin or for me. During a scrimmage at the end of Calvin's first season on the taxi squad, he injured his knee and required surgery. The operation was not successful; they found more damage than first suspected. They operated again. The results were not good; Calvin was left with a limp. He was paid for the remainder of the season, but his football career was over.

After the injury we did not hear from him for months at a time. Calvin moved from city to city, from job to job, drinking and fighting.

About two weeks before Christmas when I was in the second grade, Calvin called and said that he was in Los Angeles working as a bouncer. He asked, "Can you pick me up at the Greyhound bus station? I'm coming to visit during the holidays."

The first week went well. Calvin spent hours talking to me about his football career. I grew more determined to be a football player.

Two days before Christmas, the weather turned unusually warm. Short sleeve weather in late December—this was strange. But as the day progressed, the skies darkened and the wind picked up, blowing cold air straight out of the north. The spring-like day was about to collide with *Old Man Winter* and that meant trouble.

As thunder rolled in the background, Calvin and my farther began drinking. Both were well on their way to intoxication when the liquor ran out.

Calvin said, "Let's drive to a bar."

"No, we'll need to sober up before driving the car," my father said.

I was sitting in the kitchen watching them through the doorway to the dining room. The keys to our Ford sedan were hanging on a hook near the doorway. Calvin jumped up, grabbed the car keys, and headed out the front door with my father right behind him. I followed them outside.

War in the Front Yard

Calvin climbed into the car and put the key in the ignition. My father reached through the open window and took the keys.

Calvin's face grew bright red. "I'll beat you to a pulp if you don't give me back those keys," he yelled.

My father replied, "Stay in the car, sober up, and then we'll go to the bar."

The sky grew even darker. Lighting flashed in the distance. My father said again, "Calvin, just stay in the car, sober up, then we can go to the bar."

I watched him go back into the house. Calvin got out of the car, still red-faced, clearly looking for a fight. My father came back into the front yard with our rifle in one hand and a fist full of bullets in the other.

"Calvin, get back in the car," my father said, but Calvin would have no part of it.

Someone grabbed my arm from behind and I looked around to see my mother. She pulled me across the street into our neighbor's house. While my mother was dialing the phone, I sneaked out onto the front porch. My father was still telling Calvin to get back into the car, but Calvin was headed straight for him. There was plenty of time to load the rifle, but he threw the bullets on the ground. Just as they met in the middle of our front yard, my mother grabbed me and pulled me back into the house, then returned to the porch with our neighbor. I went out the back door, circled the house, and crouched where I could see our yard without being seen by my mother.

Both my father and Calvin were covered with blood. The rifle's wooden stock was broken. My father hit Calvin on the head with the barrel, knocking Calvin to his knees.

Finally the winter storm broke. Icy rain pelted down, instantly soaking my clothing. Lightning illuminated the dark sky directly overhead.

Calvin pulled himself to his feet and hit my father directly in the face with his fist. My father sprawled on the ground with the rifle barrel still firmly gripped in both hands. He jumped back to his feet and hit Calvin on the head with the barrel, knocking him to his knees.

I watched as they continued fighting. First Calvin fell to his knees, then my father was knocked clear off his feet. Over and over, like instant replay, this scene repeated itself. The wind blew, the lighting flashed, the thunder roared, and the icy rain poured down in sheets as, wide-eyed, I watched every blow fall.

As the distant wail of sirens grew louder, both stayed down. My father sat in the mud in the middle of our yard. Calvin crawled toward our house.

Two sheriff patrol cars and an ambulance came flying up the street.

My father stood and held out his arms. Two officers spun him around, handcuffed his hands behind his back, and shoved him into the back seat of one of the patrol cars. Another officer with a clipboard approached my mother.

I dashed across the street and ran up to the patrol car. My father was leaning forward, head bowed. His face was cut and swollen. Blood dripped from both his upper and lower lip and puddled on the car's carpet. Speechless, I stared into his bloody face. My whole body felt numb. Numb from the cold wind and rain, or from what I'd just witnessed?

"Hey, we need a rope," a medic yelled.

I turned as an officer carried a coil of rope toward our house. Were they going to tie Calvin up? I sprinted after the officer.

War in the Front Yard

Calvin lay under our front porch. Blood oozed from deep cuts covering the top of his head and formed a pool on the ground. Surely he was dead, I thought, but then I saw the movement of his chest as he breathed. Watching the two medics tie the rope around his waist, I realized Calvin was stuck underneath the porch.

The medics tugged Calvin free and took him to the hospital and the officers took my father to the county jail. It took over a hundred and fifty stitches to close Calvin's head wounds.

They kept my father in jail for three days, but when Calvin refused to press charges, he was released the day after Christmas. After his release, the three of us went to see Calvin in the hospital. My father and Calvin apologized to each other and then to my mother. A few days later, Calvin was released. We took him directly from the hospital to the bus station. That was the last time we saw him.

* * *

Mandy stared at me as if waiting for more and then yelled, "What happened to him?"

For a moment I thought maybe this was too much for Mandy, but I looked into her dark blue eyes and knew I had to continue.

"Four months and not one call from Calvin," I said. "Then we got a call early on a Monday morning from a policeman in Los Angeles. Calvin had been stabbed in the heart during a fight. After his burial, they found our phone number in the back of his wallet. We took his death very hard, especially my father. Our last living relative was gone, leaving only the three of us. This was the first in a series of unfortunate events that occurred to my family."

"This is so sad," Mandy said. Tears rolled down her cheeks.

Touched, I reached out and took her hand. Boy, this was going to be difficult. She had wonderful parents, great relatives, had been sheltered her whole life, and probably had a perfect childhood. What was I thinking, revealing all of this to her? And there was worse coming. With her tender heart, more tears were sure to flow. I knew this, but I knew, too, that I had to continue. "Are you okay?" I asked. "Do you want me to stop?"

"No!" Mandy wiped her eyes and added, "Go on. What happened next?"

Chapter Seven

Trouble with a Capital T

It had never occurred to me to soft-pedal around the truth, but I realized that I had to consider Mandy's emotions, too. She'd held up well, except for those shed tears. Without doubt, I had her undivided attention. I still had a lot to say. So when we moved into another auto theme area, I leaned against the wall, took a deep breath, and moved into rougher terrain.

* * *

After Calvin's death my father attended church more regularly. He cut back on his drinking and even went to a few AA meetings. As I began the third grade, things were looking up for my family.

My mother always seemed to be coming down with something or just getting over something else. My father often complained about the relentless doctor bills. Mom would get the flu, or have a kidney infection, or bladder infection, or some other kind of infection, but she always got well. In November my mother's health became a major concern. She lost weight, felt weak, and suffered through night sweats.

"Probably a touch of the flu," the doctor said. "A little medicine and a few days' rest should do the trick."

Weeks passed, and Mother didn't improve. She ran a fever for three days before again visiting the doctor, who sent her to the hospital for more tests. All came back negative and the medicine took care of the fever, so the doctors released her.

Another few weeks went by. She was still losing weight and feeling tired. A week before Christmas she developed a persistent cough. When she began coughing up blood, my father became very concerned.

This time the doctors took x-rays and gave her a TB skin test. The test came back positive. My mom had active tuberculosis. Both lungs were heavily infected with the disease, which was highly contagious.

"So contagious," the doctor said, "if she were to fly on an airplane, every passenger could be infected." He moved Mother to a private ward in the hospital and put her under quarantine, then notified the state department.

I didn't understand what this meant—that my life would never be the same. Behind me was the best life had to offer; in front, tough times. Change is never easy, especially when it comes on fast.

The doctors assured us that my mother's TB could become inactive with treatment, but it would take time. The nearest place for treatment was Oakville Sanitarium, which was about fifty miles north of Memphis on Highway 51. It would take two weeks to complete all the paperwork for her transfer to Oakville. Our neighbor across the street volunteered to keep me for those two weeks, but my father would have no part of it. Instead, he took two weeks' vacation.

Trouble with a Captial T

On Christmas Eve we went to the hospital to visit Mom. We could talk to her on the phone and see her through a huge plate glass window, but we couldn't enter the quarantined ward. This would be our last Christmas together.

My father and I returned home to find a huge basket full of fresh orange juice, cheese, and fruit on our front porch. A note attached to the basket said *From the State Health Department*. I watched my father pour the orange juice down the drain and throw the rest into the garbage. Then he called the health department and told them, "We don't accept charity."

Someone on the phone attempted to explain that the basket wasn't charity, but standard procedure for any family that had been exposed to active TB.

My father wouldn't listen. "This family does not take handouts," he repeated, and hung up.

During my mother's final week at the hospital, she and my father spent hours on the phone discussing me. I listened with great interest. My father had been working double shifts to cover the medical bills. He'd fallen behind on our car payments, and the bank was threatening to repossess our Ford sedan. Neighbors had volunteered to help while my father was at work, but he would have no part of that. Finally my parents reached an agreement—I would be better off in an orphanage while my mother was getting well.

On New Year's Eve we returned to the hospital to see Mother one last time before her early morning transfer to Oakville. I pressed my face to the plate glass. My tears flowed down the window until my father pulled me away.

I spent most of New Year's Day crying in my room. Finally my father came in and said, "Son, those tears will accomplish nothing; we're in for some tough times, but you have to be tougher."

The next day he helped me pack and we drove to the Porter Leath Orphanage. Although the name on the side of the large old five-story building was *The Porter Leath Orphanage*, everyone called it Porter Leath Home. Located in the oldest part of downtown Memphis at the corner of Chelsea and Manassas, my new home sat in the middle of a rather spacious piece of property surrounded by a six-foot chain-link fence topped with barbed wire.

Three blocks down Chelsea Avenue was Guthrie Elementary, and three blocks down Manassas was Humes High School. All kids at Porter Leath Home went to one of these two schools. I would come to know both schools very well.

* * *

"How long did you have to live in the orphanage?" Mandy interrupted. She wiped more tears from her eyes, then pulled a lock of hair to the side of her face and began rolling it between her fingers

Her tears didn't make my task any easier. "Well, I'm headed in that direction," I said gently, "but I don't want to jump ahead. Just let me continue. Come on," I said in a lighter tone and tugged on her arm. "This next area's called *America's Luxury Autos*."

Chapter Eight

Don't Like Your Looks

I gawked at the automobiles on display as we entered the room. "Wow, look at all these big, beautiful cars!"

"Big, I agree," Mandy replied, "but beautiful? I think not."

"What? Are you telling me these splendid Lincoln Continentals and Cadillacs aren't drop-dead gorgeous?"

"Well, I don't share your love for the American automobile, but I can appreciate your enthusiasm," Mandy said. "In fact, I enjoy seeing your eyes light up with each new encounter. But you must remember I've spent most of my life in Third World countries. In places like Manila, Jakarta, and Kuala Lumpur, with their mazes of narrow streets, large vehicles are considered excessive, wasteful, and extravagant. To me, cars are blaring horns, hair-raising intersections, traffic jams, and air pollution." She shook her head. "And we call it progress."

As she spoke, I realized just how different our backgrounds were. Never in a million years would I consider a Lincoln Continental or Cadillac wasteful or extravagant. But her viewpoint actually made sense. Okay, maybe they were extravagant and wasteful, but they *were* very pleasing to the eye.

Just then I spotted a pearl white Cadillac with black leather interior that looked identical to the one that—but that would be jumping ahead.

Mandy interrupted my daydreaming. "Have you forgotten about the orphanage?"

"Sorry," I stammered. "These extravagant cars distracted me."

Mandy grinned. "So do we need to move to another area? "

Boy, seeing that grin on her face was like a breath of fresh air. I smiled. "That's probably a good idea."

Mandy reached out and put her arm around my waist as we strolled into the next auto theme area. Feeling much more comfortable, I resumed my tale.

* * *

Before the orphanage my recollection of events could be suspect. But events after my arrival at Porter Leath Home have been etched in my memory in vivid detail. I can recall everything.

My first glimpse of the orphanage frightened me. Why was that huge old brick building so far from the road? Why was the chain-link fence so tall? And was the barbed wire to keep strangers out or to keep the kids in? All these thoughts whirled through my head as we made our way up the long drive.

We arrived at the orphanage around noon, when all the kids were at school. Two administrators showed us the grounds and ended the tour in a spacious room on the third floor of the main building.

Don't Like Your Looks

The room contained row after row of small beds. Each bed had a gray wrought-iron headboard that looked old enough to be classified as an antique. A large metal chest rested at the foot of each bed. Clothes hung on rods within small, open compartments on the front and back walls. I counted the beds as my father put his questions to the administrators. Six rows of ten beds each—sixty beds. As I turned my attention back to my father, I saw the two men walking away.

My father scooped me into his arms, held me against his chest, and told me to be strong like a man and everything would be okay. Then, all too quickly, he was gone.

I stood fighting back tears, trying to be a man, but I still felt like a little boy.

A woman pushing a large dust mop entered the room from another door. She stopped and regarded me. "Now, who do we have here?" she said.

"My name is Mark Matthews," I replied.

"So you're the new boy. Well, you can call me Marie."

I looked at the dust mop. "Are you the maid?"

"Don't you be calling me a maid. I'm the third-floor matron for the second shift. Worked this floor for the past twelve years and seen many a boy come and go."

With that said, she showed me my bed, helped put away my clothes, and took me for a tour of the floor. I gaped at the huge bathroom. Everything was in the open—no privacy there. Another large room on the floor, about half the size of the dormitory, contained only a wooden bench that ran around all four walls. Above the bench, shelves held games, a can of marbles, cards, dominoes, and more.

Marie sat me down on the bench and said, "Boy, no need for you to worry; our Lord is in control, and you're going to be just fine. Those kids will be back from school around three-thirty, and then you can make you some friends."

She sounded just like my mom. I watched her return to the dormitory to run the dust mop up and down between the rows of beds. It was one-thirty.

I sat on the bench. Two o'clock came and went. I sat on the bench. Two-thirty. I continued to sit on the bench. I was ready for those kids to show up, but as the clock inched closer to three-thirty, I became uneasy. What if they didn't like me?

Too late—I heard them clamoring up the stairs. I anxiously scanned each one as he topped the staircase. Of varying heights and ages, the boys moved all over the room, but most mingled with their own age group. There were quite a few, but not enough to fill all sixty beds. I tried to count them, but they moved around too much. I guessed there were maybe forty. In fact I learned never to keep count, because the number always varied. As Marie had said, "The boys come and go."

A small group spotted me sitting on the bench. As they headed in my direction, the tallest yelled, "Well now, look what we have here. What's your name?"

"Mark," I mumbled.

One after another, the questions came faster than I could respond.

"How old are you?"

"What grade are you in?"

"Do you have a mother?"

"Do you have a father?"

"Then, why are you here?"

Don't Like Your Looks

I attempted to answer each, but before I could reply to one question, someone was asking the next. The battery of questions continued until all had their turn. By now, the whole party had gathered around me. I continued to look them over. Suddenly, I realized I was the smallest boy in the room. This did not raise my comfort level. In fact, despite being in the middle of a crowd, I felt very alone.

A stocky boy rolled his eyes, looked me over from head to toe, and asked for the second time, "Are you really in the third grade?"

For the second time I replied, "Yep, third grade."

"You look too small to be in the third grade," he said. He backed off and stood watching me for awhile, then stepped forward and said, "I don't like your looks."

It was many years before I finally figured out why he made that statement. Okay, I'd been staring at him, and he took exception to anyone staring in his direction. He was redheaded, but his hair was actually a bright orange color. Freckles covered every exposed area of his skin. He had no neck; his head sat right on his shoulders.

But that wasn't what made me stare.

It was his hair. It grew in every direction, sticking out at all angles. Some strands sprang straight forward at a multitude of angles, some straight back at other angles, and some to one side or the other at all angles. His hair was in such total disarray that it was quite beautiful, like a bulldog that is so ugly it looks cute.

Here he was saying he didn't like my looks, while I was thinking, have you looked in the mirror lately? The possibility that my staring had hurt his feelings never crossed my mind. I was not the first, nor would I be the last person who stared too hard at Carl.

He finally said, "I think I'll beat you up."

Fear flowed into my bloodstream and pumped into all parts of my body. Carl was bigger, and he looked like he enjoyed beating on people.

Then I heard Marie say, "You kids can go out to play before supper."

Everyone started streaming down the stairs, including Carl. I tried to tell Marie I didn't want to go out to play, but she would have none of that. She herded me down the stairs with the other boys.

When I got outside, I realized the place was huge. I looked in every direction and didn't see that chain-link fence. As I searched the horizon for the fence, Carl headed toward me with a sour look on his face. I ran. Carl started running too, but I was faster. He chased me for a while, then rested, chased and then rested.

This was kind of fun. I ran slower and allowed Carl to draw near, and then I sped away. I let him get close, and then quickly changed directions. I looked back to see him trip over his feet. This was really fun! But Carl was getting madder by the minute.

As we were called to go inside and clean up for supper, I realized it might be a mistake, having so much fun at Carl's expense. When we reached the third floor, Carl could no longer contain himself. He pushed me down on one of the beds, jumped on top, and hit me repeatedly in the face with both fists. The first blows bloodied my nose. I was in for a beating.

I'd caught sight of a hammer handle lying on the bed as I fell back. It was not a hammer, just the handle. I extended my arm and with one sweeping motion, I gripped the handle. I swung with all the strength I could muster. It struck Carl on the back of his head with a loud thud.

Don't Like Your Looks

He dropped on my chest like a dead weight. I struggled out from under him. Carl was out cold. A rather large knot grew on his head as I watched. Maybe I had killed him.

After a few moments, Carl stirred. He's really going to be mad now, I thought.

To my complete surprise, Carl said, "Boy, you're pretty tough for such a small kid. What did you hit me with?"

"This hammer handle," I replied, hefting my makeshift weapon.

I had just knocked out a guy with a hammer handle and made a friend for life. Go figure.

Carl and I talked for hours that first night. His full name was Carl London. He was also in the third grade. I'd assumed he was at least in the fifth grade. As we talked, he revealed that he had failed the third grade the previous year.

When he was three years old, he told me, his parents were killed in an automobile accident while he was with a babysitter. He had no brothers or sisters, and since none of his relatives wanted him, he ended up at the orphanage. No one came to visit; he was on his own.

After hearing this, I didn't feel so bad. I had both a mother and father, and I'd be at the orphanage only until she got well. Carl was a permanent resident.

The next day I went to Guthrie Elementary with Carl. The school had two third-grade classes, but as luck would have it, I ended up sitting next to Carl. My life at the orphanage had begun.

During my mother's and father's long discussions concerning what would be best for me while she was away, my father promised her one thing. She didn't ask him to promise to stop drinking. I think she knew it was beyond his control. He promised to come to the orphanage every Sunday morning and take me to church.

I eagerly awaited that first visit. Sunday morning found me waiting patiently at the window on the third floor, watching for his car. Instead of the car, though, I saw him get off a city bus and start down the drive to the orphanage. Carl and I raced down the stairs and ran down the long drive to meet him. Our car had been repossessed, my father told me, so he'd be using the bus for transportation from now on.

"Dad, can Carl go with us?" I asked. "He's never been to church."

"Sure, he can go every week," he replied.

Two blocks up Chelsea Avenue, in the opposite direction from Guthrie Elementary, stood an old red brick building topped by a steeple with the words *First Methodist Church* inscribed above two large wooden doors. We went to both Sunday school and the church service.

The service was fine, but we did not like Sunday school. The kids in the class kept staring at Carl and me. It made me feel uncomfortable, but it made Carl mad. I told my father, and he said we would just go to church service from now on.

On the way back to the orphanage we stopped at a drugstore and ate in the soda shop. My dad let us pick out a comic book before returning to the orphanage. After we said good-bye, I ran up the stairs, sat down beside the window, and watched him until the bus drove away. Week after week we followed this same routine, including the comic book, except we didn't go to Sunday school.

Don't Like Your Looks

A couple of days after our first trip to the Methodist church, I received two letters from my mother. She had sent them a few days apart, but they arrived together. In them she told me her medicine had made her very sick at first, but after the doctors adjusted the dosage, she felt much better. Words cannot describe the joy those letters brought me. I read them over and over, until I knew every word on each page. Carl was excited too. He had me read them out loud, not once, but twice. I carefully placed each in my metal chest at the foot of the bed. Two more letters arrived a week later. I waited until the second letter arrived, then sent one reply.

That first letter was full of questions about my health and well-being, but in her second letter she described in detail how she prayed nightly for God's protection for her only son. Night after night she prayed the same prayer. After a week she awoke in the middle of the night and felt God's Presence in her room—not seeing or hearing Him, but feeling His overwhelming Presence. She felt a message being impressed upon her conscious mind: *Hazel, since I look down on you with favor, angels will be watching over your son.*

She closed that second letter and every letter thereafter with, "Son, you will be safe and protected. Angels are watching over you."

* * *

I paused and looked at Mandy. "When I was young, those words gave me comfort, but as I grew older, day-to-day struggles pushed those thoughts from my mind." I smiled and shrugged. "Besides, I have yet to see my first angel."

"But have you ever felt their presence?" Mandy asked.

"That's a good question," I replied. "No, but there have been numerous times when I was in great danger and felt the power of my mother's prayers surrounding me with protection from harm. I could give you three or four good examples, but that would be jumping ahead."

"Okay," Mandy pleaded, "but could you give me just one example now and the others as you get to them?"

I really wanted to keep events in the order they occurred, but those dark blue eyes looked so determined that I felt quite helpless. "Just one," I said.

Mandy smiled, graciously accepting her victory.

"This was while I still lived in Memphis, while going to college," I began. "Early on a Saturday morning I was running my twenty miles alone on a hilly road in the county. The few houses sat far off the road. There was little or no traffic.

"At the sixteenth mile, I heard growling as I passed a drive. I looked back to see a pack of eight dogs bounding out onto the road. All were mixed breeds of various sizes, led by a large German Shepherd. All looked lean and mean. As soon as I saw them, I felt the overwhelming presence of my mother's prayers. A feeling of peace and control replaced the fear that had been surging through my body.

"Just as the shepherd was about to grab my ankles, I spun around and kicked out soccer-style. Somehow my foot landed right under the shepherd's chin. I heard his teeth slam together while his tongue still hung out of his mouth—the teeth must have gone through his tongue in both directions. He started yelping, tucked his tail between his legs, and headed back toward the drive.

"The other dogs stopped in their tracks. They continued to bark and growl but remained in place. I ran backward up the hill, watching them closely. After I was a safe distance away, I turned and continued my run. While all this was happening, I felt as if time had gone into slow motion, and I felt engulfed in protection."

"So you have faith in the protection provided by your mother's prayers," Mandy said, "but not from angels sent in response to those prayers?"

"Yes," I replied. "Many times I've felt the presence of her prayers, but never the presence of angels."

"Very interesting," Mandy said. "Did you ever notice anything else that seemed unusual as you were growing up?"

I hesitated. "Well," I murmured, "there is one thing everyone always made a big deal over. I never seem to get sick. I have never been to see a doctor, except for checkups. I don't get colds, flu, headache, stomachache, or any other kind of ache. At the orphanage kids were always getting sick. The sickness would go from one kid to the next but somehow, it always skipped over me. Even today I run in cold, rain, sleet, and snow, but I never even get a cold."

"How do you account for this?"

"I'm physically fit," I said. "I'm a runner."

"Maybe you're the professional runner now," Mandy said, "but not back in the third grade, when you were in a big room full of snotty-nosed kids coughing all over you."

"Okay," I conceded. "You made your point."

As Mandy's dark blue eyes acknowledged yet another triumph, she said, "I have one other question, and then I'll let you continue. Where do you think the hammer handle came from?"

"I don't know," I replied. "None of the kids at the orphanage had ever seen it. That question bothered me for years."

Mandy studied me for a long moment. Then she changed the subject. "Boy, every day was a new adventure for you. What was it like, having so many boys your age to play with?"

I looked at her, puzzled. "Well, first, they weren't all my age," I said. "Besides, we didn't always play; a lot of times we fought—especially Carl. He looked for fights."

"Enough!" Mandy exclaimed. "I don't care about the fights. I just thought having so many kids to play with must have been neat." She turned away and resumed walking. "So, go ahead with your story; I want to know more about the orphanage."

As we entered another auto theme area, I considered pointing out that I hadn't let the cars distract or interrupt me in the last area. But since the sign over the entrance of that last area said *America's First Compacts*, I thought better of it.

Chapter Nine

When the Bus Failed to Stop

After the first month at the orphanage, my life settled into a routine. My mother's letters arrived twice a week. I kept every letter in the chest at the foot of my bed. Each night I reread the latest letter before going to sleep.

Every Sunday my father took Carl and me to church. We stopped every week at the drugstore to eat, picked out our comic books, and then headed back to the orphanage.

It didn't take long to discover why Carl had failed the third grade; the boy had no understanding of the concept of homework. Finally, out of desperation, I got right up in his face and said, "My father said there are a lot of things we can do without, but an education isn't one of them."

Carl wouldn't listen. At first he refused to bring his books home. When he finally started taking them back and forth to school, he still wouldn't open them. I refused to play until we both finished our homework. This got his attention. Reluctantly, he started working on the homework. Marie agreed to call out our spelling words the night before our weekly spelling test. His grades improved immediately.

School still had its problems. Carl was always one stare or one smart remark away from starting a fight, especially with kids who weren't from the orphanage.

One afternoon on the way home from school, as I stepped off the curb, the school crossing guard held out his flag to prevent us from crossing the street. I stood on the edge of the street instead of stepping back onto the sidewalk. The crossing guard, who was a fifth-grader, didn't like me waiting in the street. He punched me in the stomach with his flagpole. Before I could stop him, Carl had bloodied the crossing guard's nose. We were both suspended from school for three days.

The fights aside, Carl continued to improve in school. When the school year ended, he passed.

The arrival of summer brought something Carl had neglected to mention. Every Friday night, a group of boys from the orphanage was treated to a performance at the Memphis Opera. Half the boys on the third floor went one week, and the other half went the next. This meant Carl and I had to go to the opera every other week for the whole summer. At least we were in the same group, after Marie intervened on our behalf. And during the intermission we were given drinks, candy, and popcorn.

At some point during the performance, one of us got into trouble—it was inevitable. We considered the opera two hours of misery and torture. Everything was in Italian, including the singing. Marie tried to explain that the opera wasn't punishment for orphan kids—we attended to learn to appreciate the arts. We weren't buying any of it.

When the Bus Failed to Stop

With the fall came the fourth grade, and the opera became history. Carl finally got it into his head that when he studied, school was not nearly as difficult. For the first time in his life he received a report card that had all A's and B's and not one C.

My mother's letters still came regularly, two a week. My father never missed a Sunday to take us to church. He still rode the bus but he was saving to pay cash for his next car, so no one could take it from him. Many a Sunday he looked really rough, as if he had been on a bad drunk, but he never failed to step off that bus—until one Sunday morning in early December.

It was two weeks before Christmas—I'd been at the orphanage for nearly a year. Carl and I waited at the window, watching for the bus. It went by without stopping. We waited. The next bus failed to stop. It was now too late to go to church.

For the whole morning, I sat by the window. Finally, as my concern mounted, I went downstairs and told one of the administrators, "I think something has happened to my father."

The administrator assured me that everything was fine and there was nothing for me to worry about. I went back upstairs, but I had an uneasy feeling. Something was very wrong.

At school the next morning, during our first class, an administrator from the orphanage called our teacher, Mrs. Malone, into the hall. A moment later, she signaled for me to come into the hall. Carl followed.

Mrs. Malone said, "Mark, I'm so sorry to have to tell you this. Your father has died. You can go with Mr. Johnson."

Carl begged Mrs. Malone to let him go with me. She at first refused, but gave in when Carl began crying. At this point my memory fails me, but I do remember feeling like I was in a trance, and that this wasn't really happening.

* * *

I paused as Mandy searched her purse for another Kleenex. People stopped and stared at the tears flowing from her eyes. I bit my lip to hold back my own tears. This wasn't easy for me or for her. But we had to get through it.

"Mandy, shall we take a break?" I asked.

"No," she replied in a determined tone, "I want to hear what happened to your father."

I drew a deep breath. "Okay."

* * *

The papers said he died of an apparent heart attack—a polite way to avoid stating the real cause of death. The doctors said the alcohol in his blood was at a level greater than the human body could tolerate. In other words, he died from an overdose of alcohol.

I saw what was in the paper, heard what the doctors said, but knew the real cause of his death—pride. He wanted more for his family than he was capable of providing, so he took the easy way out and gave up. My mother said in her letters that it had been an accident, but I never bought that and still don't. He did the very thing he had taught me never to do. He gave up.

I forgave him for his drinking, but I've never forgiven him for giving up. My mother wrote many a letter trying to make me understand, but it hasn't been easy for me to forgive him for leaving me when I needed him so much.

When the Bus Failed to Stop

The funeral was at the Baptist church near our old house. My mother was not allowed to attend, but Carl was with me. I recognized a few church members and a few of his coworkers, but the room was far from full. I was determined to be a man, to present a stoic demeanor. But then, all of a sudden, the music swelled, and both Carl and I burst into tears.

Uniformed soldiers at the burial folded the American flag and handed it to me along with a small box containing his medals and ribbons—the ones I already mentioned. I still have both; they are the only items I have from my father.

The first Sunday after the funeral, Carl and I looked at each other and said in unison, "Do we go to church?"

We decided to continue, a decision that pleased my mother. Each Sunday morning we walked to church, attended the service, and returned to the orphanage. The drugstore was no longer an option; we had no money.

My mother's letters continued, but she now spent more time trying to help me understand my father. Each ended with, "Son, you will be safe and protected. Angels are watching over you."

With summer came more of the Memphis Opera, but this year, instead of hating the opera, I just disliked it. At times I actually caught myself listening to the singing. I never mentioned this to Carl or the others. In fact, every time they discussed how much they hated the opera, I joined in agreement.

Another school year found Carl and me in the fifth grade. Looking around the third floor, I realized how many of the kids who had been there on my first day were gone. There still were plenty of kids on the third floor, but most were new. As Marie said, "The boys come and go."

One boy on the floor had been at the orphanage a long time. Jeff Strong was on the third floor before Marie started working at Porter Leath Home. Now seventeen, like Carl, Jeff had no family and no visitors. He was supposed to move to the fourth floor with the high school boys when he started the ninth grade at Humes High School, but he'd wanted to stay on the floor with us. They made an exception to the rules and allowed him to stay.

There were many who told us what to do and when to do it, but Jeff was the one actually in charge of the third floor. When he said to do something, we did it immediately, without back talk. Even Carl tried not to disturb Jeff's sleep.

Jeff's last name fit him to a tee. Well over six foot, he made all-Memphis on the Humes High School football team his junior year. Every night after supper he lifted weights in our game room for an hour.

After Jeff finished with the weights, we spread out the mat in the middle of the room. Jeff knelt in the center of the mat and six or seven of us wrestled with him, attacking him from all sides. Jeff effortlessly bounced us off the mat again and again. This year, though, we were a little bigger—especially Carl—and a little wiser.

As usual, Jeff sent us one after the other to the mat. But then two or three of us latched onto one of his arms, and several more boys quickly pinned the other. To our surprise, we had Jeff flat on his back in the middle of the mat. He lunged upward, attempting to regain his feet, but we had him flat-out pinned. Now, this was kind of fun.

Jeff's face grew red. Obviously getting a little hot under the collar, he commanded us to let him up. Are you kidding me? We had spent weeks and even months being bounced off the mat. We weren't about to release

When the Bus Failed to Stop

him. By now, he was really ticked off. He called each of us by name, commanding us to turn him loose. When my name was called, I didn't release his arm. But, one by one, the others turned him loose.

There I was, holding an arm by myself. Jeff flexed the arm and I flew across the room. I bounced off the floor and skidded into the bench.

Carl ran over. "Are you okay?" he asked.

"Yes," I said, "but why did you turn him loose?"

"Well," he replied, "I didn't want to bounce across the room."

"Good point."

That was the last time we wrestled Jeff.

Chapter Ten

No More Letters

Looking back, the fifth grade was probably one of my better years at the orphanage—at worst uneventful, at best filled with hope. Carl now made passing grades, and he didn't seem to be carrying a chip around on his shoulder anymore.

As the school year ended, my mother's letters were full of hope for a new medicine. She had been at Oakville for over two years, and none of the previous medicines had stabilized the tuberculosis. This was a newly approved medicine, and tests indicated it was effective in treating extreme cases of tuberculosis.

I spent my third summer attending the opera. The first year I hated every minute, the second year I disliked most of it, but this year I actually looked forward to each play, although I'd never admit it. This was one secret I had to keep from Carl. He wouldn't understand, and I didn't want him to think less of me because of an opera. So I expressed my displeasure, just like all the other kids.

Fall brought sixth grade. My mother had been taking the new medicine for three months with some signs of improvement, but the improvement didn't meet the doctors' expectations. Finally they discussed with her the possibility of surgery. The disease was concentrated in one large area of one lung and in a smaller area of the other. If they removed those two areas, they might stabilize the disease and make it inactive. Inactive meant she could leave the hospital and lead a normal life. She would have to be tested regularly and continue to take the medicine, but she would be able to go home.

It would be an understatement to say I met this news with excitement. The possibility of going home was nearly more than I could bear. I shared my daydreams with Carl, then realized what I was saying. There he stood, beaming with joy over the possibility of me leaving him and the orphanage far behind.

That night I wrote my mother and asked if we could adopt Carl. She wrote back that I should start praying about it. If I prayed and she prayed, God would find a way to keep Carl and me together, since nothing was impossible for God. As soon as the doctors released her, she would submit the paperwork. She would then have two sons.

This was how a small boy would expect his mother to react, but looking back, I see a mother who relied on her faith to handle all situations. Mother had agreed to adopt a boy she'd never met. I didn't mention this to Carl. I didn't want to build up his hopes and have something go wrong.

Mother's operation was scheduled for the first week in November. It was major surgery that would require weeks for recovery. Then time would tell if the medicine could stabilize the disease.

For the first two weeks my mother was too weak to write, so one of the nurses wrote for her. She was doing better than even the doctors had expected. They could already see much improvement in her condition. Week by week, her letters guided me through the steps of her recovery. Her strength returned, and everything indicated the medicine was stabilizing the disease.

And then news beyond what we had hoped for arrived camouflaged in a normal white envelope. It opened just like the many other letters, but after only a few lines I knew this letter was special. Tests the first week of December and additional tests the second week of December indicated the tuberculosis was now inactive.

Her next letter brought even more good news. The doctors were going to allow her to come home Christmas. After thirty days she would be retested. If the tests were still negative, she would be fully released.

I couldn't contain myself. I told Carl of our plan—we intended to adopt him after my mother was released from the sanitarium. Carl hollered so loud, my ears rang. Sure, time does fade memories, both the good and the bad, but I'll never forget the look on Carl's face. This was nearly more than he could handle.

After three years at the orphanage, I was going home. All the boys on the third floor wished me luck, and told me not to forget them. Even Jeff gave me a high five, said he was proud of me, and that I'd be missed. We kept the possibility of adopting Carl to ourselves. We thought that might be too much for the others to take, all at once.

There is no doubt those weeks at home with my mother were special, so special that it's rather difficult bringing then up now. Carl stayed with us from Christmas until New Year's. On Sunday we visited the little Baptist church around the corner. After the service the pastor brought my mother down front and the congregation filed by, shaking her hand and welcoming her back.

No More Letters

Mother and Carl talked and talked and talked. He told me I had a great mom. She confided that Carl was a keeper. Mother had already discussed the adoption with an administrator, who assured her that it would not be a problem. It's funny—I called her Mother, and Carl called her Mom.

The day after New Year's, Carl returned to the orphanage; he had to go back to school. And speaking of school, I started attending a new school near our home. Although I didn't know a kid at Skyview Elementary, it didn't matter; Carl would be joining me soon.

I was excited as I hurried to get ready to start my second week at Skyview Elementary. Mother was going to drop me off, drive back to Oakville to sign the release papers, and pick me up after school. Both the x-rays and skin test taken the week before had come back negative. Nearly three years to the day, she was being fully released.

I watched my mother as we drove to school. For the first time that I could remember, she looked healthy and in good spirits. I thought back to all the sickness and hardships my mother had to overcome. I felt like we'd wakened from a bad dream, opening our eyes to a fresh start as a family of three.

When she left me in front of the school, I stood and watched her turn the corner before heading up the stairs.

It was close to noon when the principal called my teacher into the hall. I watched their eyes and saw both looking at me. And then, they called me into the hall.

So much, too much, maybe a dream, more like a nightmare, but then a horrid fear—this was really happening!

My mother had been on her way back from Oakville on Highway 51, about twenty miles from Memphis, when a drunk driver crossed the center line at a high rate of speed, hit my mother's car head-on, and killed them both instantly.

* * *

"Oh, I just knew it was something bad," Mandy choked out. "I knew it, I knew it, but I didn't know it would be this bad."

Suddenly, Mandy was in my arms, crying her eyes out. So there we stood, embracing in the middle of Auto World as Mandy sobbed. Sure I felt guilty, but what was I to do? I couldn't skip over the most important event of my life.

"I'm so sorry," I finally said. "If you want, we can stop for a while."

"I had to know," Mandy mumbled into my shoulder. Then she stood back, sniffling, but looking determined. "Now I'll be able to better understand you. No, we must keep going. It's bound to get easier after this."

"If you say so," I said.

* * *

The funeral at the little Baptist church was too much for me to handle. It is pretty much blocked out of my memory. Carl was with me. She was buried next to my father.

Well, I thought that first day at Porter Leath was tough, but it couldn't compare to my return after telling everyone good-bye. The first week back, no one would talk to me. When I came near, they avoided eye contact, muttered a quick "Hi, Mark," and then moved away. Even Carl had little to say. His eyes were red and swollen—a sure sign of lots of tears.

No More Letters

Gradually, everyone started treating me normally. But now I carried the same tag as Carl and Jeff: permanent resident. And there was something missing—there were no more letters.

That first Sunday back, Carl asked, "Are you going to get ready to go to church?"

I didn't look at him. "I'm not going to church anymore," I said.

He stood and looked at me for a long time, but said nothing.

Carl continued to walk to church every Sunday. I started running while he was gone. I'd circle the inside of the chain-link fence that enclosed the orphanage.

It was the same orphanage with the same third floor with the same beds and, for the most part, the same kids. But it was different, now viewed with eyes that had lost all hope and a faith diluted by events that were beyond reason. Everything looked the same, but it was like a painting that changed drastically when viewed under a different light. Light exposes flaws. Someone turned on the light, and now everything looked flawed.

I went numbly through the day-to-day routine. As days went by, I felt my despair less keenly, thanks to Carl's ability to bounce back. He pulled me along with him.

We never talked about my mother's death. Both of us knew better than to go there. The treasures in the chest at the foot of my bed, whose value was greater than any precious metals or gems, now numbered four: My father's box of medals and ribbons, the United States flag from his funeral, the bundle of my mother's letters that represented three years of hope, and finally my mother's Bible. These were the things that kept what was lost from being forgotten.

Her Bible was chock full of hidden treasures scattered from Genesis to Revelation, waiting to be uncovered by the mere turning of a page. Any space free of print was fair game for the many petitions, references, poems, praise, and prayers my mother penned throughout the Book. It was as if she knew her notes would lead me to read the Scriptures while trying to understand the diary woven throughout the pages. If this was her plan, it worked very well.

We completed the seventh grade, and summer brought more trips to the opera. Unknown to me, this was the last year that kids from the orphanage would be exposed to the arts. Someone in a position of authority decided to cancel the practice, and with a stroke of a pen he denied that opportunity to all future orphans at the Porter Leath Home.

This last year, I couldn't deny that I loved the plays, especially the tragedies. I replayed the songs in my head when I ran. I'd long since realized that one did not need to understand the words. When the songs were tragic, I felt the despair, the hopelessness, the pain, the utter desperation echoing in my mind and radiating throughout my whole being. To this day, as I run, I can still replay those songs in my head.

Carl continued going to church, and I did not. Every Sunday, we replayed the same scene.

Carl would say, "Well, I guess I'll go to church."

I would reply, "Well, I guess I'll go run."

What Carl was really saying: *I am going to go to church just as I did before, and I want you to go, too. You need to go as much as I do; in fact, maybe more.*

What I was really saying: *I am not going to church. I'm still mad at God.*

* * *

No More Letters

"And are you still mad at God? Now, as we speak?" Mandy asked.

"Well, if truth be told," I replied, "I suppose I am."

"*Suppose* is no answer—either yes, or no."

I frowned. Boy, this girl would give me no slack. "Yes," I muttered.

Mandy reached out and took my hand. "It's not that I'm trying to be critical or judgmental. I'm trying to understand." She smiled tentatively. "Flag of truce?"

I returned the smile. "Flag of truce," I replied.

"Thank you." As we resumed walking, she said, "When I was much younger, I was mad at God, too. I saw so many kids who needed so much, and we could provide so little. I asked God to do something, but He did nothing. I told my dad I was mad at God."

"And what did your father say?"

"He said that God would provide, but by *His* timetable, not mine. He said I should keep faith and pray, then God would respond."

"And did God provide?"

She bestowed that wonderful, warm smile on me again. "Always. Time and again, but never the same way. But now, I should let you continue."

"Okay." I tried to remember where I left off. "Ah, yes . . ."

* * *

Jeff graduated from high school and spent the summer lifting his weights, waiting on his birthday. Carl and I started the eighth grade. On his eighteenth birthday, Jeff joined the Marines.

During his last week at the orphanage, Jeff took each one of us to one side, offered his advice, and told us goodbye. I don't know what he said to Carl; we never talked about it. But I remember exactly what he said to me.

"Carl is the strong one, like me," Jeff told me. "But you're the tough one. Carl will protect and look after you in high school, but you'll need to be his guide and not let the wrong people influence him."

"How can you think I'm tough?" I asked. "Carl is twice my size."

"Size has nothing to do with it," Jeff replied. "Mentally, you are the toughest kid at the orphanage, me included. You take the worst life has to offer and hold it inside, never sharing it, never asking for help, never backing down, never giving in; always staying in control, and then you move on."

On his last day at the orphanage, Jeff gave his weights to Carl and passed to him the responsibility for our floor. Carl was now the biggest boy on the third floor, and all the kids fell under his authority whether they liked it or not. In turn, I made it my responsibility to insure Carl did not abuse his new position.

* * *

"What happened to Jeff after he went into the Marines?" Mandy asked.

"I don't know. We never heard from him again—no letters, no phone calls, nothing. It was as if he wanted to put the orphanage behind him and start life over."

"That's so sad," Mandy said.

"I don't know about sad," I replied. "Sure, he was missed, but we were glad for him, not sad."

Mandy thought about that, then nodded her understanding. "I'm sorry I interrupted," she said. "Please, continue."

* * *

My father had always said, "'You don't have to be the smartest in class to make the best grades. You just have to work twice as hard as the smartest."

No More Letters

At the start of the eighth grade, I decided to take my father's advice and work hard at making good grades. To my surprise, I started getting all A's. I made straight A's throughout high school, but my first year in college ended the streak. An F in freshman English was certainly a reality check—but that's jumping ahead.

By sheer willpower—my will over his power—I forced Carl to put more effort into school. To our astonishment, he started getting A's and B's. Was this the same guy who failed the third grade and had been on his way to failing a second time before he found out homework meant actually taking the book home? I was proud of Carl, but I was even prouder as I watched him instruct the younger kids on our floor on the importance of doing their homework.

At the end of the eighth grade, one other significant event occurred. With Marie's help, Carl and I were allowed to remain on the third floor, even though we were entering high school.

Chapter Eleven

Humes High

There, right in front of us, was the last auto theme area: *America's Cars of the Future.* Boy, the styles, the colors, the accessories—they were unbelievable! I extended my arm and opened the door of a candy apple red two-seater. As I prepared to climb in, I noticed Mandy. She was doubled over with laughter.

I stopped and stared at her. "What's so funny?"

"You are," she replied. "When you spied that little red car, your eyes lit up and I just knew you were about to climb in."

"So, what's wrong with that?" I asked.

She gave me a perplexed look. "Haven't you read the signs?"

"What signs?"

When she realized I wasn't joking, she said, "There are signs all over this building! They all say *Do not touch the cars.*"

"Oh, I didn't notice." I closed the car door.

Mandy grabbed the door, pulled it back open, and said, "Get in. I'll stand guard."

Humes High

I slid behind the wheel and imagined flying down the highway in this little beauty. After a few minutes of daydreaming, I came back to my senses and climbed out.

"Thanks." I tried to remember where I'd left off in my story. "High school—that's where we stopped."

"No," she replied, "that's where *you* stopped."

That tough act won't fly, I thought as I looked into those dark blue eyes, I just saw your true colors and you are a sweetheart.

***

Starting high school meant Carl and I could finally begin our football career. Numerous boys from the orphanage had gone from being just orphan kids to starters on the Humes High School team. And now it was our turn.

Carl and I spent many a night planning our emergence as star football players—Carl as a linebacker like Calvin, and I as a defensive back. Carl had long since convinced me that I was too small to be a linebacker.

Maybe I was the smallest trying out for the team, but I was also the fastest. We went through practice and more practice—Coach Mitchell believed if you couldn't get it right on the practice field, you'd never get it right during the game. Drills, plays, pushups, sit-ups, laps, and more laps; boy, was this fun.

With fall practice completed, game conditions stared us in the face. The inter-squad game, gray against gold, would determine who would make the team and who would be cut. Carl and I were both on the gold squad. Six ninth-graders from the orphanage—Carl, four boys from the fourth floor, and me—were trying out. All had been assigned to play defense, with me trying out for safety. Although Coach Mitchell tried to have Carl play defense tackle because of his size, Carl talked Coach into a fair shot at linebacker.

Humes always had excellent defense teams, and the inter-squad game ran true to form. There was little scoring with many excellent defense plays from both sides. Carl proved to be a force at his position, making solo tackle after tackle.

As the game drew to a close, I felt I'd made the team. I'd intercepted two passes—one in the end zone—slapped down numerous balls, and kept the man I was covering without a completion. I could already envision the coach starting two of his freshmen this coming year.

Then in the closing minutes of the game, the gray squad ran a play to Carl's side of the field. The running back faked left, then right, and Carl went for the second fake, missing clean. The back had an open field to the end zone, but I had the angle. He faked left and then right again, but I looked right into his chest and met him head-on. He dropped like a shot—or so they told me.

When I came to, I felt as though I were in a shallow stream, with the cool water running across my face. As my eyes cleared, I saw Carl towering above me, pouring water from a cup onto my face and praying out loud. I'd been out for more than five minutes.

I looked up at Carl and asked, "Did I stop him?"

"Yeah, you stopped him, all right," he said. "The difference was he got up, and you didn't."

After we'd showered and dressed, Coach Mitchell asked me to come into his office. Carl followed me in.

Coach said, "Son, you played a heck of a game out there. You have the quickest feet! I've never seen anyone change directions as fast as you. You covered our best pass receiver like a blanket and had him talking to himself." He paused. His somber gaze crushed my initial excitement. "We have one big problem. You're too small. I just can't take a chance on you getting hurt. You don't have parents—"

"Coach, I do have parents!" I blurted. "They just aren't living."

Coach regarded me for a moment, but not without compassion. "What I'm trying to say is, I have to deal with those Porter Leath administrators. They're looking for a reason to pull the boys from the orphanage off the team. I can't risk that happening. You understand, don't you?" As I opened my mouth to retort, he added quickly, "Son, you don't weigh a hundred and twenty pounds soaking wet. Why don't you go out for track?"

"Coach, I want to play football with Carl. If I can't play football, I won't go out for track or any other sport."

As we left Coach Mitchell's office, I said something in anger to Carl and learned a lesson that haunts me to this day. Words once spoken can never be retracted. One can say he didn't mean it. He can say he was just angry. He can make any excuse, but he can't retract a spoken word.

I said, "Carl, if you hadn't let that running back fake you and make you trip over your own two feet, I would've made the team. Don't you remember me telling you what Calvin said? Don't watch those running backs shuffle their pretty-boy feet. Look them right in the chest, and drill them between their shoulder pads."

Carl looked miserable. "I know. You're right; it was my fault. I should've made the tackle."

When we got back to the orphanage, I went up to the fourth floor and told the other ninth-graders that Coach Mitchell had cut me from the team. They gave me the real lowdown. Coach Mitchell wasn't going to let me try out, because of my size. If I were hurt, he would be in trouble with Porter Leath. Carl told him that if I wasn't

Running with Angels

allowed to try out, he would not only refuse to play, he would try to talk all the ninth-graders into quitting the team. While I was out cold, Coach Mitchell convinced Carl that I was too small.

I never told Carl I knew what he'd done. I told him I'd been angry and really didn't mean what I'd said. Carl said that it was okay, but he should never have missed the tackle. We left it at that.

I couldn't undo my words, but I learned a valuable lesson. Never say anything in anger. Words once spoken no longer belong to you. They are the property of the listener, and no matter what you do or say, you can't take them back.

Carl also learned something that day. Running backs could fake, shuffle their feet, spin, stop, start; it really didn't matter. Carl would drill them in the chest. Missed tackles were a thing of the past.

* * *

Many words and phrases could describe Humes High School. Outdated, worn out, aged, past its prime, ancient, and antiquated all come to mind. No matter how you say it, the school was old.

Yes, Humes was steeped in tradition, and many a graduate looked back at its hallowed halls with fond memories. In fact, one of those former graduates was the school's greatest claim to fame. There I sat in my ninth-grade homeroom class trying to adjust to the high school atmosphere, running my hands across the unfamiliar surface of the desk, and as I traced out five hand-carved letters, I realized what they spelled. I'd just discovered five letters of the alphabet arranged in an order that created the most famous word in the English language—E-L-V-I-S.

Humes High

It could be one of only two possibilities. Since Elvis spent four years at Humes before moving on to fame and fortune, it was possible that he knew the word *Presley* would not be required to identify the role this high school desk played in history. The other possibility was that some counterfeiter came along after Elvis graduated and, as a cruel joke, forged those most identifiable letters into the surface of the desk. I chose to believe the former over the latter.

So, my desk had belonged to Elvis. How was I going to live up to that standard?

Stories circulated around Humes about Elvis giving the school money to buy new band uniforms, new football uniforms, new ROTC uniforms, new curtains for the auditorium, and new whatever the school asked for, until the Memphis Board of Education saw the unfairness in this situation. It issued the following proclamation to Elvis: *Anytime in the future you wish to contribute to your former high school, the gift must be given to the Board of Education and then evenly divided between all the Memphis city schools.* So be it. The wise have spoken.

Long before Carl and I ever had the chance to benefit from Elvis's generosity, this unfair practice was stopped in its tracks.

We found high school gave us more independence, more responsibility, more work, more freedom, and more kids attending with us. There was less distinction between orphan kids and non-orphans. All grades mingled in the halls as the students sought their next classrooms. The pace was faster; more was required more often.

I adjusted quickly, but Carl struggled at first. We were no longer in the same classes, so Carl couldn't depend on me to tell him what needed to be done next. To his credit, he put in more effort and moved back to *A*'s and *B*'s after suffering through a rash of *C*'s.

The ninth grade brought new teachers, new classes, and new kids, but new did not always mean better. A boy named John Bradford ended up in nearly all my classes throughout high school. He wasn't from the orphanage, and no matter how you cut it; John was trouble. He was a freshman linebacker just like Carl, except he played the left side, and Carl played the right. I was correct; two freshmen did become starters on our football team—John and Carl.

John was a heavy hitter like Carl, with one big difference. Carl hit to make a good play. When John hit, he tried to inflict harm. Our team was continually flagged for hitting late or personal fouls based on John's tackles. It didn't take long to see he had a chip on his shoulder like the one Carl had when we met. He was a bully and never missed an opportunity to harass and torment his fellow classmates, with one exception.

All through high school John not only treated me fairly, but at times it appeared he actually backed down to avoid a direct confrontation. This puzzled me for years. I finally discovered why he treated me with such respect, but it would be jumping ahead. For now, I'll just say Carl made a speech to the entire football team during our freshman year, and it had a positive influence on John for many years.

* * *

"Jumping ahead or not," Mandy interjected, "please tell me now."

"Okay." I shrugged. "But it is jumping ahead."

Humes High

* * *

Right after being cut from the team, I looked for Carl in the locker room to see if he was ready to walk back to the orphanage. The next day, as the team was dressing for practice, John said, "I don't like that little shrimp hanging around the team. If he comes into our locker room again, I'm going to kick his butt."

Now, Carl would have none of this. He jumped up on a table in front of the entire team, seniors included, and yelled, "Listen up; I want everyone to hear and get this straight. If I ever hear of anyone on this team bothering Mark in any way, form, or fashion, I'll beat him to a pulp and then hurt him."

The room went dead silent. No one would confront Carl, not John or anyone else on the team.

I didn't learn of this until after we were in college. Meanwhile, John's behavior in high school always made me suspicious, though I could never put a finger on just why.

John and I were in the same shop class. As the end of our freshman year approached, we were all busy putting the finishing touches on our class projects. John still didn't have his project completely assembled. As he attempted to cut an angled section from his project, he accidentally twisted the saw. The wood split in half. I looked up just in time to see the saw fly into the air.

At the other end of the room, another boy had just completed his Philippine mahogany coffee table and was smoothing the finish with steel wool. Judging by the angle of its trajectory, that saw would either hit the boy in the back of the head, or hit the table.

"Look out!" I yelled.

The boy looked up and ducked just in time to avoid the saw, but it landed in the center of his table. With a flick of his wrist, John had destroyed the boy's coffee table. The shop teacher, Mr. Watson, was at the front of the room with his back to the class. He didn't have a clue what had just happened. Of course, no one would break the code of silence and squeal to the teacher on a classmate, including me.

To John's credit, he did apologize. I still remember the three carefully chosen words that acknowledged his fault and expressed his deepest regret and plea for pardon.

John said, "Sorry about that."

* * *

Mandy gasped. "Why was John so mean and bad-tempered?" she asked.

"Well, it took me many years before I could answer that question."

"Then I know your answer," Mandy said. "Jumping ahead—right?"

"Does that even warrant a response?" I countered. I grinned, then assured her, "Okay, and for sure I'll get there. But for now, back to high school."

* * *

In elementary school you are finding yourself, adjusting your values, deciding what you consider right and wrong, figuring out who you are and, most importantly, how you fit in. In high school fitting in becomes the most important issue. Kids hang with the kids whose values and attitudes closely match their own. For those who've not developed a strong will and character, their decisions and actions become governed by peer pressure. This is how they end up hanging with the wrong crowd and getting involved in activities that lower their standards.

Throughout high school John hung with his group, and Carl and I with ours. Well, it would be nice if I could say all the orphan kids stayed away from the wrong crowd, but that wasn't the case. For the most part, the younger ones followed Carl's and my lead, but the older ones had already found their place.

On the surface, high school is about getting an education, but beneath the surface it is about drawing lines between right and wrong and then establishing your identity. John had established his long before he met Carl and me, so we had little influence on him in high school.

Smoking, drinking, drugs—unfortunately these are a part of high school. They never tempted Carl and me, but there were other temptations. Girls were the most noteworthy.

There were girls in elementary school of course, but we'd been "those orphan boys," which made us lower than dirt when it came to attracting their interest. But in high school, Carl was the rising football star and I was his sidekick. The girls began to take notice.

Sometime during our freshman year, as I climbed into bed at lights out, Carl plopped down on the side of his bed and just sat there, staring across the room. He remained there for several minutes. I rolled over to watch, wondering, What's going on with Carl?

I was just about to ask when Carl turned toward me and said, "I need your advice."

"About what?"

After a long pause, Carl whispered, "Girls."

Like a shot, I was sitting on the side of my bed, wide awake. Of all topics, this was the one I was most interested in, but felt the most uncomfortable discussing. It was a topic about which I knew little.

Before I had time to collect my thoughts, Carl yelled, "Didn't you hear me? Girls."

* * *

I stopped and said, "Why are you laughing? This was no laughing matter."

Mandy tried in vain to stifle her giggles. "Sorry, I just found it rather cute. You go right ahead and continue. I'm very interested in what you have to say on this subject."

"First," I replied, "you've got to wipe that silly grin off your face."

"Consider it done," Mandy said, and bit her lip to keep herself from laughing.

* * *

Before I could respond, Carl rose and walked over to the window. He sat down and stared out toward the long drive. That was the very spot where we used to sit on Sunday mornings, watching for my father.

I joined him at the window. Before he could yell "Girls" again, I said, "Carl, that's a tough subject."

"Don't I know it," he said. "That's why we need to talk. I've seen you talking to that cute little cheerleader with the ponytail. Well, there are a couple of girls who have been . . . you know, kind of coming on strong."

Well, I didn't know, but I'd thought a lot about it lately. I cleared my throat, then said, "So the question is, how far do you go with a cute cheerleader?"

"Yeah," Carl replied, "especially if she has no respect for herself or her body."

Humes High

Boy, was this an awkward topic, or what? But, we somehow managed to be honest with each other and spent the next couple of hours discussing some sensitive issues. I'll spare you the details of this man-to-man—or maybe boy-to-boy—discussion. But the bottom line was, how much respect should you show a girl if she isn't looking for respect? We both agreed that mothers, sisters, and wives were women who demanded respect from all men, but what about a cute cheerleader?

After much consideration, we finally agreed it was wrong to take advantage of any girl.

* * *

"Oh, that makes me proud!" Mandy exclaimed.

"Sure," I replied wryly. "We had reached an agreement that would put us in the minority and test our willpower, but we both planned to stand by our convictions, lust notwithstanding. We'd decided all women were special and should be treated with respect." I chuckled. "Those were grand words to believe, but it took a day-to-day commitment to honor them."

* * *

By the end of the tenth grade, one thing was obvious—our football team had greatly improved. We had the first winning season in ten years, a defense that was difficult to run against, all starters on defense returning the next season—no wonder everyone was saying, "Just wait until next year!"

Carl received rave reviews in the Memphis paper for the upcoming season, but so did John. Both could flat out play defense. But who was better? From the classrooms to the halls, the debate ran: John, or Carl? How could anyone pick John over Carl, I thought, but I knew my opinion was biased. During one game the opposing team would run their plays to John's side of the field. John would have a great game and make the tackles. In the next game the team would run to Carl's side and Carl would have the great game. The word was out—you can't run against that Humes defense. There was talk of Humes challenging for the city championship the next year.

By the time we started the eleventh grade I was tired of running inside the orphanage grounds. I asked permission to run outside the gates, but the request was denied. Marie intervened on my behalf, and I received permission to leave the grounds as long as I signed in and out.

I rose early and ran in a different direction away from the city each Saturday morning. I grew to cherish my new freedom. I'd run for an hour straight out from the city, then turn and run back.

On Sundays I'd get up with Carl and leave as he started to church. He would still say, "I'm going to church," and I would reply, "I'm going to run." We had an understanding that held up over time.

During the first week of school in our junior year, the track coach—I don't remember his name—asked me to come out for track. I politely declined.

"That's what Coach Mitchell told me you would say," he said. "Have you run in any of the road races sponsored by the Memphis Runners Club?"

"No," I replied, "I've never heard of the Memphis Runners Club or their road races."

He explained that the races were for runners aged fifteen to sixty-five, or older. Everyone raced together, but you only competed against those in your age group. The groups were broken up in five-year increments—fifteen to nineteen, twenty to twenty-four, twenty-five to twenty-nine, continuing to sixty-five and older.

Now, this interested me. I'd be running for myself, against kids my own age. I had one problem, though. How would I get to and from the race?

As usual, Marie came to the rescue. So, one Saturday morning at Overton Park, I nervously waited for the starting gun along with about two hundred other runners.

Bang! We were off. During the first one hundred yards, I picked my way through the slower runners. Then the pack quickly thinned out, and I just had to find my pace. Marie and Carl were waiting at the finish line as I completed the ten-K course. To my surprise, I came in second in the fifteen-to-nineteen-year-old division.

I gave the small trophy for the second-place finish to Marie. It was the first of many I would hand over to her. To me, the race was everything; the trophies were unimportant. But to Marie, each one was like a new treasure.

The way Carl and Marie reacted, you'd have thought I won the whole race. Before I could catch my breath, they were plotting strategy for my next race. I listened patiently as they presented their ideas on what I should do next time.

This was all well and good, but I noticed all the runners had fancy running shoes. I had only high-top tennis shoes.

Two days later an administrator came up to the third floor with two new pairs of size-eight Asics running shoes. Again, Marie had come to my rescue. I never ran in tennis shoes again.

She also became my unofficial coach and, when I joined the Memphis Runners Club, she studied the road racing schedules and knew the date, starting time, and distance of every race on any given weekend.

Running with Angels

Usually, Saturday morning found just the three of us at the race. But every so often, an administrator from the orphanage accompanied us. This made Carl and me uncomfortable, but Marie made sure we stayed on our best behavior. She didn't want us to do anything that might cut off our supply of running shoes.

Carl attended each and every one of my races, and I was at each and every one of his games.

Humes had a great season, our junior year, winning all but the last two games. In the South Side game, John was ejected in the first quarter for fighting. Instantly, South Side was able to move the ball, scoring a touchdown before our defense could make adjustments. We went on to lose the game. As the game ended, I actually found myself feeling sorry for John.

Ejection, touchdown, first lost—it was plain what everyone thought. But to my surprise, instead of blaming John, Coach blamed the rest of the team. "Truly great teams overcome all obstacles and rise to the occasion," he said. After some thought, I realized Coach was right.

With only one lost game, Humes would play long-time powerhouse, Central, for the city championship. *Underdog Humes Against Mighty Central* proclaimed the newspaper headlines in the sports section.

It was a great defensive game. Neither team could move the ball. Late in the fourth quarter, it was still scoreless. Then, in the closing minutes, Central's kicker put a fifty-yard field goal right between the uprights. Our season ended with a three-nothing loss in the city championship game.

Everyone left the locker room except Carl, who sat in full uniform with his head hanging down, staring at the floor. I knew exactly what he was thinking: as a team,

Humes High

they'd let everyone down. This was going to take all my skills of persuasion.

"Do you consider me a failure if I don't win every race?" I asked him.

He looked up. "Of course not."

"So, should you consider the team a failure if you don't win every game?"

Carl said nothing, but I could tell I'd gotten through. It took a few days, but soon he joined the others in saying, "Just wait until next year."

* * *

I jumped as a booming voice announced, "Auto World will be closing in fifteen minutes."

I looked at my watch. "Mandy, do you realize it's nearly six o'clock? We have to call Kim and Janice to come and get you. I need a *To Be Continued* sign."

"No, you don't," Mandy replied. "Let's go to that new restaurant near the mall; it's open twenty-four hours a day. I'll call Kim and Janice and tell them we'll be at the restaurant until you finish. I don't care if it takes all night. Then you can take me back to my apartment."

"Are you sure?"

"Yes," she said firmly. "You're starving, right?"

Sure I was; it was nearly six o'clock and we had only eaten once. "Yes," I told her, "but I wasn't going to say anything about it. I'll call Babu and let him know."

"You can eat and talk through the night," Mandy said as we left Auto World. "I've waited patiently, right?"

"Right," I replied.

"So far, so good," she said, "but now that I'm so interested, you're not going to stop in the middle."

As we drove to the restaurant, I couldn't help thinking, So, we've gone from a casual meeting to what might be considered an actual date, and now here she is talking about spending the night together.

I didn't share these thoughts with Mandy as she sat beside me, so prim and proper. I didn't think she would find the situation as humorous as I did.

She talked while I ate, but as soon as I finished my last bite, I resumed.

* * *

So much happened during our senior year at Humes, it's hard to know where to start. In scheduling my classes, I'd somehow failed to take U.S. history; so there I was in the twelfth grade taking a tenth-grade history course. True to form, John Bradford sat next to me. All through high school, Carl and I were never in the same class, but not so with John.

It took less than a week for John to get into trouble. Right in front of the teacher he backhanded a guy who accidentally sat in his chair, and knocked him right out of the seat. John got a three-day suspension, but that was rather typical.

A week later, we had our first test. It contained one hundred questions. I'd studied, so it wasn't a big deal. Apparently no one else had cracked a book. The next day our teacher passed out the graded papers, then explained at length how disappointed she was in the poor performance of the class. Everyone had failed miserably, she said, except Matthews, who missed only two questions and made an A+.

To make matters worse, she went on to say she would've graded on the curve, but my grade eliminated that as an option. The grades would stand. This teacher was no friend of mine. In a matter of minutes, every kid in the class hated me.

As we left the room, two guys who were very proud of their leather jackets—they wore them regardless of the season—pushed me up against the lockers and described how they planned to kick my butt after school.

To my surprise, John stepped between us and said, "I'm going to give you guys some free advice. Of all the people in this school, this is the one guy you'd be wise to avoid."

I watched as fear transformed their faces, taking all the color from their skin. They both backpedaled away, stammering words of apology. John turned, strolled down the hall, and left me standing there with my mouth open. Was this the same John I'd known for three years?

I hadn't yet found out about Carl's speech to the whole football team in the ninth grade. Even after knowing about Carl's speech, I couldn't figure out what possessed John to come to my defense.

* * *

With Marie shuttling Carl and me to a road race nearly every Saturday morning, I moved my long training runs to late Saturday afternoons. I'd still run the twenty miles, but back off the pace if I'd raced that morning.

One of my favorite roads to run was Austin Peay Highway because it was long, straight, hilly, deserted, and usually void of traffic. It was anything but a highway. It ran parallel to Highway 51 to Millington and north to Oakville. Millington, a small town twenty miles north of Memphis, became a spot on the map when the United States Navy established a base there. How or why a Navy base ended up in West Tennessee, in a location devoid of water, is beyond me. I always felt the decision must have been politically motivated, but since it was a training school that didn't require ships, maybe its location could be justified.

On a Saturday afternoon in late August I'd just turned at my ten-mile mark and started back toward Memphis. In the distance, I saw a car weaving as it sped toward me. As it drew closer, I saw sailors hanging out the windows. Talk about bad timing! Suddenly, I tripped and tumbled toward the asphalt. Of all the times to fall on my face, it would be right in front of a bunch of sailors, I thought as I fell.

As the car passed, I realized a flattened aluminum beer can was heading toward me at eighty to ninety miles per hour. The can shot over the top of my head. I landed on the road with both hands and skidded along the pavement, removing hide in the process.

I lay on the ground for a few seconds, collecting my thoughts. I tried to make sense of what had just happened. Without question, the fall saved my life.

I went back and retraced my steps. The pavement was flat and smooth. I saw nothing that could have tripped me. I'd tripped on my own two feet. When we were younger, it was nothing for me to make Carl trip. But me? Never.

I continued the run back to the orphanage. When I arrived, I told Carl about the sailors, the beer can, and tripping.

He said the same thing I'd been thinking. "Mark, I've never seen you trip. What caused you to fall?"

* * *

"Yeah, that's what I want to know," Mandy interrupted. "Why did you trip?"

Humes High

"Well, that's a good question, but I have no answer. The whole episode left me with an eerie feeling. I searched diligently for an answer, but when I couldn't resolve the matter, I turned it loose."

* * *

The next Saturday we went to Overton Park for a ten-K race, but this one was different from any I'd run previously. The flier describing the race used the term *cross-country* instead of road race. We didn't have a clue what distinguished a road race from a cross-country race, but I soon found out, and it made perfect sense.

Road races are run on the road in straight north, south, east, and west directions. Cross-country races are run out across the fields in any and all directions. Someone had marked off the course for this particular race by spray-painting white arrows on the ground at irregular intervals. For most of the runners in the race, this wasn't a problem—they'd just follow the guy in front of them. But the leader had to continuously look down, searching for that next marker.

I'd won my share of races in the past year, but they were for my age group. I'd never led or been up with the leaders for a whole race.

Suddenly the starting gun fired, and a mass of humanity headed out across the fields, with me in its midst. To my surprise, I soon drew to the front of the whole pack. What was going on? I was running my normal pace, so why the heck was I in front of everyone? Before we reached the half-mile marker, it began to sink in. The leader had to find those white arrows painted on the grass.

About ten paces behind me, the famous Mahondro had settled into a comfortable stride, letting me find the markers. Mahondro was the elite runner of Memphis.

He ran in the twenty-to-twenty-five-year-old division. Not only did he always win in his age group, he usually won the whole race. He was tall, lean, and ran with an effortless stride. Never had I been near enough at the end of a race to see him cross the finish line, and yet, here I was running in the front. This continued for one mile . . . two . . . three . . . four . . . and finally five miles.

With a little more than a mile to the finish line, I led the race and still had to find every marker. At five and a half miles, Mahondro abandoned his comfortable pace and moved up to his rightful place as the leader of the race. He'd elected to take it easy, allowed me to do the dirty work, and now the victory would be his—only if I dropped dead during the last half mile. There was no way I'd let him pass after I'd had to find those stupid markers for five miles.

I picked up my pace. The race was on. With half a mile to go, we were both sprinting like we were in a hundred-yard dash.

I can't find the words to describe the pain. My chest was on fire. I couldn't get enough oxygen. I felt as if my lungs were about to explode.

Just about the time my mind started questioning whether there really was a finish line, I saw it, straight ahead. With less than a hundred yards to go, Mahondro and I sprinted side by side. Everyone was cheering. I felt like I was dying. Faster—I had to run faster! But how? Deep, deep inside, I must accept more pain. With that decision, I increased the pace and allowed pain to penetrate every living cell in my body.

Mahondro did not come with me. As I crossed the finish line, I glanced back to see him ten feet behind. I won! I won the whole race.

Marie and Carl were jumping up and down. I doubled over, gasping. Finally cool draughts of air began to reach my lungs and soon I could breathe. Next, I needed water, but as fast as Marie poured it down, I threw it back up. My chest slowly stopped burning, but I had stomach cramps for hours.

I bit my lip, attempting to hide my discomfort from Marie and Carl; they wouldn't understand. This wasn't easy, with both of them eyeing me closely. Mahondro came to my rescue when he wandered over and offered his congratulations.

"Matthews," he said—I'd no idea he knew my name, "that was a heck of a finish. I was sure you started your kick too soon and would give out, but instead of giving out, you had a second kick. That was too much for me. I was in too much pain."

I thanked him and tried to look cool. If he was in too much pain, where did he think I was?

I never ran another cross-country race. To this day, I avoid them. But I learned of a new pain level, a level where few will venture; therefore, if you go there, you win.

* * *

"Is it worth that much pain, just to win?" Mandy asked.

"No," I replied, "but if you go there to win, it clears memories that take weeks to return."

Mandy's delicate brows drew down for a moment, and she pulled on a lock of her hair. "I don't like it, but I understand."

This girl amazed me. No one had understood before, and now here was a girl who listened to my every word, absorbed it all in her tender heart, and actually understood. What could I say to show my appreciation of her willingness to listen to this relentless onslaught?

"Well," I said lamely, "I'm sure your childhood was next to perfect, so I hope this isn't too overwhelming."

Mandy shook her head. "I can see how you'd think that, but that's not the case. I've experienced nothing that can compare to the anguish and suffering you've endured, but my childhood was far from ideal. Sure, my parents are wonderful and my grandparents are a treasure. Their belief and faith have inspired me and instilled in me a love for Jesus and his work. But I grew up a lonely child. My whole childhood was spent in Third World countries. I've home schooled from the first grade to the twelfth."

I had to ask, "What is home schooled?"

Mandy smiled. "It means just what it says. All my schooling was done at home, with no classroom and no classmates. As far as education goes, it was great, but I never had kids my own age to talk to or play with."

"That's why you asked me about having so many kids to play with at the orphanage."

"Yes," she replied. "And all you wanted to talk about was boys fighting."

"Sorry," I said. "We did much more together than fight. We talked, played, planned, schemed, and dreamed. I can see how you missed a lot while growing up."

Mandy's smile faded. "Yes. I had no friends my own age until college. In college I made lots of girl friends, but no boyfriends. Every guy I met in college was pushy and arrogant, so I had nothing to do with any of them."

"So what about me?"

Mandy grinned and said, "Prideful and stubborn, yes, but not pushy or arrogant."

"So there's hope for me?" I pressed.

Mandy paused long enough to allow a heart-warming smile to adorn her face. "A lot more than hope," she said softly, then her tone turned brisk. "But we should get back to your story. I think we got side-tracked."

"Okay, let me collect my thoughts. I think I was about to get back to football."

* * *

After three games it was plain to see that Humes had a great football team in our senior year—three games, three shutouts. Our offense finally showed signs of improvement. But the real strength of the team was the defense. Seven of the eleven starters on defense were from the orphanage. That really made me proud, but then it hit me—no one from the orphanage had played offense in my four years at Humes. Why did it take me four years to see the obvious?

Carl wanted to play defense, I wanted to play defense ... but did every orphan want to play defense, for the last four years? I didn't think so.

I never told Carl or anyone else about this. I didn't want anything to detract from what they accomplished, but it was plain to me that, even though Coach Mitchell was a good coach and treated his players fairly, there was discrimination against kids from the orphanage.

The discrimination probably originated much higher than Coach Mitchell and was passed down to the coach as a suggestion. He was no fool; he knew not to rock the boat. He assigned the orphan boys to defense and left the more glamorous positions on offense to the other kids.

This year their plan didn't work. In the newspaper, the hallways, even the classrooms, our defense received praise. There was even talk of going through the entire year without giving up a point. Now, that didn't happen, but we did go through the year without allowing a team to score a touchdown on a running play.

The newspapers were already speculating about which colleges would sign Carl and John. This made me start thinking about how I could go to the same college as Carl. He would have a full football scholarship, but I'd be on my own.

Our fourth game was another shutout. And the next morning at 7:00 a.m., I was waiting for the start of the Jackson City Marathon. After the game Marie, Carl, and I drove the seventy-five miles up Interstate 40 to Jackson. We spent the night at a Holiday Inn, with Carl and me sharing a room. This was the first time we'd stayed at a motel. A Porter Leath administrator gave Marie the money she'd requested to cover our expenses. "If you don't ask, you don't get," Marie said. She asked and we got. Boy, this was great.

The racing numbers were assigned based on our fastest time in a previous marathon. We lined up based on our number, lowest to highest. Since this was my first marathon, I was near the back of the pack with racing number 911.

Mom and Dad would be so proud—my first marathon. My racing number would go in the chest with my other treasures. Then, years in the future, I'd look at this number and fond memories would flood back.

The race started at Union University, wound through countless country roads, and ended back at the school. I nervously awaited the starting gun. What could be so tough about running a marathon—twenty-six miles, 385 yards? It was only six miles and some change longer than my normal Saturday training run. But, little did I know.

The gun fired, and we were off.

I kept telling myself, Don't go out too fast... don't go out too fast. Marie and Carl had hammered that thought into my head. "Be careful the first mile, and don't get caught up in the excitement," they'd said. "Stay within yourself. Run your pace. If you go out too fast, it will do you in later in the race."

I hit the one-mile marker within five seconds of my intended pace. I was going to be okay. I'd run enough races to know how to stay on pace and stay within myself.

Unfortunately this was not a typical fall day in Tennessee. The temperature and humidity kept rising. Before the race was over, both would top ninety. Well before the twenty-mile marker, I knew we were in for trouble. At the water stops, everyone grabbed two cups of water, pouring one over their head while drinking the other, but there was no way to get enough water with the high temperature and humidity. A lot of runners dropped out of the race after the first ten miles. Every bend in the road brought into view more runners walking or sitting on the side of the road, waiting to be picked up.

Okay, I was beyond twenty miles. I'd bear down for six more miles, and I'd be home free. During those next six miles, I found out what it would be like to run down to the gates of hell and back. I knew all about the term *hitting the wall*, but since I never ran beyond twenty miles, I'd never experienced it, much less experienced it at ninety degrees with 90 percent humidity. It was kind of like how Babu knew all about driving a car without ever having driven one.

When running, the body burns carbohydrates for energy. They are consumed quickly and give off a high level of energy. There is only one slight problem for distance runners. The body does not have the capacity

Running with Angels

to store enough carbohydrates to last any runner twenty-six miles. That is what makes the race a marathon. Near twenty miles, all runners will deplete their supply of carbohydrates.

This is where the term *hitting the wall* comes from. Either the runner stops, or the body must change gears and begin burning body fat from around the muscle. It's like a fine-tuned engine running on 130-octane aviation fuel switching to a low-octane diesel fuel.

Somewhere between the twenty and twenty-one mile marker, I hit the wall. This was a different pain than that experienced by running too fast at the end of a race. For finishing a race, the pain was more physical, more on the surface, sharper, and more isolated in the chest. This pain started deep within the very core of my being, radiated through every fiber, and seeped into my mind, attempting to destroy my will to endure.

I felt like I was being eaten alive from the inside out, like a squad of flesh eaters had launched an all-out assault from within. With only stomachs and mouths with razor sharp teeth, they searched my body for any substance that contained the prize—energy.

Muscle put up a fight, but weak fat offered no defense. The flesh eaters ripped the fat from my body, devouring it to supply the precious energy for the next step. As soon as that step was completed, energy was required for the next. The cycle continued for as long as I attempted to maintain my pace.

You will yourself to continue, but with every step you have to reaffirm the supply of energy necessary to take that step. It's a mental battle of will over matter. You will it, but does it really matter? For me, it mattered. I kept running.

It was one thing to hit the wall, but hitting it when the temperature was ninety degrees was more than most of the runners could withstand. They were dropping like flies all around me.

When I reached the twenty-three-mile marker, I remember thinking, Only three miles to go. But as soon as I passed the marker, I could no longer remember what mile marker I'd passed. At twenty-four and twenty-five, the same thing happened. I was confused. At twenty-six, I could see Union University.

Only 385 yards to go.

I turned into the drive. The ninety-degree turn caused cramps to form knots in the front and back of both my legs. By the time I crossed the finish line, they were so bad, I dove onto the asphalt to take the weight off my legs.

Carl ran out and rubbed my legs to work out the cramps. Marie stood bawling her eyes out. It was a rough day for my first marathon, but it wasn't over yet.

The university had a buffet set up for the runners. As I sat under a tree drinking water, Marie urged me to get something to eat. I went through the line, filled my tray with food, and was headed for a table when everything went black.

As I fell, I thought, I don't want to drop my food. I threw the tray toward the table, and passed out. I didn't see it, but Carl and Marie said the tray landed on one side of the table, slid to the other, and stopped without even spilling the drink.

Although I was out for only a couple of minutes, they made a big deal of it. They hustled me into an ambulance and with siren wailing, sped me to the emergency room, even as I protested that I was okay. The emergency room was full of runners. We were all dehydrated. Nine pounds lighter and still a little light-headed, I waited my turn for two IVs of fluid, then I was pronounced fit and released.

To say Marie was upset would be an understatement. She asked me to promise to never run another marathon. I'd come in second in my age group and won a large trophy, but Marie didn't want it. When I suggested we leave the trophy, however, she changed her mind.

Instead of promising to never run another marathon, I promised to be better prepared and never run another in such heat. I said nothing to Carl or Marie, but I'd found a pain that could clear your mind for a very long time. And I did save my number, but instead of bringing back fond memories as I'd imagined, it brings back memories of a traumatic and difficult day. One to be marked on the calendar, because on that day I was viciously attacked from within but managed to come through it stronger and with more resolve to overcome any and all adversaries.

I've run fourteen more marathons since the one in Jackson, usually two a year. For me, no two have been alike, except all had their share of challenges. I ran one of the Memphis Federal Express marathons in a blizzard, with snow, sleet, and winds gusting from twenty to forty miles per hour. When I crossed the finish line, I had no feeling in either arm from my shoulders to my hands.

In the Boston marathon we ran straight into a headwind with a driving rain for the whole race. When I reached the hills at twenty miles, my shoes were so soaked, they felt like they weighed twenty pounds apiece.

In the Dallas Whiterock marathon, somewhere during the race I split a tooth from gritting my teeth. I didn't know until after I crossed the finish line, because the pain from the race masked the pain from the tooth. Once

I stopped and felt the cold air circulating on that open nerve, I made an emergency visit to the dentist to have the tooth extracted.

In my first Detroit marathon the race started in Canada, in a park in Windsor. We ran three miles to a tunnel under the Detroit River, through Detroit city, out into the suburbs, looped back, and finished in downtown Detroit.

At twenty-three miles, a guy waited impatiently in a Volkswagen beetle for a steady stream of runners to pass. A policeman was at the intersection with his arm extended in the universal signal to stop. The driver decided to ignore the policeman and darted across the intersection between me and a group of runners. He miscalculated either his acceleration or my speed, because we met in the middle of the intersection. As I realized I was about to be run over, I rested my left hand on the hood of the beetle and vaulted over the front of the car. I never broke stride, but the impact jarred my wrist, and by the time I reached the finish line, it was swollen double.

* * *

"What happened to the driver?" Mandy wanted to know. "Did the policeman arrest him?"

"I don't know. I looked back and saw the policeman pulling the driver out of the car by his shirt collar. The policeman looked very angry. I kept running."

Mandy looked at me incredulously. "I just don't understand why you continue to run marathons."

"They give me purpose," I said. "They give me something to live for, something to reach for. They justify all the long, hard training runs. For any runner, if you run them to your maximum ability, nothing is more difficult, but nothing is more rewarding. The pain clears your mind, and you finish with a sense of accomplishment that transcends all areas of your life."

Mandy still looked doubtful. I continued. "I'm not saying marathons are for everyone. They damage you physically. It takes up to three months for your body to fully recover from a marathon."

"Yes," Mandy said dryly. "I vividly remember the details of those little monsters eating away at your flesh."

"Okay, maybe I got a little carried away with the details."

"A little?" Mandy countered, "How about a bunch! It's a good thing I wasn't eating dinner; I'd have lost it."

Boy, she was right. I wanted to put her at the twenty-mile mark and let her experience hitting the wall. Well, I'd accomplished that, perhaps too well. "I get the point. Sorry; it won't happen again."

"Stop looking so sheepish," Mandy replied. "What about Carl? Did he try to talk you out of running marathons?"

I shook my head. "Marie tried to get Carl to persuade me to change my mind, but he said, 'You've known Mark as long as I have. Do you really think anyone on this planet is going to talk him into anything?' Marie agreed.

"Now, with Jackson behind us, I'll get back to football."

* * *

There were no two ways about it—we had a heck of a football team. Our defense was unbelievable. Game after game the opposing team would be shut out or held to field goals. But, there was another school in Memphis winning all its games, too. The city championship featured two undefeated teams, Central High School and Humes High School. This year the headlines on the sports page didn't refer to Humes as the underdog, but

Humes High

proclaimed *Powerhouse Humes Against Reigning City Champs, Central.*

Carl had a great game; John had a great game; the whole defense played a great game. Humes completed our senior year undefeated. Both John and Carl were selected all-city and state. The newspapers continued to speculate about which college had the inside track on signing them.

John committed early and signed with Memphis State. He had no choice. His girlfriend was going to attend Memphis State on a cheerleading scholarship. But Carl waited to see what I was going to do.

A few months earlier I'd asked my homeroom teacher, Colonel Hampton, how to study for the upcoming SAT test. Colonel Hampton, who was retired from the Marines, was one of my favorite teachers. I had him for general science in the ninth grade, chemistry in the tenth grade, and biology in the eleventh.

He thought about my question for a moment before responding. "I can only speak for the science portion of the SAT. Take this book, and read it from cover to cover, just like a novel, right before you take the test." He handed me my old chemistry book from the tenth grade.

I took his advice and read it from cover to cover.

When our SAT results came back, John barely passed the NCAA minimum requirements, Carl did better, and, thanks to Colonel Hampton's advice, I made the highest score in the state on the science portion of the test. What I didn't know at the time was that a company in Memphis, Southern Boiler Maker, had offered a four-year engineering scholarship to Memphis State University to the student who made the highest score on the science portion of the SAT. When I found this out, like John, my choice had to be Memphis State.

Running with Angels

I worried about Carl. When he found out, he would want to go to Memphis State with me. I wanted that too, but was that really the best place for Carl and his football future?

Sure enough, as soon as he heard the news, Carl wanted to call and tell the newspaper he'd be signing with Memphis State. I worked hard to persuade Carl to first discuss the pros and cons of his decision. He kept asking what there was to discuss. If I went to Memphis State, then he'd sign with them.

I asked him why he'd talked so much about the University of Arkansas, those razorbacks from the southwest conference, for the last two years. He finally admitted that would be his first choice, if I were not part of the picture. It took hours to convince him to consider what would be best for his future.

We stayed up half the night, but finally Carl agreed to sign with the University of Arkansas. I promised to attend every Arkansas home game.

Everything was set. We were ready to leave the orphanage and start our college careers, but we had one thing left to do before we said our farewells to Porter Leath.

Carl and I had watched Doug for months. He was only in the eighth grade but he was already bigger than me; Carl said that wasn't saying a lot. Doug seemed to treat the younger boys fairly and never picked on anyone. We decided he was our best choice.

One night during our last few days at the orphanage, we told Doug we wanted to talk to him. He was a little nervous, but he listened as we explained our plan: How would he like to stay on the third floor and look after the younger boys?

He agreed enthusiastically.

Humes High

We stressed that this was not a role to be taken lightly. He would be responsible for keeping order on the floor and he'd have to treat everyone fairly.

He wanted to do as Carl did—play football and help the younger kids stay out of trouble.

He didn't need to say anything else. Carl gave him Jeff's weights.

On our last day at Porter Leath, we told Marie about Doug. She said we'd made a good choice; she would get it approved.

High school was behind us. We were headed to college.

* * *

Mandy looked thoughtful. "You said earlier that you got straight *A*'s throughout high school. Were you the valedictorian of your graduating class at Humes?"

"No," I replied, "another boy in our graduating class had straight *A*'s and a four-point GPA. Winston Goldsmith III was chosen to give the valedictory address. As you can tell by the name, he was Jewish. Carl felt being from the orphanage put me at a disadvantage, but I disagreed. Winston was very smart. We were in a number of classes together. I worked hard to make my grades; he didn't. He was a gifted student. He went to a college in New Mexico and is now a doctor, just like his father."

My stomach rumbled. Mandy eyed me with raised brows. "Before you move on to college, would you like to eat again?"

"That's a great idea," I replied.

"First answer this question," Mandy said. "How do you eat so much and stay so little?"

"If you really want my opinion, I think it's all attitude."

Her brows fell; now she looked bemused. "What do you mean, attitude?"

"Well," I replied, "a lot of people become attached to food, as if it's their best friend. They treat it like a reward when life is good, or use it to take their minds off their troubles when life is bad. I don't become so attached. To me, it's fuel, pure and simple."

Mandy laughed. "Eat your fuel, and then we'll continue."

I thought about this lengthy narrative as I ate. Who would have imagined she wouldn't allow me to use a *To Be Continued* sign? And to be honest, I didn't want one. Once begun, my words seemed to flow and flow and flow. Nothing was contrived, schemed, designed, or diagramed; my account was just stored memories that flowed one after the other, effortlessly. Not fiction, fable, legend, or myth, just plain and simple memories that, to be sure, were difficult at times, but the worst were behind us.

As I pushed my empty plate away and prepared to continue, there she sat on the edge of her chair, eagerly awaiting the next wave. She'd already endured hour after hour of this bombardment, but still she waited impatiently for the next round. Truly amazing; this girl was truly amazing.

So, I continued.

Chapter Twelve

Memphis State

Memphis State University—so maybe it wasn't the Harvard or Princeton of the South, but it was an excellent school, and I am proud to be counted as one of its graduates.

Even so, I must be truthful and admit that there were rough spots during my first semester. On my first day in freshman English, who do you think walked through the door? None other than John Bradford. Here we go again, I thought; John's in another one of my classes. But this time it was going to be different.

I quickly realized that something was not right about this English class. First, there was not a girl in the room except for the teacher, Mrs. Fox. Second, every guy in the class was huge. And we were studying English at an elementary school level. "See Mrs. Fox run. See Mrs. Fox jump. See Mrs. Fox roll over." This was too easy. I could put English on cruise control and concentrate on my other subjects.

So you made A's in high school English. Just wait until you get to college. It quickly became obvious that these words of wisdom offered by so many had been only a scare tactic.

As I was leaving the third class, Mrs. Fox called me over and asked, "Matthews, you are on scholarship, aren't you?"

"Yes, I am."

Why did Mrs. Fox ask the question, and why did she look so puzzled by my response?

As our next class ended, she motioned for me to remain, and said, "Matthews, could you stop by my office?"

Call me innocent; call me stupid; I was still clueless. An error in paperwork, a correctable problem, nothing to worry about, a minor schedule adjustment, for athletes only—these were a few of Mrs. Fox's explanations while justifying my reassignment to another English class. I was on an academic scholarship, not an athletic scholarship. She didn't have to hit me on the head with a hammer handle; I fully understood. This was a special English class, whereas I needed a regular one.

Don't take this wrong. I understood and accepted being reassigned. I had a problem with the 7:00 a.m. class taught by Mrs. Maloney, sometimes referred to by fellow classmates as *Baloney*. She was on probation for failing every student in her class the previous semester.

The only materials required or allowed in her English class were a pen and a blue theme book. She would write a topic on the blackboard, then we would write a paper on the topic. She graded the papers and returned them at the beginning of our next class. She showed no favoritism; we all received the same grade—*F*.

On days when we didn't write the paper, she lectured on creative writing. At the start of the semester there were twenty-five students in the class but by mid-term there were less than half that number. At the end of the semester only five students showed up to take the final

Memphis State

exam. I guess we though she might pass the few who endured until the bitter end. Not one student passed the course.

Straight *A*'s in school were a thing of the past. I still made *A*'s in college, but they came with some *B*'s and even a few *C*'s. My father's theorem that the input of hard work generated an output of success was shaken to its core. After much thought and re-evaluation of his vision for success, I concluded that it was a principle to live by, but could no longer be considered an absolute law. There is some point on the graph where hard work must meet up with ability. Without that juncture the line will flatten out and no longer continue to rise.

Fortunately, that first semester, five A's with the one *F* kept my grade point above a 3.0 average; I didn't lose my scholarship. I did have to explain how I managed to combine *A*'s with an *F* in English, though.

John passed his English class with a C. I was pleased for him. In following Carl's football career through high school, I knew how hard it was to play football and excel in the classroom. And although John was well prepared for the college football field, he wasn't prepared for the classroom. He struggled and needed help adjusting to the demands of performing in class. Classes like Mrs. Fox's English might do as much harm as good, since not all teachers would bend the standards.

Another incident occurred during our first semester that caused the school to rewrite one of its rules. At Humes, football players did not have to take ROTC. At Memphis State this wasn't the case. All incoming freshmen were required to take two semesters of ROTC. I had two years of ROTC at Humes, so I knew what to expect in our first college Air Force ROTC class. Unfortunately, John wasn't as well informed.

On the first Wednesday of our freshman semester, everyone taking ROTC met on the parade grounds in full uniform. There was confusion everywhere, since many hadn't taken the program in high school. The massed students laboriously assembled into a crude formation. I fell into the front rank of a group that looked as if they halfway knew what they were doing. Everyone found a place, and it was a matter of straightening the ragged lines into a formation of the troops.

Out across the parade field, I spotted a guy meandering toward the formation. As he neared, I realized it was John.

At first I thought the sun and bright reflections played tricks on my vision. As John strolled nearer, I could see that he had not properly dressed for the occasion. His hat was on sideways; instead of pointing from front to back, it pointed from left ear to right. The sleeves of his unbuttoned jacket were three or four inches too short. The tie wrapped around his thick neck wasn't tied. His pants were shorter than ankle-beaters. His untied shoelaces dangled in the wet grass.

Taken aback by John's appearance, I belatedly realized everyone else was watching him too, including the senior cadet colonel standing in the middle of the field. I watched as the cadet colonel's expression changed from shock to disbelief.

The cadet colonel was the epitome of proper dress. Sunlight glinted on the leather bill of his cap, the many brass buttons adorning his fine tailored uniform, and the spit shine on his shoes. The guy wore his uniform with pride.

The cadet colonel took off at a double time pace towards John. As these two opposites approached one

Memphis State

another on their collision course, I leaned out to witness the confrontation.

John had settled into the front rank. The cadet colonel was in John's face with his mouth moving a mile a minute. The leather bill of his cap bounced above the tip of his nose, keeping beat with the rise and fall of his jaw.

With a suddenness that even took me by surprise, John's fist landed squarely on that moving jaw. The cadet colonel's feet lifted off the ground, and the backside of that immaculate tailored uniform landed in the wet grass. The poor guy never saw it coming. He was out cold.

John broke one of the Ten Commandments of the military—never strike an officer. They escorted John from the field and subjected him to the ultimate punishment, ejection from ROTC. Without fanfare, football players were exempt from taking ROTC the following semester.

As for football, both John and Carl became starters their freshman year. I promised to attend Carl's home games, but Fayetteville, Arkansas, was over three hundred miles from Memphis. I had money left from selling our house—not a great deal, but enough to buy a one-year-old car with less than ten thousand miles on the odometer. I drove it during the four years I attended college and the first two years at GMI. In all, I put more than 150,000 miles on that car without a major repair, just tune-ups, tires, batteries, brakes, and such. Not only did I attend all of Carl's home games for the four years, I drove to a lot of their road games, too, especially during his junior and senior year.

Carl came to Memphis and attended my races whenever possible. During football season he attended infrequently, but when the season was over, he came down every other weekend. Carl didn't have a car, but he never lacked for transportation. Everyone associated with the University of Arkansas football team, from players to coaches, willingly loaned him a car.

We never visited the orphanage. We wanted the place to stay as we remembered it, the memories unaffected by changes in our lives. When Carl was in Memphis on a Sunday morning, he would still say, "Well, I'm going to church," and I would say, "I'm going to run." Then he drove to the orphanage, parked, walked to the Methodist church, attended the service, and walked back to the car.

* * *

I paused when I saw Mandy smiling.

"Let me get this straight," Mandy said. "Carl wouldn't visit the orphanage, but he parked at the orphanage, walked to church and, after the service, walked back to his car. Why did he do that?"

"I don't know. I think he was comfortable with it."

"I think you're right," Mandy said. "He was comfortable with it just like you were comfortable with the running."

"Maybe so."

"Did he ever join the church?" Mandy asked.

"No," I answered. "As far as I know, he never joined or became involved in any of their activities. He attended the services and listened to the sermons but stayed noncommittal."

"What about Marie?" Mandy asked. "She was such a good friend to you both. Did you ever see her again?"

I sighed. That stirred up a sad memory. "Marie was a true friend," I said. "She guided Carl and me through difficult times, and we're both grateful." I looked away.

Mandy caught my evasive look and concern darkened her blue eyes. She put her hand on my arm. "What happened?"

"Not long after we left the orphanage, she retired. During college we stayed in touch. Every so often, she showed up at one of my races. And then, our senior year, she stopped coming. We would still talk on the phone, but something had changed. Finally, Carl and I decided to pay her a visit."

Mandy's hand tightened on my arm. I drew a deep breath. "We found Marie bedridden, but her sister wouldn't allow us to enter the room. 'Cancer,' her sister said. 'She doesn't want her boys to see her in this condition.'"

Mandy gasped.

"We still talked on the phone, but avoided mentioning her illness. I guess she wanted us to remember the good times from the past and not her present condition. She passed away during my first year at GMI. Carl found out two weeks after her funeral, in much the same way my family found out about Calvin from the policeman. At Marie's request, her sister waited two weeks before calling Carl."

"Why?" Mandy asked.

"I don't know," I replied. "Maybe because she remembered my mother's funeral, which was bad, really bad. That's all Carl and I could figure. We honored Marie's wishes about not seeing her bedridden, but we would've been at the funeral, if only we had known."

"She was one proud lady," Mandy said.

"That she was, for sure." I fought back tears. "Carl and I lost a friend who helped shape our lives."

I thought back to all the things Marie had done for Carl and me. She was far more than just a friend; she was one of the answers to my mother's prayers. Marie was surely missed, but she'd never be forgotten.

With some effort, I put the memory behind me. I tried a smile. "Now, where was I?"

* * *

There are two events worth mentioning that occurred at the end of our first year. The first deals with running and the other with Carl.

I was in the middle of a long run down Austin Peay Highway one Sunday morning when a dark line of low clouds rolled into the area. I'd run in many rainstorms, but as this one approached, I could actually feel the electricity in the air. The rain burst from the clouds as lightning flashed all around me. I'd run in lightning storms before, too, but now the air felt charged, as if on the verge of exploding. The storm had darkened the sky, but the lightning flashed so frequently that it kept everything illuminated.

A brand-new ivory white Cadillac approached from behind me and slowed as it drew even. The electric window hummed down, startling me. There was never much traffic on Austin Peay Highway, especially on a Sunday morning. Amidst the booming thunder, I'd been unaware of the car.

The attractive young lady seated behind the wheel wore a beautiful white gown that looked even whiter against the black-leather seats. She leaned toward the window and said, "Get in. I'll get you out of the storm."

"I don't mind running in the rain," I said.

"I mean the lightning," she said. "I'll get you out of the lightning storm."

"It's okay; I'm not afraid of lightning."

She just stared into my eyes with a perplexed look on her face.

I continued my run.

Memphis State

Oddly, instead of continuing forward, she made a U-turn and headed back in the direction she'd come. I looked back long enough to see the car had neither a license plate nor drive-out tags.

As I continued running, I thought about the lightning and God. I felt a little like I was challenging God.

God, I thought, here I am, right in the middle of this lightning storm. This is Your chance. If You are real and out there, take Your best shot. Put one of those lightning bolts in Your bow and fire it right between my eyes.

Just as that thought crossed my mind, I heard a tremendous explosion. About twenty feet off the road, a large oak tree standing isolated in a field was split down the middle by a powerful bolt of lightning. The smell of charred wood reached my nose as I stopped and watched the two halves of the tree crash to the ground.

I felt strange, as if I'd ventured into an area where I didn't belong. I stood for a few moments and tried to logically figure out what had happened, but nothing would fit into my logical boxes, so I turned it loose without working out anything in my mind.

As I continued running, the rain stopped, the skies cleared, and the sun broke out from behind the clouds. When I arrived back at my car, I tried to put the incident out of my mind.

* * *

I paused and looked at Mandy. "You're the first person to hear this. I couldn't bring myself to tell Carl. I still don't understand just what happened that morning. I'll tell you this—I have been caught in lightning storms since, but I've never again challenged God to prove He is real."

"That's amazing," Mandy said, barely above a whisper. "It gave me goose bumps. It's so amazing, I need to start a top-ten list."

"Okay, put it on your list," I said. "But for now, I'll get back to Carl."

* * *

Both Carl and John played great as freshmen. I even went to some of Memphis State's home games on the weekends Arkansas played on the road. After the last game, Carl called and asked if I would come to their football banquet to see him accept two awards, one for being the most improved player and the other for being the outstanding freshman player.

Without a doubt, I'd be there.

On Friday I headed to Fayetteville in a hard rainstorm. I arrived at the banquet at six-thirty and immediately sought Carl amidst the players. All wore tuxedos. Since I'd never seen Carl in a tuxedo, at first I thought he was somewhere in the crowd and I just didn't recognize him. The banquet started at seven, and I still hadn't found Carl. By seven-thirty, I was concerned.

Then in walked Carl in his tuxedo, soaking wet. Grease smeared the front of his white shirt. He accepted both awards without saying a word. When the MC presented the last award, Carl headed for my table.

Of course I said those famous two words, "What happened?"

Carl tried to explain, but he was so excited, he talked a mile a minute. I caught only, "On the way to the banquet ... car on side of Interstate ... hood up ... family of five." He uttered all this without taking a breath.

"Carl, you're talking too fast," I yelled to get his attention. "Slow down, and start over." This did the trick. I finally made sense of his tale.

Memphis State

While on the way to the banquet, he spotted a car on the side of the Interstate with its hood up. Of course he stopped to assist. A family of five —father, mother, two daughters, and a son—had been driving to Fayetteville when their engine sputtered and died as the car coasted to a stop. The car had half a tank of gas, but it still wouldn't start. Working in the driving rain, Carl took a chain from the trunk, hooked it under their car, and pulled them five miles to the nearest service station.

"No problem, just a wet coil and wet spark plug wires," said the attendant.

Carl waited an hour, until the car ran okay and the family continued on their way.

The father was the pastor of a church somewhere between Little Rock and Fayetteville. Their oldest daughter, Rebecca, was just a year younger than Carl. She was the most beautiful girl he had ever seen. She had beautiful, long red hair, like his.

I teased, "How could her hair be beautiful and look like yours?"

"I mean it's *red* like mine."

I started to reply that his hair was orange, not red, but decided to just let it go. I was pleased that Carl had finally met a nice girl he really liked.

There was just one problem, he admitted. His awe immobilized his brain. He didn't know her phone number, her last name, the church name, or even its denomination.

"How are you going to get in touch with her?"

After I asked the question, he paused, rolled his eyes, and then shouted, "I'm going to visit every single church between Little Rock and Fayetteville."

He made a list and, week after week, visited each church on the list. This continued until football season began.

At the first home game, I leaned over the guardrail on the second level in the stands, watching as the players out on the field warmed up and prepared for the kick off. I yelled Carl's name at the top of my lungs, trying to get his attention to let him know where I was sitting, but he didn't hear.

Someone tapped me on the shoulder. I turned and saw an attractive girl with long red hair standing beside me.

She said, "Is the Carl you are calling Carl London?"

"Yes."

"And is your name Mark?" she asked.

By now I knew who she must be. "Yes," I responded, "and is your name Rebecca?"

It was like old home week. The whole family came to the game to see Carl play, and play he did. Arkansas' first game was against a team that ran the wishbone offense—one running play after the other. By the end of the fourth quarter, Carl had set a record for the most solo tackles in a SEC game. While Carl played his record-setting game, I met and approved his new instant family.

I've seen a number of things bring joy to Carl's face, but nothing compared to the way his face lit up when he saw us together after the game.

Not only did I continue to attend all of Carl's home games for the next three years, but Rebecca and her family attended every game, too. As for Carl and Rebecca, no one could be more suited for each other than those two.

Well, to make a long story short, Rebecca's father was the pastor of Missionary Baptist Church, located about

Memphis State

twenty miles from Fayetteville. It was on Carl's list, but so were a lot of other churches that he had yet to visit. Soon Carl joined the church and was baptized. Rebecca never lost an opportunity to invite me to visit their church, but I faithfully declined. Finally, Carl told her we had an understanding and she might as well give up.

Well, I did go once, but not for a service. But that's *really* jumping ahead. I'll stop and go back to the summer.

On a Sunday morning after the Fourth of July weekend, I started a long run on Austin Peay Highway. We were in one of those weather patterns where it stayed hot and humid, even at night. There'd been no rain for weeks. The temperature ranged between eighty and a hundred degrees, sometimes climbing higher. The air was so thick and heavy it took as much effort to breathe as it did to run. With a sweatband around my forehead, no shirt, and the sun already bearing down on my back, I set a pace that took into account the relentless heat.

Out in front of me, dark clouds were rolling in and I could hear the faint sound of thunder. This occurred daily in the late evening, but without rain. This time, it looked like it meant business. With the dark clouds came incredibly cooler air. The rain couldn't follow too soon, as far as I was concerned.

I felt a stinging on my back. Instead of rain, the skies were dumping hail. I looked around and saw nothing but open road and empty fields in all directions. Boy, I was in for it this time.

Hailstones of all sizes fell around me as I ran, from the size of marbles to the size of golf balls. Huge ice balls bounced on the asphalt in front of me, behind me, and on both sides. I looked around. To my astonishment, a narrow band of smaller hailstones followed me down the road, matching my pace. It was like I had my own little private hail cloud dumping small hailstones on me while, all around, the big stuff slammed off the asphalt. This continued for what seemed like a long time, but was probably only three or four minutes. The storm stopped as quickly as it started.

Large hailstones littered the road, so many that I stopped running to keep my footing. As I walked I realized that, in this breath of time, I could have been seriously harmed. And yet, I'd made it through without getting my brains knocked out. Yes, I did feel as though I'd been shielded from real danger. Even after acknowledging that feeling of protection, I had trouble with this one. I couldn't fit it into a logical box, so I turned it loose. I kept it to myself and tried to pretend it didn't happen quite as I remembered.

* * *

Mandy looked annoyed. "So, anything you can't fit into your logical boxes, you keep to yourself. What are these *logical boxes,* as you call them?"

I thought about that for a moment. "I guess we all have a different way of understanding and handling what goes on around us. I'm most comfortable when I can fit events, problems, outcomes, conditions, results, and relationships into logical boxes and then fit those boxes together into logical patterns that form a logical solution. Once I have the logical solution, I tuck it away and accept it as fact.

"Math and computer programs fit well into this scheme. As I'm running, I can reassemble complicated math or computer problems in my mind, in logical boxes. It makes them easy to solve. Where I have trouble is with things that are not so logical."

"Oh," Mandy said archly, "do you mean things like the lady in the Cadillac, the lightning hitting the tree, the golf ball-sized hail, or maybe angels protecting you since your childhood even though you're too stubborn to admit it?"

"Yes," I replied, "but also things like God and war, God and human suffering, God and sickness, God and disease . . . "

"Well," Mandy countered, "what about Jesus, the cross, salvation?"

I hesitated, thinking. "No, I don't have trouble with that. If you are referring to the message of the New Testament, it makes perfect sense. Only God could develop a plan for salvation so faultless, so complete, so sound, and yet so simple even a child can understand."

"There's hope for you yet." She sounded relieved.

"I let you sidetrack me. I need to get back on target, or we'll never get through my story."

Was that a gentle smile on Mandy's face as she said, "Okay, go ahead. We still have the rest of the night."

* * *

During our second year of college, we fell into a routine. Both Carl and John became foundations for the improvement of their defensive teams. Each received rave reviews for consistent hard-nosed play, week after week. I continued to drive to each of Carl's home games. Rebecca and her family were there with me every week, rooting for Carl.

On weekends when Arkansas was on the road and Memphis State was at home, I went to the Memphis State game to see John play. Although we hardly spoke to each other, I still wanted John to do well.

Near the middle of the sophomore season, who do you think called me on the phone? Yeah, none other than John Bradford. Why would he call me?

Struggling in a couple of courses, might need a little help, how about it? This was the gist of our conversation.

With running six days a week, holding down a part-time job, taking fifteen credit hours of course work, and attending all those weekend football games, I already had a full plate. I wanted to tell him, "Sorry, too busy." But just the fact he called and the sound of his voice told me he needed more help than he admitted. We agreed to meet three times a week; I'd cut back on the part-time job.

He wasn't just struggling in a few of his courses, he was downright failing all of them. What had I gotten myself into? He needed more help than I could give. He needed Mrs. Fox to take over those classes. Since that wasn't an option, it fell on John and me to turn this around.

And turn it around we did. I have to give John credit. He was not your stereotypical, dumb football player. He reminded me of Carl, back when I first came to the orphanage. Now in his second year of college, John had never learned how to study. To my surprise, he really caught on fast. He had an excellent memory; he followed directions; and he wasn't afraid of hard work. By the end of the semester all his teachers were asking, "Who is this guy? Is this the same person who started the class?" John passed every course. Talk about proud, he was one proud guy. I was pleased, to say the least.

John and I never developed a close friendship. I helped because he asked and because we went to high school together. I didn't dislike John, but I didn't care for the guys he hung with.

Memphis State

I did ask him one question. Why did he take so many cheap shots when he was such a good defensive player?

His response left me baffled. "First, the referee is not going to call every foul. Second, when you play rough and dirty, it makes the offensive player so mad that it takes him out of his game. You get into his head, and he loses his concentration. Then he starts making mistakes."

I always thought John's rough play was due to extreme aggressiveness. I had no idea it was a planned tactic.

He volunteered one more of his strategies, which pretty much floored me. After a tackle that ended in a pile-up, John would bite the offensive player on the leg, but not hard enough to bring blood. This tactic guaranteed the attention of the offensive player.

This piece of information left me speechless. I tried unsuccessfully to come up with an appropriate response.

I helped John at the beginning of the next semester, but soon it became obvious that he no longer needed my services. At our last agreed session I finally had to ask one more question.

I said, "Do you remember that time in the hallway outside our history class at Humes, when you stepped in and defended me from the guys in the leather jackets?"

"Yeah, I remember."

"Why did you do that?"

"It was weird, real weird," he said. "I kind of heard this voice in my head."

"What? You kind of heard what?"

It never made any sense, he said, and he knew it sounded strange, but he heard this *Commanding Voice* that said, "Stop them from bothering Mark." So he did.

That was definitely not the answer I expected.

* * *

"Yes," Mandy said as she pulled on a lock of her hair, "and it is one worthy of my list."

"Speaking of the list," I said, "something happened the summer after our second year at Memphis State that might make the top."

* * *

It was another long, hot summer in Memphis, with no rain for weeks. On a Saturday morning I ran a race, then headed to Fayetteville to meet Carl and Rebecca.

I was late, nearly out of gas, and traveling a bit beyond the speed limit when I spotted an Exxon service station sign. As I pulled off the Interstate, it started raining. This was no light shower; it poured. The exit road went down a long hill to an intersection with a traffic light, and on the other side of the intersection, to the right, was my destination, the Exxon station.

Oil residue had built up on the road during the many weeks without rain, and the sudden rain floated the oil to the surface. The hill was long and steep, and I still hadn't slowed enough from my speed on the Interstate. The light at the intersection changed to red, and as I touched the brakes, the car's tires climbed onto the oil.

The steering wheel went from being a device for navigating to a brace I desperately clung to while the car spun in circles through the intersection. Round and round I hurtled, right through the red light with traffic flying past me in both directions. When I cleared the intersection, the car completed one last spin and continued skidding backwards. I turned around in the seat to see where I was headed. As if the car knew my intentions, it slid off the road into the drive of the Exxon station.

Not only was I going backward, but I was headed toward another vehicle in front of a full-service island.

Memphis State

Just as my car attempted to claim its rightful place in front of the pump, the other vehicle pulled away in the opposite direction. I came to rest perfectly aligned with the gas pump, in the exact position held by the car that had just left.

I still had my head turned, looking toward the rear of the car.

There, standing beside the pump with the gas nozzle still in his hand, was an elderly gentleman wearing an Exxon ball cap. He stared at me with his mouth open and eyes wide with amazement.

The only thing I could think to say was, "Fill 'er up."

We both broke out laughing. As he pumped the gas, I thought, This is going to cost big bucks. Here I was running on empty and having the tank filled at the full-service pump.

As I attempted to hand the attendant a twenty-dollar bill, he said, "Son, this one is on me."

"No, sir," I said, "I'll pay for my gas. Why would *you* want to pay?"

"Son, I am seventy-five years old," he replied. "I'm retired from the railroad, work at the station part-time to stay busy, and I've been a deacon at my church for more than thirty years. In all my years I've never witnessed a miracle. I not only just witnessed one, but I feel like I was part of it. I watched as you came down that hill too fast. I watched as the light changed to red. I watched as your car spun out of control through the intersection. I saw the two tractor-trailers heading in opposite directions through the intersection with your car in their path. I saw your car align to its narrowest position as the two rigs passed on each side. With just one extra coat of paint, your car would've been too wide to avoid contact. Not only did it align to its narrowest position, it seemed to pause as the two rigs flew by, then it continued spinning.

"I'm here to say someone was looking out for you today. Someone is watching over you for a reason. I want to pay for this gas so that I can feel a part of it. I can't wait to get home to tell my wife. Son, I don't know how many years I have left, but I'm going to pray for you daily until I meet my Maker in glory. It has been an honor meeting you."

I didn't know what to say. I thanked him and drove away without even getting his name.

* * *

"Did you also keep this to yourself?" Mandy asked. She sounded annoyed.

"Well, yes and no. I told Carl every detail about spinning through the intersection and sliding up to the gas pump. I didn't tell him about the man or our conversation."

With a look of flat-out disapproval, Mandy said, "And why not, may I dare to ask?"

"I didn't feel comfortable with it."

"You mean you couldn't tuck it comfortably into one of your logical boxes. Right?"

"I guess you could say that," I replied.

Mandy sniffed. "Just like I thought. You know, this one makes the top of my list."

"Yeah, I figured it would. That's why I told you. Another event similar to that occurred during our last year of college, but that—"

"I know, I know." Mandy waved her hand in dismissal. "You don't even need to say it."

"There's not a lot to go over between our second and fourth year of college. Remember Beth, John's girlfriend from Humes who was a cheerleader for Memphis State?"

Memphis State

"Sure, I remember you mentioning her."

* * *

During the summer before the start of our senior year, John and Beth were married. She was with child. I guess that's a polite way to put it. She dropped out of school for the fall semester and had a baby girl.

Now, this really changed John. He was crazy about his daughter and her mother. Soon, he stopped hanging with his drinking buddies and settled into the responsibilities of being a husband and a father. Carl and I were both proud of how John reacted to his new role.

John and Carl played great football during their senior year. Arkansas was in a battle to win the Southwest Conference and a major bowl bid. Carl was in the running for the Southwest Conference defensive player of the year. John didn't get the press attention like Carl, since Memphis State was not in a major conference and was having another average season. But, now as a married man, John stepped up his game and was the best defensive player Memphis State had seen in many a year.

By this time I'd become so involved with football, I cut back on my racing. Every weekend I attended a game—if not Carl's, then John's. Even on weekends when both Memphis State and Arkansas were on the road, I drove to whichever game was closer to Memphis.

This brings me to an event similar to the wild ride into the Exxon station.

Arkansas' last conference game was at the University of Texas. The winner would be the Southwest Conference champion, which meant they would play in the Cotton Bowl on New Year's Day. I couldn't miss this game. I left early on a Saturday morning and drove to Texas.

Texas ran the wishbone offense and ran it well. Carl was all over the field making tackles. Still, the outcome of the game would not be determined by Carl's defensive skills, but rather by his offense heroics.

With less than two minutes left in the game, Texas had the ball on our twenty-yard line. They had a six-point lead and were in the process of grinding out another touchdown to put the game out of reach. Then came the play of the game. Texas ran a play to Carl's side of the field with the halfback running the ball behind their big fullback. It was obvious to me that the fullback was about to level Carl and clear an open path to the end zone. Carl wouldn't get around the big fullback and have a shot at the running back.

I was correct. Carl met the fullback head-on. You could hear the collision all over the stadium. But, instead of flattening Carl, the fullback was driven back into the running back with such force that the ball was knocked loose, and after one bounce on the ground it landed in Carl's outstretched arms.

I would like to say Carl raced down the sidelines to score the winning touchdown, but that was not the case. He did score the winning touchdown, and to hear him tell it, he did race to the end zone. As I saw it, he rambled for sixty yards down the center of the field and, with three Texas players hanging on, he lumbered the last twenty yards into the end zone.

Arkansas won by one point and was the Southwest Conference champion. Carl was named the Southwest Conference defensive player of the year. But, after years of discussion, he still thinks he should have been named the Southwest Conference offensive player of the year.

With the game over, I could either check into a motel or drive straight back. Why waste money on a motel? At ten-thirty I started the nine-hour drive back to Memphis.

Memphis State

With the evolution of the modern Interstate you would think accidents on the highways would become a thing of the past. All traffic on one side flows along in the same direction. All traffic on the other side flows together in the other direction. With such vehicle segregation, travelers should be able to travel in harmony down the Interstate without hostility, conflict, or wrecks. There is one factor that prevents this theory from becoming a law or principal—the unexpected.

At 5:00 a.m. I was closing on Little Rock, Arkansas, at a speed in excess of eighty miles per hour. Up ahead an old panel truck sat on the right-hand shoulder of the road. As I rapidly closed the distance, the truck pulled out on the Interstate, crossed over into the left lane, backfired, and came to an abrupt stop. In a matter of a few seconds I went from being a weary driver heading down the open highway to being a driver who was within inches of hitting a stationary object at eighty-plus miles per hour.

I jerked the wheel hard to the right and nearly ran up under a truck driving in the right lane at about sixty miles per hour. I immediately jerked the wheel back to the left.

When a car is moving at more than eighty miles an hour, if you jerk the wheel hard to the right and immediately hard to the left, the centrifugal forces become confused, and the center of mass and the center of gravity shift into an unstable state. That is my feeble attempt to logically explain what happened to my car. The two tires on the passenger side lifted into the air, and the car balanced on two wheels at a forty-five degree angle to the road. The car knifed between the two trucks without touching either vehicle.

I looked back and saw that the car had gone between the trucks in a space that was only half its width.

I continued down the Interstate, riding on two wheels for the length of a football field. Gravity ever so gently took control and pulled the wheels softly down to the pavement. My first thought was that a stunt driver in the movies couldn't have done better.

As I reflected on those riveting few minutes, I realized that I'd had nothing to do with what happened. Yes, I was the one holding onto the steering wheel for dear life, but I wasn't the one in control of the vehicle. No, I never told Carl. Yes, I felt that protection, but nothing made sense, so I had to turn it loose.

* * *

"Well, I'll tell you one thing," Mandy said. "It made plenty of sense. You mean it wouldn't fit nicely into one of your logical boxes."

"Okay," I admitted, "it was another in a long line of events that are difficult to understand and even harder to explain."

Mandy declared loudly, "At times, I think you just don't get it. No matter the danger you entertain, you come out of it unscathed. Don't you realize this is not typical, common, or normal?

"When I was a teenager, I dropped a bowl, and it fell straight to the floor without pausing along the way to allow me to move my foot. It broke my big toe and hurt like the dickens. If you had dropped the same bowl, it would've stopped a few inches above your toe, hung suspended in mid-air, and waited while you moved your foot and contemplated how to fit this event into one of your logical boxes."

"Okay," I replied, "I get your point. Don't make fun of me."

"I'm not making fun of you. I'm just saying that so many miracles happen in your life, they've become nearly commonplace to you. I see them one after the other. You try to logically figure them out, and when that becomes too difficult, your solution is to push them from your mind. That doesn't dismiss them from having happened, and it doesn't matter whether you view it as divine protection generated by your mother's prayers or as a band of protective angels. It just allows you to accept those things that are perfectly logical and to run away from those things that are not."

"Okay," I said, "I understand what you are saying. Really, until talking to you, I'd never looked at all of this together. The truth is, there were many incidents that I skipped. I recounted only those I could recall in detail. Other things happened that I've half forgotten. I didn't place much significance in them individually, especially when I was younger. But I'm close to wrapping this up, so let's not dwell on the issue right now."

"Indeed, let's continue. I want to know what happened to Carl and Rebecca, and John and Beth. But," she warned, "we are not finished with these issues, that's for sure."

Chapter Thirteen

Graduation and Beyond

Well, it never occurred to me that what started out harmlessly enough would grow into a full-scale marathon—no pun intended. But I was pleased. We had made a night of it and, with daybreak approaching, all that remained were a few odds and ends. And to be sure, I had told my story straight and true.

Okay, maybe I'd included a bit too much detail about football. Since there was more to come, I asked, "Be honest; am I boring you with all this football talk?"

Mandy laughed and said, "Since you used the word *bored*, I shall defend myself from that accusation. I can tell you live and breathe football. And even though you were unfairly denied participation, you stayed involved through your friends. Now, do I understand American football? I don't think so. In fact, I've never seen the game played."

"Are you kidding me?" I blurted. "You never saw—not even one game?"

"I never had the opportunity, prior to college. And by then, I had no interest."

This was worse than I'd imagined. "Then all this football talk must have been confusing, to say the least."

Graduation and Beyond

Mandy studied me for a moment. "Well, I surely don't understand the rules. When you described carrying the ball and catching the ball, I thought that was illegal, but I guess the rules for American football are somewhat different than those for soccer."

"Quite different," I replied. "So you know the rules for soccer?"

Mandy's face lit up. "Oh, yes. I've been to countless soccer games. In fact, my dad and I have attended two World Cup matches."

Just when I thought I was gaining ground, she knocked my feet right out from under me. "At least you weren't bored," I said lamely.

"Bored? No. Fascinated? Yes. I enjoyed every minute you talked about football, even though I don't understand the silly rules." She shook her head, perplexed. "Who ever heard of catching or carrying the ball? That seems so unfair. But one thing is for sure, the game develops character, just like soccer, and that's a good thing. It had a positive influence on you, Carl, and even John, I think."

That I couldn't deny. This girl could see much that was hidden. How? I didn't know, but it was a fact that I now accepted. As for John, she didn't know the half of it. But, by the time I finished, the truth of her words would come to light.

I asked, "Is there anything else we need to discuss or clarify before I wrap this up?"

Mandy lingered as if in deep thought. "Remember when I said that I was lonely as a child?" she finally asked. "Well, I don't want you to think that I was also unhappy. Sure, I missed friends my own age, but the Lord provided much to fill the void.

"When I was quite young, I visited my grandparents during the summer. Gary would read children's Bible stories to me right before bedtime. Then, I would repeat the story but had to include myself as a character. Soon, I could include myself in any story. As I grew older this provided me with hours of enjoyment and a multitude of companions.

"And I always looked forward to our frequent visits to the surrounding towns. Every village had new friends waiting to meet me. While mom and dad were drawing the attention of the adults, I sought out the kids my age.

"When I was younger, we played without a care in the world. As I grew older the kids became more quiet and reserved. I studied their faces, looking for what was lost. Finally, I found it in their eyes. They had lost their hope. This made me sad. But, with each trip they listened more and more to my mom and dad. I watched their eyes." She paused and shook her head again, in wonder. "It was so wonderful. I saw it time and again."

"What did you see?" I asked.

"As they accepted the truth of God's word, I saw their hope restored." Her eyes strayed toward the window. "Do you realize it's daybreak?" she exclaimed. "We've talked through the night! Sorry—I got carried away. Back to you."

"Okay," I replied. "I think I can finish this up."

* * *

After four years of college life filled with both good and trying times, John, Carl, and I reached another milestone—graduation. With great expectations and a sense of accomplishment, we accepted our diplomas. Carl attended our commencement at Memphis State and I, in turn, attended his at the University of Arkansas. Beth

Graduation and Beyond

graduated the following spring, since she missed a semester. Rebecca was a freshman at Arkansas when we were sophomores; she graduated the following fall.

We have covered my move to Michigan, GMI, and Babu; now I only need to bring you up to date on Carl and John. As you probably guessed, Carl and Rebecca were married at their church by Rebecca's father. And I was proud for them, especially for Carl. To start life totally alone and then be brought into a loving family was all he could have hoped for, and more.

On top of this, the Washington Redskins selected Carl in the second round of the draft. It wasn't the Chicago Bears, but we had dreamed about this since the third grade. I knew Carl would make a heck of a professional football player.

But sometimes things don't work out as planned, especially if your values and priorities change.

On the day Washington called and offered Carl a significant signing bonus, he called me and said, "We need to talk."

"Okay," I said, "talk."

"Not on the phone." He asked me to skip the race that Saturday and spend the weekend with them. This was serious.

Carl wanted to know if I'd be disappointed and think less of him if he turned down the football contract. I admit this shocked me, but as I stood and looked at my lifelong friend, I saw a man who didn't need fame and glory. He already had it all.

I had to convince Carl that I understood. After many hours of discussion, we reached agreement on a lot of issues. Carl planned to become the youth director at their church. He also interviewed for a position as the director of the Fayetteville recreation center. He'd been offered the job, but he waited until after our discussion before accepting.

Carl and Rebecca begged me to look for a job in Fayetteville or Little Rock. I knew they meant well and wanted me near, but they had their family and church. I didn't want to impose and have them fit me into their life. I stood my ground and wouldn't give in. Carl finally told Rebecca to give up. He said I was sometimes too stubborn for my own good. At least we finally reached an agreement on that.

* * *

With a little bit too much enthusiasm, Mandy said, "Well, I agree with that, too."

"Agree with what?"

"With Carl's comment," Mandy answered. "That you're too stubborn for your own good."

"Now, that's not what I meant," I said.

"I know," Mandy said, "but I couldn't pass on this opportunity to confirm Carl's assessment. You are *stubborn*." She saw my face and covered a smirk with her hand. "Sorry—continue."

I regarded her for a moment, then shrugged and proceeded with my story.

* * *

John was not drafted. Playing at Memphis State didn't make his name a household word in professional football circles. But when we were juniors, a Memphis State defensive coach left the school to accept a position on the Denver Broncos coaching staff. After the draft he called John and invited him to their training camp to try out as a free agent.

Graduation and Beyond

John not only made the team, he ended up a starter by the end of the pre-season. By the middle of the year, all the newspapers called him the sleeper of the draft. Everyone seemed to ignore the fact that John wasn't even drafted. Every time a Denver game was on national television, Carl called to make sure I knew to watch.

At the end of the season John came in second in the voting for rookie of the year. A fancy-footed rookie quarterback won, but for John to be second was a great achievement. Because of his outstanding season, Denver tore up the contract and replaced it with one containing a significant bonus.

The fourth game of his second season was the Monday night game of the week against the Oakland Raiders. Near the end of the first half John made an outstanding play, tackling the running back behind the line of scrimmage. At the end of the play one of Oakland's huge offensive lineman fell on the back of John's leg while it was twisted and pinned by another player.

As soon as I saw the play, I knew John's leg was hurt bad, real bad. I jumped up and tried to call Carl, but his phone was busy. Of course he'd seen the play and was trying to call me. As they carried John off the field, I finally got Carl on the phone.

All I could think was, Here we go again. First Calvin, and now John. Something had to be done to save John from the same fate as Calvin, but what?

Both Carl and I called John regularly while he was recovering from the surgery. The doctors agreed that John would never play football again. This left him very depressed, and nothing we said could cheer him up.

I reminded him about his family and how much they needed him. John kept saying that football was all he knew, and he didn't see how he could live without it. I kept thinking about Calvin. Finally, in desperation, I asked John to visit Carl when he got out of the hospital. I told him to find out why Carl turned his back on a football career and never looked back.

To my complete surprise, John followed my suggestion. When he left the hospital, he took Beth and their baby girl to Fayetteville, Arkansas. They spent two weeks with Carl and Rebecca.

John's visit with Carl was only a mild surprise compared to the phone call I received a short time later. John Bradford, the terror of Humes High, was going back to school to become an evangelist. Yes, you heard me right, an evangelist. He is in his second year at a seminary school in Kansas. Of all the people I grew up with, John would've been my last choice to become a preacher.

* * *

Mandy beamed. "That is wonderful, just wonderful," she said. "What did Carl say? How did he accomplish this in just two weeks?"

"It was more than wonderful; it was downright remarkable," I said. "I don't see how it could be accomplished in two years, much less two weeks. I don't know what Carl said, but John was a changed man."

"Well, I guess you and Carl had more influence on John than you thought."

"Carl did," I corrected her. "I had nothing to do with it."

"You're wrong," Mandy replied. "You don't give yourself credit. You had a tremendous influence on how Carl's life turned out."

I thought about that. "No, I don't agree. My life is messed up. They have their acts together despite me, not because of me."

Mandy shook her head and looked about to argue, then seemed to change her mind. "We'll drop the issue for now . . . please, continue."

Easy for her to say, I thought. What else was there? We'd covered GMI and Babu in our hours of conversation on the phone. "There's not a great deal left to tell you," I said.

"What about Fayetteville?" Mandy asked. "Have you gone back to visit Carl and Rebecca since moving?"

"Yes, twice. The first time I attended Rebecca's graduation. Then I went last year, when their baby was born."

"You didn't tell me they had a baby!"

"I hadn't got that far. Plus, I forgot," I added.

"Forgot!" Mandy cried. "How could you forget something that important? Tell me all about it; I want to know every detail."

Now she was confusing the issue. "I didn't mean I forgot they had a baby," I explained. "I meant I forgot I hadn't told you."

"Okay, so tell me."

I'll confess she was right; this was significant and worthy to be told. Also, it contained another event that might make her top-ten list. So I began with, "It occurred last year, on the fourth of April, the same day Martin Luther King was shot in Memphis, back in 1968. The day is also significant because during the drive to Fayetteville I went through Memphis, and something happened. I guess it could've happened to anyone, so maybe it won't make your list, except for the cross in the glass."

"The cross in the glass?" Mandy asked, but I held up my hand.

"Carl kept me posted on the timing. I wanted to be in Fayetteville when the baby was born, not a few days after. With the due date only a couple days away, we decided I should head for Fayetteville. Now that is one long drive, between fifteen and sixteen hours."

Mandy looked incredulous. "Are you telling me you drove from Flushing to Fayetteville without stopping?"

"No," I replied. "I stopped three or four times for gas."

"That's not what I meant," Mandy said impatiently. "Have you ever heard of *airplanes*? They take you long distances in a short period of time. That's how I traveled from Malaysia to Nashville, from Nashville to Flint, and on many, many other long trips."

"Okay, I know," I protested. "But I don't mind driving."

"Sure," Mandy said, "and I bet you drove straight through for Rebecca's graduation and straight through going back."

"So what's the big deal?" I asked. "Isn't that why we have Interstates crisscrossing the country?"

Mandy sighed and shook her head in exasperation. "Never mind. Tell me more about this cross in the glass."

* * *

I reached Memphis at 7:00 p.m. As I exited the Interstate to fill up, I noticed three black teenage boys standing on an overpass. As I went under the overpass to return to the Interstate, I heard a loud bang that rocked the car. Looking back, I saw a twenty to thirty pound boulder bouncing along the side of the road. I looked beyond the boulder to the overpass, and saw the teenage boys staring in my direction. When I turned back, the front windshield had two cracks directly in front of the driver's seat. They formed a perfect cross.

Graduation and Beyond

I pulled to the curb and jumped out of the car. There was a huge dent in the roof right above the driver's seat. The boulder hit a couple of inches behind the windshield with such force, the glass cracked.

I got back in the car and continued the drive to Fayetteville. I remember thinking, Boy, what a close call! As I drove, I kept staring at the cross in the glass. It was perfect. You couldn't have carved one any better by hand.

Before I left Fayetteville to return to Flushing, I had the roof fixed and the windshield replaced. The repairman was so impressed by the cross, he took pictures of the windshield. He said he had replaced windshields for twenty years, and had never seen a window crack in two separate directions like this one. Maybe a flaw in the glass at the intersection of the two cracks could explain it. That sounded good to me.

* * *

"I guess you know this does make my list," Mandy said. "Did you report the incident to the police?"

"Not that night. I called the Memphis Police Department the next day from Fayetteville, since I needed an accident report for the insurance. They said there was always trouble and unrest in Memphis on the anniversary of Martin Luther King's death. That shot cut short the life of the man, but it did not silence his voice. His words are permanently etched in the heart and conscience of our great nation. Now, Memphis is my hometown, and I know its citizens aren't responsible for that tragedy. But, since it happened in Memphis, it's left a cloud of shame over my hometown that will take more than our lifetime to dissipate.

"Now, I'll go back to when I arrived in Fayetteville."

* * *

When I pulled into Carl's drive, I saw an elderly man sitting on the porch, reading a newspaper. He stood, picked up a cane, and limped toward my car. He wore a ball cap similar to that worn by the man at the Exxon station, except instead of saying Exxon, it said *101st Airborne*. I rolled down the window as he slowly approached.

"Land mine," he shouted as he reached the vehicle. "This here limp is a souvenir from World War II, but that's a long story. I reckon you must be Mark."

"Yes, sir."

He leaned against the car to shift the weight from his bad leg. "I'm the Londons' neighbor. They're fine folk—yes sir, fine folk. They asked me to keep an eye out for you. So I just fetched my paper and camped out on their front porch."

"Where are they?" I interrupted.

He straightened up, shifting his weight again. "Oh, Miss Rebecca went into labor and they rushed her to the hospital."

"How long ago?"

I waited while he took off the ball cap, rubbed his head, and returned the cap before saying, "I reckon it's been near an hour—yep, just about an hour."

"Thank you." I restarted the engine.

"Son, one last thing," he said as he stepped away from the car. "Where did you get that pretty cross in that there windshield?"

As I backed out of the drive, I yelled, "Sir, it's a long story."

He nodded as I pulled away.

Graduation and Beyond

At the hospital I found Carl pacing and sweating bullets. Boy, I had timed it close. After about thirty minutes a nurse approached us and reported, "Rebecca is doing fine, but it's going to be another hour or two."

Carl nodded, then turned to me. "I bet you haven't had a bite to eat today."

"No big deal, I'm fine."

Wrong answer. He insisted that I go and eat at the restaurant down the street, since it was still going to be a while. I reluctantly agreed; I was actually starving.

But when I walked into the restaurant, the manager rushed up and said, "Get back to the hospital. The baby is coming."

I rushed for the door. "How did you know to tell me?" I yelled just before I left.

He laughed. "Because you look like you've been driving for two days without sleep."

Okay, I could buy that. I *was* dead tired.

I arrived at the hospital just in time to hear the nurse announce the arrival of a beautiful, red-haired baby girl. Carl was one proud dad. I was proud too, but when Rebecca told me they had named her Hazel Marie London, I went misty-eyed.

Hazel looked just like her mother. Carl asked if I thought she had any of her dad's features.

I said, "Sure, her red hair."

He was not satisfied. Rebecca also had red hair. "What about her eyes, her mouth, her nose?"

Well, I did see a slight, ever so slight, resemblance. That was just enough to satisfy him. I didn't tell Carl that I'd feared the baby would have no neck, like someone else in the family. She had a beautiful neck, and she was in perfect health.

I stayed for a few days, then headed back to Flushing.

* * *

"How much did she weigh?" Mandy demanded.

You would think, as much as I deal with numbers, I'd have the answer on the tip of my tongue. "I don't remember." I motioned with my hands, trying to indicate size. "She was kind of small."

"All babies are kind of small," Mandy snapped. "You don't even remember how many pounds she weighed?"

"Sure I do," I said. "She weighed seven pounds and some ounces."

Mandy frowned. "That's not small for a girl. It's about average."

"Okay," I replied, "but they let me hold her, and she looked awfully small to me. That was the first time I ever held a baby."

Mandy's dark blue eyes sparkled. "That's wonderful. A baby is a blessing, a true blessing to any family."

I paused to collect my thoughts. "I believe I've covered everything that had an impact on my life. I know it's been a long ordeal, but I needed to give you a straightforward account of my life. I mean, one hundred percent real; both the good times and the bad. I'll admit the bad got a jump start on the good, and still continues to extend its lead."

"Well," Mandy suggested, "don't you think it's about time we turn that around?"

"For sure," I replied. "For the first time I see a glimmer of hope. You have been extremely patient and understanding. It's difficult to find the words to express my gratitude. But I really don't know where we go from here." I searched Mandy's eyes, looking for a clue.

Graduation and Beyond

She said, "Don't worry. We are committed; we'll find the answer together. I have five more weeks at the mission. Let's use them wisely and see if we can resolve some of your spiritual concerns and issues first."

I nodded, but I must have looked skeptical, because she added, "You knew John very well. You saw what happened to his life. If he can make such a drastic change, there is surely hope for you. Maybe in these next few weeks you can declare a truce with God. That would be a great starting point."

A feeling of release swept through my entire body. I was glad I was sitting down; I felt weak-kneed. "You're right. There may be hope for me after all. Just going over all of this has helped. I feel like a weight has been lifted from my shoulders." I paused, searching within myself, then said, "I know my biggest problem is zero faith. How could my mother have so much, and I end up with so little?"

Mandy shook her head, but her gentle smile took some of the sting out of the movement. "You question everything, and if you can't fit it into one of your logical boxes, you run away from it. You can't put God in a logical box. He is infinite, and you are trying to make Him finite. It doesn't work. That's where faith comes in. Without it there are no answers. Don't worry. We'll work together. Can you adjust your work schedule so we can meet each day for an hour-and-a-half lunch?"

"Sure," I said. "I can come in early or work late. That won't be a problem."

"I want to have lunch with you and Babu on Monday, with Babu on Tuesday and Wednesday, and with you the remainder of the week."

Boy, this girl had a plan and did not intend to waste any time implementing it. "Whatever you say," I replied. "You'll like Babu. He is one great guy."

Mandy's smile widened. "I already like Babu. Now I want to meet him and get to know him better."

I nodded. "Let's call it a night—or should I say, day and night? It's nearly 8:00 a.m. I'm sure you're worn out; let me take you to your apartment."

"No," Mandy said, "I want to call Kim and Janice. Drop me at the mission. I'll meet them for the early service, then I'll take a long, long nap. I won't ask you to go with me. I know you have a lot of things to work out. I'll wait until you tell me you're ready."

"Thank you for being so understanding. Don't give up on me. For the first time in my life I have a reason to get my act together."

"Listen," Mandy said, "Carl never gave up on you, and you'd better believe I won't either. I do have one question. After you drop me off, are you planning on going to your apartment for a nap, or back to the U of M recreation center to run?"

How the heck did she know that? I replied, "First a run and then the nap. I've got a lot of things to work out."

Chapter Fourteen

The Whirlwind

Sooner or later, one reaches a pivotal point in life. It could be called a crossroads, a fork in the road, or a turning point. From my perspective, it was a point requiring a complete change in direction, like maybe a U-turn.

I'd been running away from God since the sixth grade, and now I wanted to run toward Him. Without a doubt, after talking through the night with Mandy, I'd settled this in my mind.

Although I'd known Mandy for only a few weeks, I loved her with all my heart and soul. How could I consider expressing those feelings to a person whose life was completely in tune with God's agenda? Before I could even consider that possibility, I had to change.

Maybe I knew about God. I read His book. I even argued with Him almost daily. But I wanted to know God as Mandy knew Him. This girl had a personal relationship with our almighty God. I'd long ago grown tired of feeling separated from Him, but how could I begin those first steps of change? What separated me from God?

The answer to that question was well within my reach. Sin is what separates anyone from Him.

What sin stood in my path? Drugs, drinking, sexual immorality, stealing, lying—those sins trip many, but it required only a casual glance inward for me to see that mine was *pride*.

I'm not talking about a spoonful of pride. This pride filled the whole container and continuously spilled out without ever reducing the supply. Mental discipline and a strong will are key to developing integrity and resisting many temptations, but when combined with excessive pride, the result is a person who accepts help from no one. For me, "no one" included God Himself.

In the Old Testament, a person of this nature was called stiff-necked. Carl called me stubborn and hardheaded. And Mandy agreed. Looking back, there on the side of the road in the middle of a lighting storm stood one defiant guy. One so full of pride, so stubborn and stiff-necked, he would rather God strike him dead with a bolt of lightning than ask for help and submit to His authority.

Seeing the need for change and actually seeking to change are not the same. First Carl, then Babu, and even John had pointed out the need. But now I wanted to change. How could I stop depending on myself and relinquish control to God?

For a guy with a natural gift for questioning everything, it's hard to accept that *why* sometimes has no answer—or maybe the answer is beyond this lifetime.

God can, and at rare times has, made His presence directly felt in people's lives. Does He glide in on a gentle breeze? No. There is no doubt when this occurs. He comes in on a whirlwind and turns your life upside down. That's exactly what happened to me.

The Whirlwind

During the next few weeks much happened, so be advised and be prepared. Time jumped from its slow, day-to-day pace over into the fast lane. Events occurred rapidly and carried Mandy and me along at breathtaking speed.

By the time Mandy and I had lunch that Friday, she knew more about Babu than I'd learned in three years. Yes, they hit it off big-time. Babu had nothing but good to say about their two lunches together. With some prompting, he did reveal that Mandy had very deep feelings for me.

During our Friday lunch, Mandy shocked me by casually telling me Babu was about to take four weeks' vacation to visit his family in India. Why did she know this, and I didn't? One would have thought his best friend for the past three years would be the first to know. She also knew why he had waited this long to return to India and why he decided to go now. She did not elect to share this information with me until later. In fact, she and Babu had shared much that would be revealed to me in the weeks ahead.

On Saturday and Sunday all of us—Babu, Mandy, Kim, Janice, and I—went to lunch and talked for hours. Having Babu and Mandy together, I attempted to pry more information out of them about why Babu was suddenly going to India. Neither one talked. I sensed there was much more to this sudden vacation, but I couldn't put a finger on it.

So, every day for the next two weeks, Mandy and I met for lunch. On Friday, with only two weeks remaining, we took Babu to the airport. As Babu boarded the plane, even with Mandy standing by my side, an overwhelming feeling of loneliness rushed through me.

So this is what it would feel like without him, I thought. How much worse would it be without Mandy? I shivered.

After leaving the airport, we drove to a nice restaurant for dinner. I eyed her as she sat beside me in the car, admiring how radiant and beautiful she looked in her long, flowing dress. As she allowed me to help her out of the car, held my hand, and let me help with her chair, I thought, Now this is more like a real date.

We talked freely during dinner. Then, out of the blue, Mandy asked, "Have you ever flown in an airplane?"

This innocent question caught me rather flat-footed. Then again, was it so innocent? I finally answered, "No."

"Would you be offended if I pursue the subject?" she asked quickly.

Pursue what subject? I wondered. Aloud I cautiously replied, "No problem."

Mandy watched my face. "I know you think nothing of driving anywhere and everywhere. I know there's little you fear. But, are you afraid of flying?"

Wow, this girl was relentless. She left nothing unexposed. I answered her question with a question while I composed my thoughts. "Where did that come from?"

"I don't know." Mandy shrugged. "I have a feeling flying might make you uncomfortable."

Okay, how the heck did she figure this out? I felt trapped. "I've always avoided it. In fact, *avoid* is probably not the correct word. *Fear* may be more appropriate," I admitted. "Yes, I guess I am afraid of flying. I have never feared death, but when a pilot is in the cockpit at the controls, well, that's a different matter. I can't explain it, but I do admit it."

The Whirlwind

Mandy gave me one of her reassuring looks and said, "You don't have to explain. I understand; it makes perfect sense to me. It's a matter of who is in control. As long as you are in control, it's okay; but when something is beyond your control, it's not okay. It really boils down to a simple matter of faith—or should I say, your lack of faith."

I thought about that. "You're right; I understand. Since you asked me a question that has been bothering you, would you be offended if I ask one of you?"

"I think we know each other very well. Ask your question."

"We surely do." I smiled. "We've met many times, and I've never seen you in a dress that doesn't touch the floor. Do you own a dress that is shorter than ankle-length?"

"Oh! I think I understand." Mandy laughed. "Let me stand and show you . . . "

I quickly shouted, "Put down your dress!"

"Oh," Mandy said ever so cleverly, "weren't you implying I've been hiding my legs? Do they pass your inspection?"

"Yes," I stammered, "they are very attractive. They have very good form, like a runner's legs. But I didn't mean for you to pull your dress above your waist in the middle of this restaurant."

"Well, it wasn't quite that high. I wanted you to have a good view, to see if they met your approval."

"Okay, you win," I said. "I was totally out of line. I apologize."

Mandy smirked as she sat back down. "Your apology is accepted. Now I'll answer the question. I own dresses that come just below my knees, shorts, and even swimsuits, but there's no way I'm going to wear them here in this bitter cold."

I laughed. "Clever. You never cease to amaze me. Whoever marries you will be one lucky guy."

"Luck will have nothing to do with it," Mandy said softly.

After I dropped Mandy off at her apartment, I wrestled with the idea of telling her I was ready to go to church on Sunday morning. I knew she was patiently waiting for me to come forward with this declaration. I wanted to go badly, but felt it should come as confirmation of a dramatic change.

Mandy was too special. I could not and would not be less than totally honest. Even if it meant losing her, I would never alter the truth, and I was still struggling. I knew it, and knowing Mandy, she knew it. Was it pride, stubbornness, stupidity, lack of faith, disobedience, or all of the above? Whatever the case, I'd wait.

After running on Saturday morning, I called Mandy. Kim said Mandy had a bad headache and was lying down with a towel over her eyes. I recalled a couple of times when Mandy mentioned having a headache. In fact, I remembered her complaining about eyestrain and the possibility of needing glasses.

I told Kim, "Don't disturb her; I'll check back later."

I decided to make a trip to the store for some groceries. I stopped at Babu's apartment to see if he wanted to go with me and was about to knock on the door when I realized he was gone. I went on my way. First the gas station, then the cleaners, and finally the store turned my quick trip into a two-hour excursion.

The phone rang as I opened my apartment door. When I heard Kim's voice, I knew something was terribly wrong. Kim was sobbing so hard, her breath came in short gasps. Her voice kept breaking.

The Whirlwind

I was able to make out "emergency room" and "McLaren Hospital." That confirmed my worst fears. Indeed, something was wrong. I tried to get Kim to put Mandy on the phone. Instead, Janice started talking. She was crying softly, but I understood what she said.

They were at McLaren Regional Medical Center in Flint. No more than thirty minutes after my call, Mandy sat up in bed, started crying, and said she was seeing bright flashes of light. Then she said she couldn't see anything except the flashes of light. They called my apartment, but when there was no answer, they headed for the emergency room at McLaren. The doctors were with Mandy now.

Fear swept through my body. I interrupted Janice. "We can talk later. I'm on my way."

While I drove to the hospital, I prayed over and over, Lord, our Almighty God, not Mandy. She is one of your special children. Not Mandy—anyone but Mandy.

I had no trouble finding McLaren. I passed it every day as I went to and from work. As I drove from the top of the hill all the way down to the intersection, I watched a red neon sign flash the words *Emergency Entrance*. How many times had I driven right past the entrance and never once thought about the patients inside, whose lives were at risk, or the doctors who toiled to save them? I was well aware of it, this Saturday afternoon at 1:15 p.m. I followed the sign, little knowing and ill prepared for the worst of it.

The doctors had taken Mandy up for tests. Janice was still filling out admittance papers. As I listened intently, Kim went over every detail. She confirmed that Mandy had complained for weeks about her eyes, headaches, and the possibility of needing glasses.

After Kim finished bringing me up to date, we decided to call Mandy's grandparents. Kim made the call, since she had spoken to them many times. Gary answered the phone.

After Kim went through the details again, Janice and I could tell what Gary was asking from Kim's answers. Had we talked to any of the doctors? When exactly did Mandy first mention problems with her eyes? What type of hospital was McLaren? Who was at the hospital with her? His tone seemed to calm Kim, because her voice lost its quaver.

When Kim hung up the phone, she reported that Gary would contact Mary and David, and then book tickets to Flint on the next available flight. He'd asked for a number at the hospital, said he would call from the airport, and told us to keep faith that God was aware of this great need.

At 2:15 p.m., a doctor came into the waiting room, said he was the head neurosurgeon at McLaren Regional Medical Center, and asked if we were relatives. We said her family was on the way, but we were close friends.

We listened intently as the doctor gave us grave news. Everything indicated Mandy had a brain tumor that was putting pressure on her optic nerve. They were running additional tests to better determine the type and location.

Never had I faced a crisis of this magnitude. Fear consumed my whole being. At the same time, I felt tremendous guilt. I had pushed God's patience beyond the limit. Mandy's condition was the result of my stubborn pride. This much I knew.

The ring of the waiting room phone interrupted my thoughts. Mandy's family was already at the airport in Nashville. The plane would arrive in Detroit at five-thirty, but there would be a three-hour wait for the connecting

The Whirlwind

flight to Flint. I told Kim to tell Gary that I would meet them at the airport and bring them to Flint—to just look for a guy holding a sign that said *Mandy.*

The drive to Detroit was filled with soul-searching and tears. Did it have to come to this? Would God take one of his special children to humble a man who was consumed with pride?

For the first time since my mother's death, I prayed from the bottom of my heart—real prayer; no arguing, no questioning, no doubting. I had no desire to fight with God anymore.

I surrender, I thought. God one hundred, Mark zero. God, You win. Mark, you lose.

My eyes were finally open. I felt like the man who had been given sight by Jesus. When the Pharisees asked him what happened, he said, *I was blind, and now I see.* One can try to make it more complicated, but it all boils down to that one simple truth: *I was blind, and now I see.*

I knew I had to surrender my will to God absolutely and irrevocably—but was it too late?

There I stood in the Detroit airport, clutching my little sign as Gary, Brenda, and Adam arrived. Our introductions were brief; we were anxious to get to McLaren. During the trip, Gary said that David and Mary were not at the mission when he called; they were visiting an orphanage on an island and would not be back for three days. He left a message for them to call, but did not leave any details or stress the urgency.

I quickly saw how Mandy had developed so many fine qualities and such character.

During the drive, I went over what the doctor had said about a brain tumor putting pressure on her optic nerve. When I finished, they all joined hands and prayed for Mandy, one after the other. The last time I'd heard such prayers of faith, they'd come from my mother. Just hearing them pray gave me my first hope for Mandy's condition.

When we got back to McLaren, Mandy was in a room, but the doctors wanted to bring us up to date on her condition before we saw her. Two doctors took us to an office to talk.

The news was anything but good. Mandy had an astrocytoma, a brain tumor. The location of the tumor was indeed putting pressure on the optic nerve. Astrocytic tumors are classified according to histologic grade. The tumor's grade determines the prognosis of the tumor. Astrocytomas are graded from one to four, with grade one being the slowest growing and grade four the most rapidly growing.

The test results so far indicated Mandy had a grade four astrocytoma.

I thought the news could not be any worse, until they told us the prognosis—on average, seventeen weeks' survival after diagnosis without treatment; thirty weeks average with biopsy followed by radiation therapy; thirty-seven weeks average following surgical removal of most of the tissue component of the tumor and radiation therapy; fifty-one weeks average following stereotactic volumetric resection of the tumor tissue component and radiation therapy.

They recommended that Mandy be transferred to the Henry Ford Hospital in Detroit, which had one of the top four departments of neurosurgery in the nation. They had already talked to Mark L. Rosenblum, the chairman of the department. Gary expressed his thanks for all their efforts and said we wanted to meet with Mandy before making any decisions.

The Whirlwind

Only two visitors per patient were allowed in the room, but Mandy's nurse agreed to allow the four of us in for a short time, since we had just arrived. Kim and Janice went to the waiting room. Gary, Brenda, and Adam rushed up to the bed to console Mandy. I stayed back to allow her to be with her family.

Mandy called my name, and I hurried over to the bed. She grabbed my hand and held on. I sat down next to the bed and let her squeeze my hand.

As Gary spoke gently to Mandy, I marveled at his words. Somehow, they took the sting out of the doctor's prognosis and replaced it with a glimmer of hope. Still squeezing my hand, Mandy listened intently.

Mandy didn't want to go to Henry Ford Hospital. Whatever had to be done could be done back home, she said. She wanted to go to Vanderbilt Hospital in Nashville. Gary, Brenda, and Adam agreed. Vanderbilt had an excellent department of neurosurgery. She would be close to Murfreesboro and all her loved ones.

"May I talk to Mark alone for a few minutes?" Mandy asked.

Gary nodded. "We'll go talk to the doctors about Vanderbilt instead of Henry Ford."

Mandy continued squeezing my hand as they filed out of the room. I had yet to say one word. I was afraid to open my mouth. I feared that I would start crying, and boy, would that cheer her up.

Sensing I needed help, she said, "We have a lot to talk about and not much time. I admit I'm afraid, for myself and also for you. Beyond the fear, I have faith that God is in control. I have to find His will, and no matter the outcome, peace will be with me and will carry me through."

"This is not between God and you," I told her in a voice thick with emotion. "It's between God and I. My pride was so great, the only way God could humble me and bring me to my knees was through you."

Mandy shook her head. "I was having trouble with headaches and my eyes six months before I ever met you. I was afraid I needed glasses, so I ignored it. I didn't want to have to wear glasses."

"All right," I said, "but don't you think God knows what is going to happen six months in advance?"

Her expression made it clear that this part of our conversation should end. "I don't want to spend our time and energy discussing who or what brought us to this place."

"Okay," I said, "I'm sorry. Let's move on. There's so much I need to say and so little time in which to say it." I paused and drew a deep breath. "Mandy, I've loved you with all my heart since that day when you walked into the GMI library and sat down across from me."

"I know," she said. "I felt the same way. When I got back to my apartment that night, I told Kim and Janice I'd just met the man I would probably marry."

I was stunned. Surely I'd hoped for this announcement, but it was totally unexpected. "Are you serious?" I stammered. "You would consider marrying me, knowing how I've locked God out of my life?"

Mandy smiled. "I felt and still feel that God brought us together for a purpose that is bigger than life itself. I knew God was working in your heart and soul, and that He would eventually open your eyes and breathe His life into your spirit. That's why I told Babu to go ahead and go back home. I told him you wouldn't be alone, that we would be married before he returned."

The Whirlwind

I felt my jaw drop open. Again I blurted, "Are you serious?"

"I'm lying here in a hospital bed, and I can't see." She sounded a little annoyed. "Don't you think I'm serious?"

Boy, did that set me straight. "I didn't mean it that way," I said sheepishly. "You told Babu to go to India and told him we were going to be married. Why didn't you tell me some of this?"

"The friend who wrote Babu is a girl. Years ago, her father and Babu's father made a marriage agreement. Babu knew that when he went back, the marriage would take place, and he would have to move back to India. He didn't want to leave you alone, so he refused to return, even when his parents insisted."

Again I felt my jaw sag in amazement. "You mean he stayed because of me?" "Yes," Mandy said. "He thinks the world of you. He would rather disobey his father than leave you here alone."

I shook my head in disbelief. He would do that for me? "How did you persuade him to go?" I asked.

Mandy wore a glib smile. "I told you—I told him not to worry, that I was not leaving here without you. We would be married before he saw you again."

I frowned as realization dawned—Babu had returned to India to marry. "Is he coming back?"

"Yes. In four weeks — but alone. He wants to come back to see you, give his notice at GMI, sell his car, and ship his stuff back to India."

"Now, how in the world did you find out so much about Babu in such a short time?" I asked.

Her smile grew wider. "He liked me and thought I was the best thing that ever happened to you."

I laughed. "You know, the guy is a genius; you should be honored." Then I added, "I guess you know I'm flying with you to Nashville."

"I know you would fly with me, but I think it would be better if you drove your car," Mandy replied. "You'll be able to get around better, and you'll feel more comfortable."

"Are you sure? I'll fly with you."

"I know," Mandy said, "but this time you drive. After we're married, you'll have plenty of opportunities to fly."

Since she'd brought the topic up, I said, "Speaking of marriage, let's get married as soon as possible."

"We'll see," she replied.

I sighed. "Okay. I'd better get out of here and let some of the others come in to see you."

"Would you kiss me before you leave?" Mandy asked. "We have never kissed . . . on the lips, not the forehead."

"Oh, sorry," I said, and leaned toward her again.

There are many things that will fade from my memory as I grow older, but that kiss will not be one of them. When our lips touched, it was as though our two bodies became one. I felt our spirits join; nothing would separate us, not even death. She would be part of me forever.

The others were all waiting patiently. Gary had talked to the doctors, who agreed that Vanderbilt Hospital was an excellent choice, especially since Mandy would be near her family. In fact, I learned that they had already contacted Vanderbilt and made the arrangements. The sooner the transfer took place, the better. Gary booked the flight for the next morning at eight-thirty. I told Gary that I'd be driving to Nashville.

Had it only been yesterday that Mandy and I were at the airport with Babu? So much had happened so fast. Never could I have imagined the events that brought me

The Whirlwind

together with Mandy's family in this waiting room at McLaren hospital. As I studied the sober faces of others gathered in the large room, wondering what circumstance brought each to this place, one of Mandy's doctors entered. He approached and told us they were going to give Mandy a mild sedative to insure a good night's sleep prior to the flight. We could first tell her goodnight, but only one person could spend the night in her room. Everyone volunteered, but Brenda won out.

All of us crowded into the room. First Kim spoke briefly to Mandy, then Janice, Brenda, Adam, then Gary. Finally I approached the bed.

"If I drive, I'll need to leave tonight so I can be at the Nashville airport when you arrive," I told her. I held her close and told her good-bye. I could no longer contain the tears; they flowed freely down my face.

Mandy whispered, "God loves us and will see us through this to the end."

Here was Mandy lying in a hospital bed, blind, facing possible death, and *she* was comforting *me*.

Before we left the room, Adam had everyone place a hand on Mandy. Then he prayed—about God being our Refuge, about not knowing His will, about staying true to God, about trusting in God, and about healing purchased by the sacred blood of Jesus. Boy, this whole family could pray.

This was only the second time I had been in a hospital, not counting when I was born. Hospitals are not warm, friendly places. They are sterile, cold, and void of color. There is no comfort in them, no signs in the rooms that say *Home Sweet Home*. Mandy's room was no exception—until Adam began praying. As he prayed, I felt a protective presence spreading, like a vapor, throughout the room. I had the same feeling I had discussed with Mandy.

As I left the hospital, I stopped to talk to Kim and Janice. I wanted to thank them, tell them I'd keep in touch, and say good-bye. But before I could speak, Kim said that she had something she needed to say. This tragedy made her want to face a tragedy from her past. She described the events that prompted her parents to quit the casino and join the Sandia Catholic Mission.

As she finished, Janice cleared her throat nervously. "I have something to say, too," she admitted. And she told us about her tour of the Netherlands, and why she'd put her nursing career on hold and entered the missionary training program.

Wow, I felt honored, having both confide in me. Mandy would be interested in these revelations. But right now, I had much to do and little time. I hugged each good-bye and told them I'd call from Nashville and keep them posted on Mandy's condition.

When I arrived at my apartment I called Chuck, my department manager at GMI, and told him about Mandy and that I had to go to Nashville. I wanted to be perfectly truthful, I told him; no matter how things turned out, I probably would be leaving GMI. If possible, I would try to get back when Babu returned from India and work a few weeks to help in the transition.

He understood. He told me to call if I needed anything done while I was in Nashville. He also revealed that he knew Babu would be working only a short time before returning to India. Everybody and his brother knew about Babu going to India to be married. Wait until I saw him again. He'd have some explaining to do.

185

The Whirlwind

Next I called Carl. I had already told him and Rebecca that I'd met Mandy, and they'd been pleased. They said my meeting her was an answered prayer. Now I had to tell them this terrible news.

As I went over the day's events, from the trip to the emergency room, to meeting Gary, Brenda, and Adam, and finally to the doctor's prognosis, I heard Rebecca weeping on their other phone. She interrupted as Carl was asking me a question.

"Stay on the line," she said. "Carl, watch Hazel; I'll be right back."

"Where is she going?" I asked Carl.

He had no idea, but he'd heard her squeal the tires while leaving the driveway. We continued to talk for another ten minutes. Then Carl said, "I don't know where she went in such a hurry, but she just came flying back into the driveway."

Rebecca was out of breath when she came back on the phone. She'd gone to talk to her father, who lived only two blocks away. At ten-thirty tomorrow morning, she announced, their whole church would pray continuously for Mandy instead of having a sermon. During our conversation I'd held up very well, but when I heard what Rebecca had done, the tears flowed again.

We talked for another thirty minutes, then I said I had to go. I quickly packed and headed out the door.

The plane was scheduled to land in Nashville tomorrow morning at 11:40 a.m. It was already 11:30 p.m., and I still needed to stop and get gas. I could make it— Nashville is not nearly as far as Memphis—but I'd talked on the phone longer than I'd intended. I tried to estimate the difference in distance and time between Memphis and Nashville. It took close to fifteen hours to go from Memphis to Flint, so I estimated eleven hours to Nashville. Boy, I didn't have any time to spare. Maybe I could make up some of it during the night on the Interstate.

That did not turn out to be the case.

One thing did happen as I drove through the night. I reflected over my life and the last month, in particular. I could now see and comprehend clearly those things that before were hidden from my view and understanding. Did it take Mandy's blindness to open my eyes? Perish the thought.

Still, everything was now clear. My whole being was entrenched in human pride, in stubbornness, in ignorance to truth—all combined with a lack of faith and no understanding of forgiveness. I questioned everything. I blamed my father for his death and for leaving me alone. I'd never accepted my mother's death. Even worse, I blamed her death on God. How would I react now concerning Mandy?

I prayed for God to heal her.

My answer showed me I was finally ready to change. I knew that, no matter what the future held for Mandy and me, my life would never be the same. If we were allowed one month or one year, I'd be thankful for each day. Mandy said that, with God, anything was possible. If she were taken from me, I'd live my life to honor her. Now I had to determine God's will and live my life accordingly. Questioning, blaming, running from God—these were of the past. In the future I would seek God's direction, find His path for my life, and follow it daily.

I could hardly wait to tell Mandy, who had waited patiently for so long. I was ready to go to church.

My immediate problem was the weather, which I'd not considered in my calculations. As I left Michigan, I ran into snow. It fell lightly at first, but it soon turned

The Whirlwind

into a full-scale snowstorm. This was not everyday snow. It included thunder and lighting. I'd never heard thunder or seen lightning during a snowstorm. It was snowing so hard, the traffic slowed to thirty miles an hour, and still it was difficult to see the road. I drove for hours at this slow pace. I knew I wouldn't beat Mandy and her family to Nashville. What I'd estimated as eleven hours turned into a fourteen-hour trip.

Somewhere in Kentucky, I drove out of the snow into clear skies and sunlight. It was an abrupt transition, coming from thunder, lightning, snow, and clouds into bright sun. Even more amazing was seeing the clouds clearing to reveal a beautiful rainbow stretched across the horizon. Thunder and lightning with no rain, a rainbow without rain—these were new to me.

After 2:00 p.m. I finally reached downtown Nashville. There was no need to go to the airport. I headed straight to Vanderbilt Hospital. I could hardly wait to see Mandy. No matter what she faced, we would face it together. I was prepared for the worst but prayed for the best.

I had no idea the answer to all our prayers had arrived on a whirlwind while I was driving out of a snowstorm toward a beautiful rainbow.

Chapter Fifteen

New Light

Vanderbilt Hospital and Medical Center is on 22nd Avenue in downtown Nashville, near Vanderbilt University. I ran three or four races in Nashville while at Memphis State, so I knew my way around downtown fairly well. I'd never been to the hospital, but one of the races started at the university and looped past the main entrance of the medical center.

As I parked and headed into the building, I studied the streets and buildings surrounding the hospital complex. There were quite a few restaurants and fast-food outlets within walking distance.

I was mentally preparing for a long stay. One thing was for sure, no matter how long Mandy was in this hospital, I planned to be here for the duration. I'd stay in her room, a visitors' area, the waiting room, or even a broom closet—any of these would be fine. Anyplace I could stretch out would be my home. In fact, I might get a plaque to hang that said *Home Sweet Home*.

New Light

Yes, I was told at the desk, Mandy had checked into a room on the fourth floor around noon. It was after two-thirty and I was late, big time. I supposed they were wondering what was taking me so long. I'd not even thought about calling.

The door to Mandy's room was open. Anticipating a solemn occasion, I was ill prepared for a room full of happy people. Last night at McLaren there were four of us in the room; now, not counting Mandy in the bed, there were twelve. Three of the twelve were not strangers; Gary, Brenda, and Adam were all smiling, laughing, and talking.

Brenda saw me first. She rushed forward, grabbed my arm, and pulled me to Mandy's bedside. "It's Mark," she exclaimed. "Mark is here."

Mandy turned and looked in my direction. Now, it had been just a few hours since we were together, but she looked different. She was downright gorgeous; her beaming face nearly glowed. Sure, I'd like to say I had an idea what she was about to say. But that wouldn't be true.

Mandy sat straight up in the bed, looked at me with those dark blue eyes, and shouted, "I can see! I can see! I can see!"

I stood for a moment, speechless. Well, it was actually longer than a moment. As I stood dumbfounded, Mandy asked everyone to leave the room. She wanted to talk to me alone.

Through my shock, as if from far away, I heard her voice saying, "Do you hear me?" Without waiting for a reply she said, "I said you look normal."

What did she mean by I look normal? Maybe I looked amazed, astonished, or even bewildered, but not normal. She probably meant I looked okay. With that worked out, I replied, "I'm okay. I just ran into one heck of a snowstorm that took forever to get through."

Clearly frustrated by my answer, she said, "That's not what I'm talking about. Let me slow down and start from the beginning."

Now, that sounded like an excellent idea. One thing was for certain; she definitely had my undivided attention. "Okay," I replied. "I'll try to listen as well as you listened when I talked through the night." Boy, I had a lot of questions. But I'd let Mandy have her say.

"It won't take near that long, but I do have a lot to tell you."

"Have you already seen the doctors here?" I blurted.

She smiled and wagged a finger at me. "Now, I didn't interrupt you, so please listen patiently. When I'm through, you can ask all the questions you want."

"Fair enough. Talk and I'll listen." I sat down at the foot of the bed.

"We were sitting in first class during the flight," she began. "When the airline learned of my condition, it upgraded our tickets." She chuckled. "I've flown all over the world, but that was my first time in first class, and I couldn't even see! I had an aisle seat. Brenda sat next to the window. Gary and Adam were sitting directly behind us.

"It was just another typical flight, except every five minutes the stewardess asked if I needed anything. At 11:00 a.m., the pilot announced we were starting our descent for our landing at the Nashville airport. We were ten minutes ahead of schedule, with a landing time of eleven-thirty.

New Light

"I suddenly felt a tingling sensation in the back of my head. It started faintly at first, then grew from a tingle into what could best be described as an electrical current. As it grew stronger, it grew warmer. When it felt hot, I began to see light, faint at first, but soon I could distinguish forms and actual images.

"There right in front of me stood the stewardess, again asking if I needed anything. Everything about her looked perfectly normal except for her face. I could see everything in sharp, crisp detail, but her face—let me continue, and then I'll come back and discuss her face, okay?"

Now, I had no idea what she meant about the stewardess' face; maybe it was blurry. "Sure," I replied, "but there is one thing I'd like to say. At the same time this was happening to you, I was driving out of one bad snowstorm. It was odd. Instead of raining, it was snowing, thundering, and lightning. A few minutes after 11:00 a.m., as I left the storm, I saw a beautiful rainbow. Can you believe a rainbow without rain?"

Mandy smiled. "After today, I can believe anything."

Well, I had interrupted again. "Sorry; I broke your train of thought."

To my surprise, she said, "That's okay. I'm struggling. I'm having trouble putting things in the proper order. I'm not as good a storyteller as you."

"You're doing great."

"I'll tell you what Gary, Brenda, Adam, and the doctors know, and then I'll come back and tell you more that they *don't* know. How about that?"

I still had no idea what she was talking about. "That sounds fine to me."

"Just bear with me, and you will understand." Mandy pulled on a lock of her hair as she resumed. "I told Gary, Brenda, and Adam that God had just healed me—I could see! Gary and Adam jumped to their feet and shouted, 'Praise the Lord.' With tears of joy streaming down her face, Brenda gave me a bear hug. Word spread faster than a brush fire throughout the plane. Passengers came down the aisle to express their joy. Even the pilot came back to talk to me. Before he could speak, I said, 'You are a devout Christian, aren't you?'

"He smiled and said, 'Yes, and I'm honored to have God perform a miracle on my plane.'"

I just had to ask, "How did you know he was a Christian?"

Mandy studied me for a moment. "I'll get back to that," she said. "An ambulance was waiting at the airport. With the siren blaring and lights flashing, we sped through the streets of downtown Nashville. We flew through the admittance area without stopping to sign papers. Within minutes of our arrival they were running tests, just like at McLaren.

"Four doctors performed the tests—one test after another for two solid hours, until finally they brought me to my room. Each doctor talked to Gary and Adam, but only one came to my room. His name was Dr. William Lee Morton. Dr. Morton said they could find absolutely nothing wrong with me—no blindness, no tumor, nothing whatsoever. I was one healthy girl.

"I said, 'You are a devout Christian, aren't you?'

"He said yes. 'I'm just a doctor,' he said; 'sometimes the Great Physician intervenes and shows us what healing is all about.' He said not to worry; I was healed. But his three associates were having difficulty accepting this. They continued calling and faxing McLaren.

New Light

"Dr. Morton said, 'They want to run some additional tests in the morning. Be patient. They will run out of ideas and release you before noon.'

"About thirty minutes later, you walked into the room."

All this time—in fact, all my life—I questioned, I doubted, I disbelieved. Now, all at once, I got it. Yes, it took my whole life, but I got it. This opened the gates to a new world, one where Mandy already lived. I felt like I had just stumbled and groped my way out of absolute darkness into light. For reasons known only to God, my life had just been blessed.

Humbled, awestruck, and nearly speechless, I looked into her blue eyes and mumbled, "This is beyond my greatest expectations. You are a treasure. Beyond that, I can hardly say more. I have one question, though. How did you know the pilot and doctor were Christians?"

"Okay, here goes," Mandy said, then warned me, "I haven't told this to anyone. We will keep this totally to ourselves, okay? No, we need to tell Gary. But for now, just the two of us will know."

I rolled my eyes. How easily she left me in a state of total confusion! "I've no idea what you're talking about, but if you say to keep it to ourselves, it will never leave my lips."

Reassured, Mandy continued. "As the light grew, I saw the outline of the stewardess. Then my eyes cleared, and I could focus. All her features were sharply defined and distinct." She hesitated. "I know your logical brain and logical boxes will not want to accept what I'm about to say."

Before today, she would have been right. But, by thunder, I reckoned she was now dead wrong. "Say it," I prompted. "Give me a chance."

"All right. When I looked into the stewardess' face, I saw light radiating outward in all directions. Her features were sharp and distinct, but it was as if I could see beneath the surface, to an inner glow that sprang forth and leaped outward as light. This was not normal light; it was bright and vivid. The source of the light generated a sensation of warmth, love, and compassion." She paused again. "I hope this is making sense."

Before this day it would have been well beyond my reach, but now, no problem. This was just another in a long line of miracles. In fact, I'd always felt Mandy could see right through me, so this was not a big stretch. "You're making sense," I said. "What else did you see?"

Mandy looked pleased by my response. "When I turned to Gary and Adam, they had the same light radiating from beneath the surface of their faces. Their light was much brighter than the light from the stewardess' face. In fact, their light filled the first class section of the plane. I rubbed my eyes, tried to refocus, and turned to look at Brenda. She had the same beautiful glow radiating from beneath her face. They all gave off different degrees of light that radiated in all directions.

"I turned to look at the four people sitting across the aisle. Each was surrounded by a—well, it's hard to describe. It was as though a dark cloud engulfed their whole being. Even as they laughed and talked, each had a look of hopelessness and despair. A gloomy, dark shadow seemed to surround their person. The light from Gary, Brenda, and Adam that filled the first class section of the plane did not penetrate these clouds of darkness. Every adult on the plane either radiated the light or was enveloped in the darkness.

New Light

"That's the reason I asked the pilot if he was a Christian. I saw in him the same level of light as Gary and Adam. Later I asked the stewardess if she had recently become a Christian. She replied, 'How did you know? I was saved three months ago.'

"Every adult I see is either one or the other, including the doctors. The one who came into my room to tell me I was healed looked just like Gary. The cloud of darkness surrounded the other doctors. I've told no one, because I don't want the doctors to think something is still physically wrong with me."

Did she say 'adult'? "What about children?" I asked.

She looked me over from head to toe. "All the children I've seen look like you. You are the only adult who looks normal. As I waited for you to arrive, I kept going over in my mind all the events since we took Babu to the airport two days ago. When you came into my room and I saw your face, I realized you were right."

Finally we agree on something, I thought. Aloud I said, "I was right. This is all about me."

And would you believe she replied, "Yes, you were. Now I agree."

Wow, things were becoming clear that before, were such a reach. "Mandy," I said, "you were physically blind, and now you can see. I was spiritually blind, and now I see. I'm finally ready to accept Jesus Christ as my Lord and Savior."

Before I could finish, she said, "Mark, I know you are, but before you do, I want to tell Gary about this. Then I want us to meet with Gary, but not around the clock. We can take two or three hours each evening after supper. I don't care if it takes two days or two weeks. You ask Gary every question you ever had about God, creation, sickness, hunger, faith, your father's death, your mother's death—question after question. Even if it is no longer an issue for you, bring up everything that created doubt in your mind. Why God has moved in and taken things into His own hands is beyond our understanding, but I feel strongly this is what He wants us to do."

Now, this seemed like an excellent idea. "You are so right. I don't know why God reached out and extend His hand a little further just for me, but surely He has, and my eyes are open to see. Maybe it's because He found such favor in my mother, or maybe because of you; maybe a combination of the two. Whatever the reason, I'm just thankful for His patience and mercy."

"Maybe He saw a small boy whose mother passed down to him an abundance of favorable qualities like kindness, fairness, and truthfulness," she suggested. "Maybe He saw a boy lose everyone he loved, who turned his back on God when he had nowhere else to turn. Maybe He saw a boy who developed tremendous willpower and mental discipline to cope with being alone. Maybe He found so much favor in the boy's mother that He responded to her petition and sent a band of protective angels. Maybe He saw a man who had all the qualifications to be one of His saints, yet was so full of pride and stubbornness, he was constantly running from Him."

"Maybe so, but do you want me to go over every issue, even those things that are now settled in my mind?"

"Yes, I certainly do," she said. "I want you to ask Gary everything you ever questioned. I agree; God has extended His hand a little further, so let's not leave a stone unturned."

New Light

"I think you're right. I'll be ready. The sooner, the better." Things were falling rapidly into place. I drew a deep breath, closed my eyes, and took a moment to thank God for allowing me to become one of his children.

As I opened my eyes, Mandy said, "Have Gary come back into the room, and I'll talk to him. We'll start tomorrow afternoon, if they release me in the morning. There was one other thing that I forgot to tell you. The nurse who brought me back to the room after the testing overheard Adam and me talking about how the whole congregation at CFC was praying for me during service this morning. She told me she also lived in Murfreesboro. She said she was a Christian and had attended a Methodist church for the past twenty years. I saw she wasn't a Christian, and I invited her to visit CFC next Sunday. She said after seeing what happened to me, she would be there. I couldn't bring myself to tell her she wasn't saved. Did I do wrong?"

I hesitated, trying to determine an appropriate response. "I think you've opened a door of opportunity for her. It will be up to her to respond, just as I've been given this opportunity." Then I stood up, took Mandy's hand, and said, "I'm ready, but I see why it's important to have Gary help settle the issues that have stood between God and me for so long. I'll go and tell him to come back into the room."

"After you talk to Gary, have Adam take you to his home. You haven't had any sleep for two days. You can stay with Adam, and I'll stay with Gary and Brenda."

"No," I said, "I'm going to stay at this hospital until they release you."

"Listen," she countered, "I'm in better shape right now than you are. You look very tired. I want you well rested for tomorrow afternoon."

My first impulse was to stand my ground, but she was right; I was dead tired. "Okay, I'll go," I said.

As I turned to leave the room, Mandy shouted, "First I want you to kiss me! And not on the forehead."

* * *

Before Adam and I left the hospital, I called Carl and Rebecca. I related in detail everything Mandy told me concerning the flight, having her sight restored, the tests at the hospital, and Dr. Morton's announcement that she had been healed. Staying true to my promise, I didn't mention her ability to see a person's very spirit.

Carl and Rebecca were so overjoyed, they both cried. I joined them. Whether from heartbreak or joy, crying releases confined emotions and has a soothing effect on the whole body. I'd shed enough tears in the last couple of days to last a lifetime.

Carl added that, after talking to me, they'd called John and told him about Mandy. John said he would have everyone in the Sunday morning church service pray for her.

As soon as I finished with Carl and Rebecca, I called Kim and Janice. They, too, were overjoyed. Plus, they volunteered that at 11:00 everyone in the mission church prayed for Mandy. So, at 11:00 a.m., when I was praying for Mandy, church services in Arkansas, Tennessee, Kansas, and Flint were praying for her. Now, that's a lot of prayer focused on the same petition.

Quite often, my mother wrote in her letters about the power of prayer. She wrote that when we pray, it is not to change God to respond to our petition. We pray to change ourselves. God wants to pour out His blessing, but we must change to align ourselves to His will. Once

New Light

we are aligned to His will, the blessings rain down upon us. I never really understood what she was saying, but now it made sense.

With Adam leading the way and me following in my car, we headed down Interstate 24 to Murfreesboro. After about thirty miles we exited near Adam's home. I'd never been to Murfreesboro and knew little about it. As we passed a sign that said *Stones River National Battlefield*, I remembered Murfreesboro was where one of the bloodiest battles of the Civil War took place. So many soldiers were killed at the battle of Stones River, they say the river turned red with blood. When we'd studied this in U.S. history in high school, I remember thinking, What a waste of human life. The unnecessary loss of just one life is too much, but what about thousands from war?

This was a question for Gary.

Going to sleep in unfamiliar surroundings is usually difficult for me, but not this time. As soon as my head hit the pillow, I was out.

* * *

Dr. Morton was correct. After a few more tests, some head shaking, and looks of bewilderment, the three doctors gave up. Mandy was pronounced well. In fact, they said she was the healthiest person in the hospital.

For Mandy and her family, this miraculous healing was within their vision of possible answers from above. For me—*O ye of little faith*—this had been beyond all expectations. Sure, I prayed for and wanted the best. The difference was, they prayed with the belief that it could be realized. Their hope was entrenched in faith with far-reaching roots that had been watered and nourished over time. My hope was crippled by logic, rootless. It just blew in the wind.

After my third and final trip carrying flowers from the room to the car, I headed back to get Mandy. As I entered the room, Dr. Morton and a distinguished-looking gentleman followed me in. The man was Indian, but older than Babu. He had an imposing appearance that demanded instant respect.

As Dr. Morton began speaking, I glanced at Mandy. She sat on the side of the bed, staring, mouth agape. I cleared my throat to get her attention. It did no good whatsoever. She continued to stare at the gentleman. If he was anything like Carl when we were kids, Mandy was about to make him mad.

As I looked back into his face, I could tell anger was not even part of this man's nature.

Dr. Morton said, "Before you two leave, I want to introduce you to a friend whom I consider a saint. This is Dr. M. A. Thomas, the founder of *Christ for India*. I met Dr. Thomas many years ago while visiting India with a group of Christian doctors. He has been visiting for a short time but is about to return home. I told him about the two of you, and he wanted to meet you."

Now, I have met Indian professors, deans, and even a university president, but none could hold a candle to this man. In a soft, gentle voice he said, "I have known William for many years. He is a mighty soldier in God's army and a pretty good doctor, as well. I'm just a humble man who has compassion for the poor and needy. In 1978 we opened our first Emmanuel Orphanage for a few of the hundreds of thousands of orphans and unwanted children who live in the streets of India. Today there are more than twenty Emmanuel Orphanages scattered across India. We not only provide food, clothing, shelter, medicine, education, and the Gospel of Jesus Christ, but we also challenge the children to become full-time

New Light

pastors and preachers all over India, or to work in our orphanages to give other children the same opportunity they received.

"I brought several copies of a small book, *Evangelizing India through God's Orphan Army*, from India. I gave away all except one. I had many ask for that last copy, but the Lord pressed it on my heart to wait until He showed me what to do with the last book. Last night William told me about you. As I listened, I knew the book was to be given to you."

Dr. Thomas placed the book in my hand, bowed, and left the room with Dr. Morton following.

I looked at Mandy. To my amazement, her mouth was still open. After a few seconds, l finally said, "Mandy, why are you sitting there staring with your mouth hanging open?"

Mechanically, she closed her mouth, paused as if to get her bearings, then said, "Well, what did you see when you were looking at Dr. Thomas?"

Now, that was simple enough for me to answer. "It was like Dr. Morton said. The man looked like a saint."

"If his face looked like a saint to you, what do you think I saw?"

Her words reminded me of what she'd told me the day before, about her ability to see the inner light or the dark clouds surrounding people. I wanted to know what made Mandy sit dumbfounded while Dr. Thomas was in the room. "Sorry, I forgot. Tell me."

"To tell you the truth, I don't think words could do justice to this man's appearance. Let's just say I saw the spirit of a true saint, and it is a wonderful sight to behold. This man's spirit is so filled with light; it fills the whole room with brightness, and a feeling of love, and peace. What an honor to meet such a man of God."

Chapter Sixteen

Round One

Monday afternoon, as six o'clock and my first meeting with Gary rapidly approached, I wondered with some apprehension if this was such a good idea. I felt somewhat as I had on that first day at the orphanage, when I waited for the kids to get back from school—not fear so much as an uneasy feeling of anticipation.

On top of that, Mandy had been staring at me ever since we checked out of the hospital. And every time I caught her staring, she gave me one of those heart-melting smiles that left me speechless.

Understand I had spent the whole day pondering what questions to ask. Mandy said to bring up any and every issue, even those now resolved in my mind. But, for the life of me, I felt ill prepared. As I followed Gary and Mandy into the study, still washed in a wave of anxiety, I renewed my determination to make the best of this opportunity and make Mandy proud.

As Mandy steered me toward a chair, I was caught up in the width and depth of this massive room that dwarfed the remainder of the house. What particularly took my fancy were the dark wooden bookshelves that reached

Round One

from floor to twelve-foot ceiling on three entire walls. As I peered closer, I realized the shelves were made of the same wood as the coffee table John had destroyed in our shop class in high school. This study was a garden of Philippine mahogany. Mandy's chair, my chair, Gary's chair, his massive desk, and the beautiful hardwood floors all could have come from the same tree that had provided the wood for the bookshelves.

Never had I seen so many books outside of a university library. As I was swept away in this sea of books, someone—Gary or Mandy, I'm not sure which—spoke to me. It took me a moment to recover and say, "Sorry; I was distracted by your vast collection of books." Not a good start.

Gary leaned back in his chair, surveyed the room as if admiring each book as a treasure, and said, "Yes, they are a comfort. As I grow older, I depend on them more and more to share their knowledge."

"Where did you get all this beautiful wood?"

Gary again surveyed the room. "Some years ago, Mandy's parents shipped the wood from the Philippines. After a little work in my wood shop, it ended up here in this study." Then he leaned forward. "I'm honored that Mandy and you chose me as a spokesman for God's truth. I surely don't have all the answers to the questions and issues you've struggled with, but with much prayer and the able assistance of the Holy Spirit, I'm prepared to respond."

He looked at Mandy. "I've been an eyewitness to the events of the past few days. There is much I don't understand, but without question the Lord has become directly involved in your lives. Mandy, I'll respect your wishes not to reveal your God-given ability to see a person's very spirit to anyone outside this room." His gaze swung back to me. "Now, let's begin."

All day, I'd had no idea what I would say, but now it was all there. Was it Gary, the study, Mandy's eyes, or something beyond this room? I began with a pivotal point in my life—my mother's tragic death. This subject had been off limits for Carl and me. But Kim had a tragic event in her life that was off limits, and she'd faced it. I must do the same.

"For many years after my mother's death there were two questions that constantly surfaced in my mind, yet could never be resolved," I said. "Is there a God? And if there is a God, then why my mother's death?"

Before I'd finished the last words, Gary said, "With such a loss as a small child, it is well within reason to have doubts concerning God and His existence. In fact, all of us go through periods of uncertainly, apprehension, and doubt in our lives. So your question concerning God's very existence is understandable.

"Let's look at—or better yet, *search* for God. Many do not have a genuine desire to find the truth about God. They simply wish to argue, or are sure that what they can't taste, see, feel, smell, or touch could not exist. These people will not find God, but for those who truly search, the truth is all around us. What evidence, then, is there for the existence of God?

"Have you ever awakened in the middle of the night and considered the fact that you exist?"

I hadn't realized he would respond with an inquiry of his own. I hesitated, then replied, "Many times. And at times as I drifted off to sleep, I considered my sense of awareness. At daybreak would I still exist and return from this state of unconsciousness?"

Round One

"Haven't we all," Gary said. "So the evidence of our very existence, the fact we are in relation to the fact He is—the great I Am. Who can really believe we are the result of blind coincidence? Can anyone truly believe that inanimate, nonrational, everlastingly existent matter produced our minds, our intelligence, and even our ability for enjoyment? What nonsense! Our ability to reason is limited to time, space, and matter. Dealing with things beyond these limits cripples our ability to even comprehend, so there must surely be something greater, outside these limits that is our Source."

Again Gary fired a question at me. "Have you ever looked up into the heavens in amazement and thought, how can this be?"

"Yeah," I replied. "Sometimes Carl and I would lie on a blanket on a hillside, look up into the night sky, and attempt the impossible—to number the stars."

"Yes," Gary said. "The evidence of the grand design of our universe, the fact it all fits together, is beyond coincidence. Can one sensibly argue that the universe, with all its intricate patterns, with so many events at just the right time, in just the right way, all result from the accidental explosion of matter?"

I thought about it. Gary's explanation made sense. "So you're saying, how can one choose coincidence, when the inference that someone controlled and brought about our situation is much more realistic?"

"Very well put." Gary looked pleased. "Now let's look at right and wrong. Aren't we all aware of right and wrong? Don't you always try to be fair and do the right thing? Mandy gave me many examples from your life, so this requires no response. Doesn't the evidence of the conscience, our knowledge of right and wrong, imperfect as it may be, demand a moral source? How do we explain man's awareness of right and wrong? In our most inward being we know it is not true that morals are just a convenience. Forget morals that contribute to our well-being."

"So you mean that deep within us is a sense of right and wrong, one governed by a consciousness of the existence of a Source Who will call us to account."

"I couldn't have said it better," Gary replied. "Let's next consider the very nature of man, the quest for some meaning to life. Do we not all try to find meaning in our existence? Why do we reach out for God at all?"

I considered his question. "I guess to justify our existence."

Gary continued. "So why is this question of His existence important, deep down, to so many people? Is life just an empty and futile experience in which we grab what enjoyment we can and never look ahead or back? Man reaches out to God because something within him cries out for satisfaction that can be found only in a Higher Source.

"And finally, there's the supreme evidence, the life and teachings of Jesus. Without question, this supports the existence of God. How can Jesus be explained without admitting the existence of God? It is my genuine conviction that no one can read the life of Jesus with a sincere desire to know the truth and fail to see Him as the Son of the living God. Once you absorb His life and teachings, then you can ask yourself, *Is He not my Lord and my God*? So if you really wish to know God, you must seek Him through Jesus.

"Would this response be appropriate when you were just a lad? Certainly not, but you are now a young man and hopefully I have given you some food for thought."

Round One

Wow, I was not prepared for the depth and dimension of Gary's answer. But, after a few moments, I regained my composure. "You're right—when I was a small boy, your answer would've gone over my head. Now, though, you've given me a multitude of reasons to believe in the existence of God. But I already managed to clear that hurdle on my own.

"After that day in the storm when I challenged God to prove He was real and the lightning struck the tree, I no longer doubted the existence of God. I continued to be mad at God and constantly took issue with Him about allowing human suffering, disease, hunger, war, sin, and even death. But I no longer questioned His existence.

"There is one other point I would like to make before we continue. After painstakingly studying each page of my mother's Bible, I do believe He is the one eternal Creator who brought the entire universe into existence by His spoken Word. I also believe the Bible is His very Word, infallible and authoritative in the highest degree. Once these two basic truths are accepted—there is a God, and the Bible is His Word—the arguments concerning its complete accuracy seem rather foolish, at best.

"Whether a second is ten thousand years, or a day is an age or era, or a day is an ordinary twenty-four hours, is not an issue for me. If the writer of Genesis says creation took six days, then who am I to question the numbering scheme applied? A God who can create something from nothing and who can breathe life into a handful of dirt can do everything exactly as stated in the Bible. To disbelieve based on my intellect as compared to His written Word would be utterly ridiculous.

"With this said, I still have always struggled with *Why God? Why this? Why that? Why did you allow my mother's untimely death? Why?*"

"You have planted your feet on solid ground with your acceptance of His existence, His Word, and the creation," Gary replied. "This foundation makes a good starting point for addressing your questions. To be perfectly honest, your first question is difficult, to say the least. And my response must be viewed over time to make it real in your life. I will say your mother's death was not punishment for you or your mother. God would never punish us like that. He clearly states this in the Bible. I could say people get drunk, as the driver who hit your mother did, and bad things happen to good people. Instead I will say God allowed your mother's death, just as He allowed sin in the world.

"Why did God allow her life to be taken? Let's look at your life as a journey down a long road with forks, detours, hills, valleys, and even a few bridges out. God has a plan, a road map for your journey, but unless you know His will daily, how can you expect to stay on course? You can't, and so you veer off course.

"Near the beginning of your journey, your mother's life was taken. This occurred in a snippet of time in relation to your life. You focused on this snippet of time without taking into account the before or the after. In fact, you couldn't see ahead to the *after* and as a small child you couldn't relate to the *before*. God is not limited by time. He sees the *before* and the *after*. We can both agree that this snippet influenced your journey. Your path was altered. You didn't understand. You became angry with God. In fact, you declared war on God.

"Still, your path was altered. You traveled a different road, met people, influenced people, befriended people, and loved people along this road. You developed a special compassion for orphans and had a deep understanding of their hopes and dreams. Your journey wasn't over, but you were on a different path."

"Maybe this new path was part of God's plan for your life," Mandy suggested, and glanced at Gary for his reaction.

Gary nodded. "Yes. Would you have found it on your own without that snippet of tragedy? Is God through dealing with you, or has He just begun? Do you know what lies ahead—or, better: do you know God's will for Mandy and you? Would you even have met Mandy if that snippet of tragedy had not occurred? I don't have the answers, but God does. How much farther down the road do you need to travel before you can look back and begin to see God's plan for your life?"

Mandy was right; these sessions were going to be worthwhile. I now felt comfortable with what we were about. I looked at Mandy. She sat on the edge of her seat, taking in every word. Then I looked at Gary, who had leaned back in his chair, waiting. "Why didn't I meet you sooner? It could've saved me much pain and grief."

Gary studied me for a moment, then said, "Maybe I'm at a fork in your road, as God intended. Maybe you could've reached this point sooner, except you veered off the path a few times. Maybe you missed more than one opportunity because of your strong will and plain stubbornness. Don't feel you are the exception; we all get sidetracked and stray from God's will for our lives."

"Yes," I replied, "but I guess some of us stray a lot further."

Gary chuckled. "Yes, maybe so. But God always shows us the path back."

With this settled in my mind, I was prepared to move on. "We mentioned sin," I said. "When I was at Humes, I saw good kids mess up their lives by getting involved in drugs, drinking, and things they knew were flat-out wrong. With sin being so attractive and appealing, I wonder why God allows it in this world."

"Well," Gary said, "let's discuss God's sovereignty, His plan, man's free will, and salvation. God's sovereignty is His absolute and exclusive right to exercise authority in the universe. He holds this position because He is its Creator and Governor. As Creator, His decrees are final. As Governor, He is to be obeyed by all.

"He decreed an eternal purpose for this world. The creation of all, including angels and humans; permitting the fall of Satan, his angels, and Adam; providing salvation for all people; electing some who believe and leaving condemnation to those who do not believe; applying salvation to all who believe—all of these comprise His purpose.

"Allowing man free will and providing a plan for salvation are the two greatest gifts God gave man. Without free will we would be like robots, reacting in a controlled manner without room for original thinking. Instead we were given the ability to choose."

I sat up straighter as comprehension suddenly dawned. "Oh, I see! To exercise our ability, we needed something to choose. So God allowed for both good and evil."

"Yes," Gary replied. "God permitted sin, but God does not cause or necessitate it. What other purpose could be served by His permitting sin in the world?"

I thought for a moment, then gave up. "I don't know."

"First, that man might recognize it's evil. Second, that God might demonstrate His grace. Third, that man would be provided a clear path from sin and evil to salvation—that path was the death and resurrection of His Son, Jesus Christ—and finally, that the principles of sin and

Round One

evil be brought into complete and final judgment for all who do not believe."

I'd never considered sin in relation to our free will. This made sense. "I understand. I don't know why this was so difficult and is now becoming so clear."

Gary smiled. "Maybe your eyes have opened and you are allowing the Holy Spirit to reveal truth. I'm pleased by our progress. As you can tell, Mandy has given me a detailed account of your life."

I glanced over at Mandy, who sat all prim and proper in her oversized chair. She looked pleased and I felt we were making excellent progress.

"I have never understood why God allows so much human suffering in this world," I said. "Even in my earliest memories, I watched my mother suffer. My dad's drinking and his temper, her constant sickness, her separation from our family, my father's death—it all weighed on her shoulders. It seems so unfair. She was such a good woman and deserved a better life. And it's not just her; everywhere, people suffer broken homes, broken lives, sickness, disease, and pain. Suffering is not limited to evil people. Sometimes it appears the good suffer more. My mother suffered with sickness all her life. I've never been able to understand."

Gary's eyes were full of compassion. "You make a good point, especially concerning your mother. I can't respond with a single answer that covers the mystery of suffering. I think there are many factors to be examined.

"We have already discussed God's gift of free will. Our poor choices can bring suffering upon us. In some cases it may not be as punishment for our actions, but rather, permitted based on those actions. We don't necessarily suffer according to our own sinfulness. We need to be aware of the bigger picture before we can begin to understand suffering, that sometimes it is associated with things well beyond our human understanding. It can be brought on us by the bad choices of others, including those of previous generations. The consequences of bad choices sometimes affect many—family, friends, and even nations, for two and three generations.

"Fear of the Lord is our wisdom, and to depart from evil is our path to understanding. We must remember that God is just, and when we turn away from God's goodness through sin, God can discipline us for our own good. In this case, suffering can produce benefits greater than the suffering itself. It can strengthen us, help us appreciate righteous living, lead us to greater faith, and be a tool to influence others. Suffering can produce perseverance, character, and hope. Our faith is strengthened as we rely on God to see us through troubling times. In this case, we suffer so that we might be restored.

"Finally, some may suffer as did your mother and Job in the Old Testament. Job was a righteous man who suffered disaster after disaster. He lost all his possessions one after the other, then his children in a great calamity, and then he was smitten by illness and covered with boils; yet he held true to his faith and confidence in the Lord.

"There are powers and forces at work in this ungodly world of which we are unaware. The forces of evil bring pain and suffering, but we must place our trust in the righteousness and power of God, because all will be revealed in the end. We must learn to not question God's ways, which are beyond our understanding."

I frowned in concentration. "So, you're saying things happen for a reason, but the explanation may not necessarily be one that we comprehend."

Round One

"Correct," Gary replied. "It's impossible for us to fully understand the ways of a God Who puts our faith to such strenuous tests. Does this make sense?"

"Yes, I think so," I said. "I appreciate your comparison of my mother's suffering to Job's in the Old testament. You have a great understanding of the ways of God."

"I'm no different from you," Gary said. "I seek the Lord, and sometimes I stumble. I get up and seek the Lord, and again I may stumble, but I always seek the Lord."

As Gary spoke, Brenda entered the study. When he finished she said, "I hate to interrupt, but Mary and David are on the phone."

This brought an end to our first meeting. "We're at a good breaking point," Gary said. "We'll continue tomorrow afternoon."

I came away with more than I could've imagined.

Mary and David had just returned to the mission and received Gary's message to call. He had left no information, but they feared something had happened to Mandy. Their voices were full of concern.

Mandy grabbed the phone and began to bring them up to date. Suddenly, she paused in mid-sentence and said, "Mom, I'd have to write a book to relate all that has happened in these last few days. Instead I'll wait until you arrive and give you every last detail. I hope you and Dad can come to Murfreesboro as soon as possible. I plan to be married, and I won't start without you. I already told you in my letters about meeting Mark and how I knew from that first day he was the man I would marry. Well, he is, and we are only waiting on the bride's parents to begin the ceremony."

You could have knocked me over with a feather—her silence in the study and then this. I thought her mother would question Mandy about the suddenness of the wedding plans, but she was overjoyed. She told Mandy they'd adjust their schedule and head for Murfreesboro within a week.

"A week is fine," Mandy said. "We have a lot to do yet, and we still need to apply for the marriage license." Then she turned to me. "They want to speak to you."

I was somewhat apprehensive as I took the phone. I'd envisioned meeting her parents and letting them get to know me before asking them for her hand in marriage.

Mandy was not one to drag her feet about anything, including our wedding plans. When she decided, she moved. Sure, I was ready, but I thought things would move a little more slowly. But we were on a fast track, and it looked as if Mandy planned to keep us there.

I relaxed after speaking to her parents for only a few moments. They told me not to worry, that Mandy was not an ordinary girl who believed in custom, tradition, or due process. They said she paid little attention to guys in college, but she'd always said that when she met the right guy, she'd know it. Therefore, they knew I was that special one, and they were going to be proud to call me "son."

I knew they were great parents, and told them so. How else could Mandy have developed such great character and love for life? Then I passed the phone to Gary and Brenda.

No one told them anything other than the wedding plans.

Chapter Seventeen

Round Two

As I reviewed the day at 6:00 p.m., I decided that, all in all, Tuesday had been a productive day. That morning, I'd casually inquired about Gary's wood shop, and I'd promptly been invited on the grand tour. Mandy declined the invitation, so I waved good-bye and followed Gary. From their back door I could barely see the building nestled in a stand of pine trees. But as we neared, I saw what appeared to be a small house attached to the shop.

Neither of us had spoken on our way to the building, but now I broke the silence. "Does anyone live in that house?"

"Oh, yeah, Travis lives in the guest house, but he's out of town and won't be back until tomorrow."

I had no idea who Travis was, but since he lived back in the woods, and since no one mentioned him, I decided to ask no more questions.

The wood shop was spacious. It contained every woodworking tool known to man. Gary revealed that he had made every piece of furniture in their house and the guesthouse, including the kitchen cabinets.

As we wandered around the shop, I watched the passion that animated Gary's face as he described working with the raw timber, how he first cut and shaped it, then molded it into a finished piece that still retained all of its natural beauty. As I listened, I realized that Gary's time in this shop with just God and the wood was far more valuable than the finished product.

He moved among the stacks of timber, caressing one piece after the other, and I marveled at his love for what I'd considered mere lumber. Then I thought about the vast collection of books in his study. Hidden within those books was knowledge. Gary had a passion for the truth in those volumes resting on the Philippine mahogany bookshelves, but why?

"How did you come to acquire such an impressive library?" I asked.

Gary turned his attention from the lumber, glanced back toward the house, and said, "That would be a long but interesting story. Do you think you are up for it?"

"Sure."

Gary motioned for me to pull up a stool, and he did likewise. Then he said, "Well over thirty years ago, when David was just a young pup and Adam was still in diapers, the only book in our home was a Bible. At that time, its primary purpose was to collect dust. Although we attended church, the Bible remained on a small table in our living room. Though we attended church regularly, neither of us was saved. Except for a few brief moments during the weekly service, thoughts of God, Jesus, or salvation were rare.

"Now, Brenda is not one to complain, but she obviously didn't feel well. Since it took an act of congress to get her to a doctor, I mentioned her yearly checkup,

Round Two

which was long overdue. The physical led to additional tests, a specialist, more extensive tests, another specialist, all to confirm the worst—cancer.

"The doctors agreed; the cancer was spreading rapidly. They gave her three to six months, and told her to get her life in order. But the Mayo Clinic had developed a new treatment that could add months to the life expectancy of terminally ill patients. We decided to try the treatment.

"On our flight to the clinic, I started to pray. How could I raise these boys without their mother? How do I prepare myself? While I was petitioning for an answer, Brenda was seeking a sign from God, one that would prove He is real so it could be passed on to the boys. Neither of us considered or prayed for healing.

"When the head doctor at Mayo Clinic asked us if we were pulling some kind of joke, we didn't understand. What joke? 'There is no cancer!' he told us. Why were we wasting his valuable time?

"Brenda was healed. We didn't ask for it, expect it, or understand it, but right out of nowhere, she was healed. Have you ever been given something of great value that was undeserved? Maybe this miracle was undeserved, but for sure it was appreciated and life changing.

"First we were saved and then we quickly moved from believers to followers of Christ. We got real with a real God. Our eyes and ears were opened to God's involvement in our new lives. Brenda accepted the healing as a sign from God to be passed to our sons. Daily, she shared the wonders of God with our children. I had prayed for guidance and found it in His Book. Soon my whole being was engulfed in a burning desire to study His Word and learn the ways of our almighty God. One by one, my collection of books grew. And you are a witness to their numbers."

Gary paused as we both heard Mandy's voice, faint with distance. "It's a good thing I've finished my story," he said. "Mandy is calling us to lunch."

Could it really be time for lunch? What seemed like a few minutes had actually been more than two hours. Those two hours in the shop, casually talking with Gary, had been worthwhile. I now felt more comfortable around him, and I was eager to begin our next session that evening.

Mandy continued to stare at me throughout the day. When I noticed, she just smiled.

What the heck is going on? I wondered. I couldn't confront her. When she smiled, I melted. She left me speechless.

Gary had answered my questions during our first meeting with remarkable wisdom and understanding. Everything he said made perfect sense. Mandy was pleased, I was pleased, and I was sure God was pleased. As we entered the study for a second round, I considered my first question. Okay, I had lived my life denying the possibility of spiritual influence. The issue baffled me as a child and followed me consistently until I met Mandy. Why not give Gary a chance to shed some light in this area?

So when we were comfortably settled in our chairs, I said, "In reading the Bible it is clear that angels, evil spirits, and Satan himself have been present throughout biblical history. My whole life, I've had encounter after encounter with a form of spiritual protection. I tried to logically reason through these encounters. I even tried to compromise and accept them as a shield of protection

219

Round Two

from my mother's prayers. Every letter from my mother ended with, 'Son, you will be safe and protected. Angels are watching over you.'

"Mandy had no problem whatsoever accepting that God honored my mother's prayers and sent a band of protective angels. After these last few days I no longer have a problem believing as Mandy does. I value your wisdom and understanding of God's ways. What is your belief concerning angels, evil spirits, and Satan in the twentieth century as compared to biblical times?"

"That's a broad question," Gary said. "I'll need to break it up into smaller portions to give an adequate response. First, time does not apply to God. Therefore whatever was possible during biblical times is still possible today. Satan was there to tempt Jesus, and you can be sure the deceiver is at work in the world today, attempting to destroy lives, families, communities, and even nations. Spiritual warfare is a reality today, as it was then.

"Ephesians 6:12 states, 'For we do not wrestle against flesh and blood, but against principalities, against powers, against the rulers of the darkness of this age, against spiritual hosts of wickedness in heavenly places.' Yes, most definitely God's angels and the devil's host of evil spirits abound in our world today. Satan and his host of evil spirits are powerful, dangerous adversaries to be respected, but we should not consider them equal to God and His angels. Their power is nothing compared to that of the sovereign God. Although subtle and cunning, Satan is a defeated foe who continues to resist God furiously until the time when he will be sealed in hell forever.

"There are many unbelievers today who either do not believe there is a God or are totally unconcerned with His presence. They laugh at the existence of angels, evil spirits, and Satan himself. Unfortunately there are those who do believe there is a God but also doubt the existence of angels, evil spirits, and Satan. Many churches avoid the subject altogether.

"Satan stalks the path of every believer, offering a storehouse of enticements to lure the Christian away from his faithful walk with Christ. How better prepared the believer would be if he could recognize the source of this temptation, if more of us understood that our spiritual struggle involves more than sinful desires and psychological disorders! Evil spirits and the powers of darkness wage war against our very minds. If we as Christians are to win these spiritual conflicts and gain freedom, we must be aware of the source of these attacks. This is an area where there is much misconception. Since many churches fail to take a stand on the existence of Satan and his evil spirits, confusion among many believers keeps them in bondage to a power they refuse to acknowledge.

"I must make one more comment on this issue before we go to your next question. As Mandy described your life, I marveled at this stubborn boy who would not give an inch to anyone or anything. You argued with God daily and left yourself wide open to the attacks of Satan and his host of demons. Instead of allowing Satan to take control of your mind, you had such a strong will, he was not even allowed to enter. Yes, you constantly ran from God, but still you harbored no evil and treated everyone fairly.

"Mandy told me how you repeatedly walked away from danger, unscathed. Maybe you are the one to speak with authority on the subject of angels. Yes, you surely had a band of angels protecting you from harm, but they were protecting your body, not your mind. That you guarded for yourself. If this was your character before

Round Two

following Christ, what a mighty warrior you will make in Christ's army! I see why Mandy is determined to be your wife."

Mandy interrupted. "Thank you. That's exactly what I've been trying to tell him for weeks. I actually believe when he's running, angels hover over both his shoulders. It's truly amazing."

I was not about to take Mandy to task for her unsolicited input. And I couldn't argue with Gary's response that confirmed what she had been trying to tell me for weeks. Although heaven and hell did creep into almost every sermon I'd heard during my childhood, Satan was pretty much kept confined to his fiery pit. And the weekly message never associated angels or evil spirits with the living. So, I found Gary's answer enlightening. But this first question was only a warm-up compared to an issue that had bothered me since high school.

"On my first day at Humes, in the middle of the ninth grade English classroom, four empty desks surrounded one occupied by a boy wearing a little round black cap. Since these were the only empty seats in the room, I sat down next to Winston Goldsmith III and introduced myself. For the next four years I witnessed classmates and some teachers harass and persecute this Jewish boy. Why was this allowed? I studied my mother's Bible, attempting to understand the relationship between God and these chosen people. I understand the Jewish people failed to meet the terms of God's covenant, so God scattered them throughout the earth and allowed them to be persecuted in every generation. As the Bible predicted and with history as an eyewitness, the Jewish people have suffered dire consequences for their disobedience. What I fail to understand is why a God of love and mercy would allow millions of His chosen people to be annihilated during the Holocaust."

Gary was silent for a while. I waited. Finally he said, "I could say God is not only a God of love and mercy, but He is a jealous God and a just God, and He works in ways that we sometimes can't understand. That would be an answer, but you already know this, so I will try to paint a picture that takes into account not only God's character but also the complex nature and heritage of His chosen people.

"First, the history of the Jewish people is not only an ongoing miracle but also a continuing fulfillment of biblical prophecy. How do we account for the survival of the Jewish people as a race? No matter the country—Russia, Poland, Hungary, France, Holland, Belgium, or the United States—they live within each as a separate people who keep their identity intact. Take your Winston as an example. You schooled together for four years. His Jewish culture and tradition were handed down from one generation to another, not for hundreds of years, but for thousands. This allowed him to retain his identity and heritage."

"I understand," I said. "God has carefully preserved them, even in unbelief, throughout history."

"Most certainly," Gary replied. "That Jerusalem lay in ruins and the chosen people were scattered over the world did not mean God's promise to Israel in the Old Testament couldn't be fulfilled.

"What would it take to sway the votes necessary in the UN to establish the State of Israel? Would it take convictions of shame, guilt, and compassion to produce those yes votes at that moment in time?

Round Two

"From 1939 to 1945 World War II raged throughout Europe. Under the cover of this war, the Nazi regime attempted to systematically wipe out the Jewish race in Europe. Six million Jews were murdered in Nazi labor and concentration camps for no other reason than their race. On May 8, 1945, World War II ended in Europe. At war's end there were only about 200,000 surviving Jews in the Nazi camps, from a population of about 6.5 million. A wave of revulsion spread across Europe and the United States at news of the death camps. The horror stories of the survivors influenced public opinion around the world. Many have struggled with your question: Where was God? His silence while His chosen people were nearly wiped out raised many painful questions.

"I am not defining an answer. I'm just painting a picture. Hopefully we can look at the canvas and find an answer—one to hold onto until God reveals all.

"In 1947, two years after the end of World War II, the reality of the Holocaust's horrors had settled upon the conscience of many nations. And that is when the UN proposed the establishment of the Jewish state of Israel. Its existence was proclaimed on May 14, 1948. Less than twenty-four hours later, the armies of Egypt, Jordan, Syria, Lebanon, and Iraq invaded the country, forcing Israel to defend their one-day-old sovereignty. In Israel's War of Independence, the newly formed, poorly equipped Israel Defense Forces—the IDF—repulsed the invaders. The fierce fighting lasted some fifteen months and claimed over six thousand Israeli lives."

"So God's promise was fulfilled," I supplied.

"Most assuredly," Gary replied. "The Jewish people now had a country to return to—and return they have. From all over the world, they've come back to their Promised Land. Still, the borders of this new Israel encompassed far less than those of their ancestors.

"On June 5, 1967, Israel found itself surrounded by hostile Arab armies and launched a strike against Egypt in the south, followed by a counterattack against Jordan in the east and the routing of the Syrian forces entrenched on the Golan Heights in the north. The war lasted six days. Now Judea, Samaria, Gaza, the Sinai Peninsula, and the Golan Heights were under Israel's control. As a result, the northern villages were freed from nineteen years of recurrent Syrian shelling; the passage of Israeli and Israel-bound shipping through the Straits of Tiran was ensured; and Jerusalem was reunified under Israel's authority."

Gary paused and regarded me. "I know that is quite a bit of historical information, but I think it is very important that Christians understand the Jewish people and their homeland as much as possible. Now, can we look at this and find an answer to your question? Did the evil deeds of evil men open the door for the fulfillment of God's promise to Israel? I don't have the answer. I just painted the picture."

Time out! Gary's response left me numb. Never had I considered that the wicked deeds of evil men had been used to open the door for the fulfillment of God's promise to Israel. It would take a long run with some deep thought for me to come to terms with his response.

Round Two

"I must confess, your answer nearly overwhelmed me," I said. "But I do see your picture, and I understand there is no simple response to such a complex issue. Shall we pause and continue tomorrow afternoon? While it's fresh on my mind, I'd like to think this one over."

"That's an excellent idea," Gary replied. "I don't want to overwhelm you, but you touched on a subject that is very dear to my heart. I hope I didn't get too carried away with facts concerning the history of Israel. Our lives and the future of this world are so tied to this nation. For more than 1,900 years, Israel has taken a back seat while Christianity took center stage in the Lord's affairs of the Gospel. Nevertheless, God has carefully preserved the Jewish people and is returning them to their homeland. Thus they have not been forgotten in God's plan.

"In the end, God will restore Israel to center stage on the world's theater, so we must recognize what God is doing with Israel, not shrink from it as though our own interests will be overshadowed."

"We should rejoice in these developments," Mandy pitched in.

"Yes, we should," Gary said, "with full assurance that our own redemption draws ever nearer. So with the Bible as our guide, we focus our attention on this holy land knowing full well that God has preordained Israel to be the cradle through which He will *rock* this world."

Chapter Eighteen

Round Three

Wednesday. As it neared six o'clock, I eagerly awaited our next round of questions.

Well before dawn, I'd headed out for a long run. I was intentionally under-dressed for the cool night air; otherwise, I'd have been burning up after just one mile. I started at the foot of a steep hill and had to lean forward to overcome the pull of gravity as I scaled the slope. My breathing quickened and my lungs burned as I gulped in cold oxygen. After a half mile of steady climbing, I topped the crest. Now warm, I settled into a comfortable pace and recalled last night's session. There were issues raised by Gary's response that must be resolved. So I thought back to high school.

I admired and respected Winston. We had many interesting discussions that went over the heads of most of our classmates. I always treated him fairly. So, why did I feel so guilty? Because I let peer pressure keep me from being his friend. And did I ever stand up for him, as Carl and even John had stood up for me? I wish the answer were yes, or sometimes, or even every now and then. But it was no, never.

Round Three

You can't change the past. There was nothing I could do about that now. But as I topped another hill, an answer came to me. I would write Winston a letter, apologize for not being the friend he deserved, and ask for his forgiveness. With that settled, I felt better. But, what about the blockbuster Gary dropped on my head, that God used the wicked deeds of evil men to fulfill His promise to Israel?

Hill after hill, I attempted to come to terms with this issue, but this just did not seem right. As I reached a zone where my mind was freed from the labor of running, I realized that I was only seeing this from my point of view. Gary had learned the ways of God; therefore he saw it from God's viewpoint. And what would that look like? Maybe in the grand scheme, if evil is to be allowed, how could God counteract this evil? As I turned into Adam's drive, I accepted Gary's answer: Create good from those wicked deeds to defeat their purpose.

After the early morning run and then breakfast with Adam, Mandy and I went for blood tests, then to apply for the marriage license.

I did finally build up nerve to ask, "Why do you keep watching me so closely?" This was a more polite way of asking what I'd been thinking for three days: Why are you constantly staring at me?

Her response skirted the issue. She mumbled something about marveling at how I was growing and responding to Gary's insight. I didn't buy it. Something was going on, and Mandy was in the know, and I was not.

After a busy morning, we arrived at Gary's in time for lunch. A rather large man who appeared to be in his early thirties joined us. Gary made the formal introductions, and Travis Hall rose to shake my hand. Just as the circulation in my right hand completely shut down, Travis released his grip. I looked up at Travis and realized *rather large* did not do him justice. At six-six and 250 pounds, he made Carl and John look small.

This was Mandy's first meeting with Travis, but she already knew all about him. I found lunch and the next few hours most interesting and enlightening, as Brenda and Gary related how Travis came to live in their guesthouse.

On a cold Saturday morning about a year ago—nearly a year to the day—Brenda was in Nashville picking up supplies for the wood shop. As she turned at 8th and Broadway, she spied a most pitiful man standing on the corner, holding a sign that read *Will work for food*. He was tall and thin, with pleasing features, but clothed in a patchwork of rags that left most of his skin exposed to the frigid air. Although she had just caught a quick glimpse, the sight was unforgettable—not that of the worn rags hanging from his frail body, but the lost look radiating from his eyes.

Brenda prayed, *Lord what would you have me do?* She got her answer. Brenda circled the block, rolled down the window, and said, "Sir, I have plenty of work and food. Will you come to Murfreesboro?"

Instantly this homeless man folded his long, lanky body into the seat beside Brenda. Although startled by his quick acceptance, Brenda maintained her composure and began their thirty-mile trip to Murfreesboro.

Again, Brenda prayed, *Lord, how do I communicate with this poor man?*

Immediately the answer was there: *slowly*. So, slowly, she began. "What is your name?" It was the only question asked during the drive.

After a long pause, he replied, "Travis. Travis Hall."

Round Three

Brenda told him her name and briefly described her life and marriage to Gary. To this Travis volunteered that he had been living in a cardboard box under a bridge near the Cumberland River for the last three and a half years.

Brenda was shocked by the mere thought of living in a box under a bridge, but she continued talking as she drove, neither expecting nor receiving another response from Travis. She told him about Gary's wood shop, the attached guesthouse, and the shipment of wood that had just arrived. And about her good fortune in finding a man who needed work. It would take Gary well over a week to move the wood into the lumber bins in the wood shop. And Gary was too hardheaded to ask for help. So, the Lord had answered her prayers and provided just what was needed at just the right time.

Although Travis did not reply, he smiled for the first time and nodded his approval.

After being introduced to Gary, Travis moved into the guesthouse.

I marveled at how Gary quickly and fully accepted Brenda's decision to bring a stranger to their home.

Within two days, the wood was in the lumber bins and the work was done. But when Gary found out that Travis had been a licensed electrician, he convinced the big man to stay and do some wiring in the shop. One week stretched into two, and then to three. Not once during those first few weeks did Gary or Brenda pry or pressure Travis for information; they only listened to what he volunteered.

On that first day, Gary had asked Brenda how he should approach Travis.

She replied, "Slowly."

Running with Angels

But as each day went by, Travis shared more and more about his life and how he ended up living in a cardboard box under a bridge. During the last few days of his tour in Vietnam, his squad was ambushed behind enemy lines. Every squad member was killed except for Travis. He was left for dead, but managed to crawl back to base camp. Once in the United States, heavy drinking and drugs did little to help him deal with the memories. A long succession of lost jobs and lost hope led him into the streets.

During that first month, neither Brenda nor Gary attempted to give Travis advice; they only listened. But, on a Saturday night four weeks from the day he arrived, Travis asked Brenda if he could ask a couple of questions. First, why had they befriended him? And second, why did they go to church three and four times a week?

"Because you are one of God's children," Brenda replied. "Besides that, God specifically told us to. As to why we go to church regularly, why don't you come with us and find out?"

After a long pause, Travis said, "Okay, I will."

And, true to his word, he did. After each church service, he met with Brenda and asked more questions. This was not just casual interest; he hung on every word. This continued for weeks, until Travis asked Gary to attend one of their meetings.

With his new Bible clutched in his right hand, Travis stood and said, "Three months ago, you welcomed me into your guesthouse. During this time I have remained drug and alcohol free, mainly out of respect for the two of you. You had something I wanted, but I did not understand what it was or how to receive it. So, I watched and listened. And now I know that it is *truth*. You live it; you breathe it; you share it. And I now know the source

Round Three

is our almighty God and the path is through Jesus and the Cross. I wasted all these years because I felt tremendous guilt over being alive when the rest of my squad died in a remote jungle in Vietnam. But now I understand that my life was spared for a reason. God has a purpose for my life. I intend to find it and live it."

The following Sunday morning, Travis accepted Christ and was baptized after the evening service. Soon after, the VA hospital in Murfreesboro hired him as an electrician. With Gary's help, he began teaching a twelve-step recovery class on Thursday nights at the church.

After one Sunday morning service, Travis casually asked Brenda about the attractive single mother with the two small children he'd seen. Playing matchmaker, Brenda invited Rachel to dinner. More dinners followed and three months later, to Brenda's delight, Travis announced their engagement.

For the past six months, Travis had been working afternoons and weekends, constructing their house. In the spring, when the house was complete, Rachel and Travis planned to marry.

Now, that is a fair account of what they told me, except for a most interesting event that deserves a bit more detail.

Not long after Travis joined the church, Adam asked him to give his testimony during the Sunday evening service. Travis spoke for forty-five minutes. When he concluded, there were few dry eyes in the sanctuary.

As soon as service ended, a lady rushed up to Gary and said, "I do not mean to sound critical, but do you think helping one homeless man can really have a significant impact, considering the hundreds of homeless in all the cities in our country?"

Adam's morning message had been *Significance in God's Kingdom*. After a short pause, Gary replied, "I really don't know about significance, but I do know one thing; it sure meant a lot to Travis."

Boy, did that hit home. I needed a long run to fully absorb the truth contained in that little exchange. But for now, I needed to focus on my next session.

As we three entered the study, I searched for my first question. During my morning run I'd taken inventory and attempted to organize potential issues. There was this three-letter word that kept popping up—sin, not sex. Sure, we are all born with a nature to sin because of Adam, but once saved, shouldn't we rapidly eliminate it from our lives?

I remembered when Carl and I endured the Sunday school class at the Methodist church. In a class full of Christians, or at least the kids of Christians, we were treated bad, big time! Was this the way Christians acted?

I also wondered about the difference in the divorce rate between Christian couples and non-Christian couples. Everything I'd read indicated this difference was insignificant. How could this be?

Hoping Gary could shed some light on these issues, I said, "I know that salvation brings one's spirit to life, providing a dwelling place for the Holy Spirit. But, even with the presence and guidance of the Holy Spirit, why do we continue to sin and have ungodly thoughts?"

Gary leaned back in his chair. "Let's consider a person as a vessel," he said, "with his spirit the center, the mind the command post, and containing a multitude of compartments. Now, think of the Holy Spirit as light. When one is saved, his dead spirit is brought to life and filled with the light of the Holy Spirit.

Round Three

"Each of the many compartments contains a facet of the old nature. Together they are who we really are, not who we pretend to be. One compartment may contain compassion, another gentleness, and another love. The light of the Spirit flows into these compartments and radiates back out, but other compartments are filled with sin like jealousy, pride, and lust. Sin—darkness—and the Holy Spirit—light—cannot exist together, so these areas stay dark, and we now have a believer whose old nature is restricting the light. How is this Christ believer going to become a Christ follower?"

"He must replace the darkness with light," I answered. "But, how?"

Mandy leaned forward in her chair, as eager as I to hear his reply.

Gary smiled and said, "The light of the Spirit focuses on one of the compartments containing sin. The believer is convicted of the sin and recognizes the need to remove it from his life. As soon as it has been released, the light flows into the compartment and radiates outward. This process is repeated over and over as one matures in Christ. Sure, occasionally a compartment full of light will give way to darkness as a new sin creates a stronghold, but for the believer who is seeking God daily in his life, it is a steady journey toward being a Christ follower."

"I've never thought of it this way," I admitted. "You actually make it sound logical. Boy, can I relate to these compartments of sin. Without doubt, I have a compartment stuffed full of pride. I've been convicted. With time, light is going to overcome this stronghold."

"Very good," Gary replied. "Now, let's look a little closer at that special compartment, the command post. The Holy Spirit resides in the believer as a Counselor to guide and direct the believer along God's chosen path.

In order to accomplish that task, the Spirit must flow into the command post, which continuously retrieves and stores from the network of compartments.

"When the command post retrieves compassion, the Holy Spirit flows into the command post along with the compassion, but when the command post retrieves lust, the Holy Spirit moves out. Remember, lust is sin; sin is darkness; the Holy Spirit is light; light and darkness cannot coexist. From this we can see that, if a person has evil or sinful thoughts, the Holy Spirit is nowhere to be found, but if a person has godly thoughts, the Counselor is there to assist in every decision.

"Now, what is the difference between a new Christian and one of God's saints?"

"Ask Mandy," I said immediately. "She can give you an eyewitness account." Maybe I spoke out of hand, but both Gary and Mandy smiled.

"A new Christian is one of God's children," Gary said, "but there are many areas still without the light. One of God's saints has so many compartments filled with the light, it radiates from his whole being."

"Like Dr. Thomas, or Mother Teresa."

"Excellent examples," Gary replied, "but only one man received the Holy Spirit, and the light filled each and every compartment. Jesus was totally without sin, so when the Holy Spirit came down like a dove, Jesus became the Light for the world. Does this answer your question?"

I had to give Gary credit. He made this sound so logical. I could relate to his answer. "Yes, I think I understand. But you mentioned *believer* and *follower*. In fact, the name of your church is Christ Followers Church. How exactly do you distinguish between a Christian, a Christ believer, and a Christ follower?"

Round Three

"Well now," Gary said, "Let's start with a Christian. For centuries, people who have declared themselves Christians have equally declared that others are certainly not Christians, and the others have returned the accusation. What, then, is the test? What is the minimum level of response necessary to make a person so? It's not an easy question to answer. The simple answer, of course, is to believe in Jesus. Well, that raises another question. What does this mean?"

"To believe in Jesus is to believe Jesus is the Son of the almighty God," Mandy supplied. "He was born of the Virgin Mary. He was crucified on a cross. He died and was buried for three days. He arose from the grave and ascended into heaven to sit at the right hand of God. Through His death on the cross, his burial, and his resurrection, He provided purification for our sins so that whoever believes may have everlasting life."

I smiled at her, impressed by her succinct answer.

Gary nodded his approval of Mandy's input, then continued. "The Bible says in John 1:12, 'To those who received Him, to them He gave the right to become children of God, even to those who believed on His name,' but certainly more than intellectual belief is required. When Jesus speaks of believing, He clearly means a genuine response of the heart to Him and His teachings, a response that changes lives. As He said in Matthew 7:16–20, 'By their fruits you will know them.'

"The thief on the cross was a wrongdoer and knew little about Jesus, but on the cross he recognized that here was One sent from God Who in some way could offer him mercy. He responded as his life ebbed away, and learned that his salvation was assured.

"Are we to believe that he accepted the full divinity of Christ? Certainly not. Such a question would hardly have sprung to his mind. Did he understand the mystery of his atonement? Again the answer must be no, but he recognized Jesus was from God in some special way, and that He was able to offer him forgiveness and salvation, and he genuinely accepted that forgiveness and his salvation.

"In the end, we must stand by this. Those who genuinely believe in and respond to Jesus and His teachings, recognizing that through His work on the cross He has created access to God, will find acceptance with Him. We must always strive to ensure that our faith is not just a bundle of doctrines but a genuine response. Then we can have confidence in our salvation. This is the reason most churches have the new Christian come forward and respond in front of the congregation, declaring that he accepts Jesus as his Lord and Savior.

"It would be nice if we could say believers were new Christians and followers were those who have been Christians for a time, but unfortunately that is not the case. A believer has accepted Christ as his savior, so his spirit is alive and filled with the Holy Spirit. When the Holy Spirit focuses on areas of his old nature that need change, the believer who is not growing and maturing allows the old nature to stay in control and does not heed the conviction of the Counselor.

"The believer is like a newborn baby crying for his milk. That's okay for a new Christian, but babies grow and soon walk and eat solid food. The believer is still looking for his next bottle.

"Now, let me ask you a question. Do you think Christ believers have found God's will for their lives?"

Round Three

After a prolonged period of silence, I realized he was waiting for me to respond. Caught totally off guard, I answered his question with one of my own. "Huh? What do you mean?"

Gary smiled. "How can believers know God's will for their lives when they can't even feed themselves? How are they going to feed someone else? Are believers saved? Surely they are saved. Are they becoming more Christ-like? If only believers and not followers, I don't think so. They may attend church regularly, but sitting in church every Sunday morning does not make them grow or become more holy. If it did, the pews would be more holy than they are.

"A Christ follower is on a journey to become just like Jesus. Surely he will never complete the journey, but as each season comes and goes, he becomes more Christ-like. When the Counselor convicts him of an area of his old nature, he strives to remove it from his character and let the light of the Holy Spirit flow in. He is not content with hearing the Good News; he wants to share it with others.

"Christ did not say, 'Believe in me, come into My Church, and rest your weary souls.' He did not say, 'Believe in me, come into My Church, and pastors and clergymen, go out and spread the Good News.' He said, 'Believe in me and go out into the world and spread the Good News.' All Christians are commissioned to tell others so that they may have the same opportunity to be saved."

I interrupted with, "So, a Christian is anyone who believes and has responded to Christ's offer of salvation. A Christ believer who is not maturing is a Christian who is still drinking bottled milk instead of taking solid food.

A Christ follower is a Christian who is maturing in Christ and has accepted the responsibility for spreading the message of salvation."

"Very good. But this raises another question that I will ask for you. Can a man be saved and then lost?"

Boy, this was one I'd struggled with all my life. My mother believed *Once Saved, Always Saved*, but I was unsure. I answered, "My mother would say yes, but me?" I shrugged.

"Let's take a closer look at this idea of *Once Saved, Always Saved*," Gary said. "We are always a little concerned about this phrase, because it carries with it the danger of complacency. While we believe the statement is true, we must include 'as long as a person is really saved, and the only true test of that, from the perspective of the Bible, is his life.'

"This salvation is accomplished by an act of faith and commitment. As a person genuinely recognizes his need to be saved from sin, he commits himself completely to the One who saves and trusts Him to carry out the work, knowing that once He has begun a good work, He will carry it out to the end. We are then saved and have also entered the process of being saved.

"This guarantee of salvation is confirmed in a number of verses. In Philippians 1:6 Paul speaks of 'being confident of this very thing, that He who has begun a good work in you will perform it until the day of Jesus Christ.' The assumption is that God's work will produce results, slowly but surely, because He is doing it.

"This aspect of the security of the Christian is found in the words of Jesus. In John 10:28 Jesus summarizes the Christian's position in these words: 'My sheep hear

Round Three

My voice, and I know them, and they follow Me, and I give to them eternal life, and they shall never perish, neither shall any pluck them from My hand.'

"This verse is packed through with certainty—the gift of eternal life, the safety in His hand, and the guarantee that they will never be allowed to wander away and perish. This is Christ's promise, but notice the test to ensure we are His sheep. His sheep hear His voice and follow Him. So perhaps we should say *Once Saved*—hear his voice and follow Him—*Always Saved*."

I shook my head, overwhelmed. "Wow, that's a ton of information. Should we call it a night before I suffer information overload?"

This brought a smile to Gary's lips. "Yes, we can pick it up again tomorrow evening. I hope I'm not losing you in the details. I want to be thorough, but at the same time, I don't want to over-answer your question."

I must confess, his answers required my undivided attention, but they were most enlightening. "Your answers are right on the mark," I assured him. "Don't change a thing. My eyes are finally open, and I'm understanding and absorbing all you say."

"Excellent, excellent," Gary said. "We will talk again tomorrow. I'm really enjoying our discussions."

Chapter Nineteen

Round Four

It finally dawned on me Thursday morning, with Mandy making wedding plans left and right, that I needed to go about the procurement of a wedding ring. I decided to discuss this important issue with Brenda, but Mandy was not letting me out of her sight. She still watched me constantly, still favoring me with that beautiful smile whenever I caught her looking.

Finally I said, "I need to talk to Brenda."

To my surprise, she left the two of us alone in the kitchen.

I told Brenda that I needed her advice on buying the ring. "Should I go to Nashville and pick out a ring on my own, or should I discuss it with Mandy and see if she wants to select the ring?"

"Mandy would be overjoyed, either way," Brenda replied.

Now that was comforting, but it did little to solve my problem. "Okay," I said, "but that doesn't answer my question."

Brenda rested her chin in the palm of her hand. I could tell by the expression on her face that she was deep in thought. As I waited, she closed her eyes. Suddenly, she

Round Four

opened them and said, "Well, there is a man at CFC who is a retired jeweler. He still makes rings for close friends. He has known Mandy since she was born, and I'm sure he would be interested in sharing his expert advice."

"Great. Let's give him a call."

Saying Mr. Wilson would be interested was an understatement. When I told him of my dilemma, he took command of the situation. He would come right over, he said, and bring a bag of select stones that had just arrived from a supplier in New York.

In response to my stunned silence, he explained that he was preparing to make a ring for another couple. Whenever he agreed to make a ring, he had a selection of stones of varying sizes shipped in, asked the couple to make their choice, and then returned the remaining stones to the supplier. He always wanted the woman involved in selecting the stone. She was the one who would be wearing it, hopefully for life, and this was not a time for surprises. He wanted Mandy to look through the stones and make her choice.

This sounded perfect to me. I called Mandy into the room and brought her up to date on the game plan. Her eyes lit up with joy.

Mr. Wilson arrived with a bag full of beautiful diamonds varying in size from one-fourth carat to two carats. At first Mandy attempted to select the smallest diamond in the bag. Mr. Wilson came to my rescue and told her to select the one she liked best and not worry about price. He intended to sell the diamond to us for his cost and make the ring as a wedding gift. The diamond was an investment; it would only go up in value, so she should find the one that suited her best.

Mandy selected a beautiful pear-shaped diamond that weighed 1.47 carats. Her choice elated Mr. Wilson. He said she had selected the clearest and brightest diamond in the bag. Others were larger, but this was the best of the lot.

Next, Mandy looked through Mr. Wilson's catalogue and selected the ring style. He measured her finger, and with that little effort, the procurement of the wedding ring was complete. He told us he'd finish the ring within a week.

With this behind us, Mandy brought up the wedding itself. She didn't want a big wedding. She wanted only family to attend. That was fine with me, but I had four people I wanted to invite, and none of them were family.

She pushed me away in mock exasperation. "I'm not talking about your side!" she exclaimed. "Of course you can invite Carl, Rebecca, John, and Beth!"

We scheduled the wedding two weeks from Saturday, counting on her parents arriving as planned. We called Carl and John, but actually talked to Rebecca and Beth. They were both elated, and told us they would begin making arrangements to attend.

With so many things happening so rapidly, I reckoned I'd better plan the next step. I asked where she wanted to go for the honeymoon. Not surprisingly, a honeymoon was of little concern to Mandy. We would probably have plenty of opportunities to travel after we were married. She suggested that we spend our wedding weekend in the honeymoon suite at the Opryland Hotel in Nashville. I couldn't argue with that, but the thought of emerging from a limousine and making a grand entrance in full wedding attire to check in made me nervous.

Round Four

That evening, as the three of us went into the study for the next round in our discussions, I attempted to focus on the next issue to raise with Gary. Finding questions was getting harder. Gary's responses were so thorough, they covered a multitude of questions. I still had a couple of issues that I'd never been able to work out, though. I knew I'd have difficulty expressing one, in particular. If I could just get my point across, I was confident Gary could handle it.

After thinking for a moment, I said, "Gary, this question may be easier for you to answer than for me to express. I'll attempt to clarify the question with an example. Salvation is available to all, but a child has no control over his birth." At Gary's nod of encouragement, I pressed on. "Yet his birth weighs heavily on his ability to find God and salvation. We have no control over where we are born, whether our parents are Christians or atheists, wealthy or poor, good or evil. Does a pastor's son have a better opportunity for seeking God and finding salvation than an orphan who doesn't even know his parents? I have always questioned, *Why, God*? This seems so unfair.

"Both Mandy and Carl love the Lord and have found salvation through Jesus. How much easier was this for Mandy than for Carl? Did Carl have mountains to climb to find salvation and Mandy have it run over her as she stooped down to smell the roses? Don't take this wrong. I'm proud for both, and I know each had to reach out to receive, but Carl had to reach so much farther." I glanced at Mandy, then added, "I hope this makes sense."

"Yes; excellent, excellent, Gary replied. "It makes good sense. To answer, I'll need to give you some insight into the character of God." He leaned forward and clasped his hands on the desktop. "We want to see God as a God of love and mercy, but there is much more to His character than this. When Adam and Eve sinned, they immediately suffered spiritual death—the separation of the soul from God—and they gradually suffered physical death—the separation of the soul from the body. This penalty affects all humankind, because Adam's sin was charged to our account.

"We can't separate ourselves from Adam. He was created with a physical body, a soul—or mind—and a spirit. All three worked together in harmony, as God intended. Since Adam's fall, we are born with a physical body and a soul, but with a dead spirit. The results of Adam's sin are continuously transmitted to us through his ancestors.

"It really doesn't matter in what generation we are born. We still come from Adam. Therefore, we start life with this mark already on our account. This mark is in reality a curse handed down from generation to generation. God has made provisions so that we may rise above it, but he does not declare 'fresh start' and wipe the slate clean for each new generation.

"When God tested Abraham with the life of his son Isaac and Abraham obeyed through faith, God marked the account of Abraham and all his descendants. This mark on his descendants' account is a blessing handed down from generation to generation."

Gary paused and looked at me. "Is this making sense?"

I frowned in concentration. "It does, but this concept of blessings and curses following us from generation to generation is new to me."

"God has made provisions for his chosen people to be blessed, but they can fall far below those blessings to the point of being cursed for generations," Gary explained. "Obey and be blessed; sin and be cursed. Still,

Round Four

each of us is born with that free will, so he can move from curse to blessing or from blessing to curse. It is an individual's choice, no matter when and where that individual is born.

"What causes curses is exactly opposite to that of blessings. Blessings result from hearing God's voice and obeying. Curses result from not listening to God and not obeying. In Exodus 20:4–5, in the second of the Ten Commandments, God explicitly forbids the making of any kind of idol or image for religious purposes and warns that those who break this commandment will bring judgment—a curse—not only on themselves but also on at least three generations following. In this we can see that God's character is not only one of love and mercy, but of judgment, as well.

"Nations are blessed based on past generations, but nations can become so wicked and evil that they curse the next generation. If this wickedness reaches a certain point, it can become intolerable to God and provoke Him into destroying that nation. How wicked were Sodom and Gomorrah compared to our country today? As we promote and practice the right to abortion in this generation, are we cursing the next generation?

"Now, how much is too much in God's sight?"

Gary paused as I considered the question. Finally I said, "You make an excellent point. I don't know. But if our nation continues to move away from our godly heritage, this land is going to suffer a catastrophic event allowed by God. Would this serve as punishment or would it happen to get our attention? I don't know that answer, either. But, based on what I've learned from our previous sessions, He could allow the wicked deeds of evil men to bring this about."

"Very good point," Gary said. "Travis and I have spent many an evening discussing this very issue concerning our nation. In fact, we pray for our nation and its leaders daily. So, let's get back to your question. Now, with insight into God's character, let's consider an individual born in either poverty or wealth, one who is healthy or sick, with Christian or non-Christian parents, in or out of wedlock. Does the child have any control over being brought into this world? Surely not, but is he not of a certain generation, from a certain nation, from a certain family? Surely he is. This is his starting point, based on those who came before him. He can rise above his birth and be blessed, or he can sink below it and be cursed. It is his choice.

"I agree; going from blessings to more blessings is an easier journey than going from curses to blessings, but God cannot apply love and mercy and hold back judgment, just as God cannot apply judgment and hold back love and mercy. God is true and just, so it is impossible for Him to hold back one over the other. Is this making sense?"

Wow, did that make sense? You better believe it. That was an awesome answer. "Yes, for the first time I understand. No one gets a fresh start. We are all tied to the past, but that doesn't prevent us from determining our future. Everyone is born under the curse handed down from Adam. It's like God designed a perfectly balanced, three-cylinder automobile, but because of Adam's sin, each of us is born running on two cylinders. Until a person's spirit comes alive, he is flawed and out of balance. Everyone has a starting point in life that's tied not only to his parents but to his generation, his nation, his community, and even to past generations."

Round Four

"Very good, very good indeed. Now, what is your next question?"

As Gary waited, I searched my memory. "I'm rapidly emptying my box of questions. This is not actually a question, but more a matter of not fully understanding. When I was a child, my mother talked about worshiping one God. Then, in the next sentence she referred to God as Father, Son, and Holy Ghost. This always confused me. In the orphanage, as I read my mother's Bible, I attempted to solve this mystery. The Bible repeatedly states that there is but one God, but also references God the Father, God the Son, and God the Holy Spirit. I still don't understand this paradox. How can one be three?"

Gary chuckled. "Well now, the doctrine of the Trinity—God the Father, Son, and Holy Spirit—is not easy to fit into your logical boxes, but it is the very foundation of Christian truth. Logic is a good thing. In fact, many people could use more of it, but in dealing with Godly and spiritual issues, logic can actually keep you from the truth. There is a point where we have to release logic and grab hold of faith. Logic is tied to science; faith is tied to God.

"God wants us to use our free will and continually move toward Him based on faith, not logic. Hebrews 11:6 says 'But without faith it is impossible to please Him, for he who comes to God must believe that He is, and that He is a rewarder of those who diligently seek Him.'

"Now I'll attempt to answer the question. The Trinity of the Godhead is found in both the Old and New Testaments. The idea that there is but one God is found throughout Scriptures. In Isaiah 45:21–22 we see 'and there is no other God beside Me, a just God and a Savior; there is none beside Me. Look to Me, and be saved, all you ends of the earth! For I am God and there is no other.'

"The three persons of the Godhead are also noted throughout the Scriptures. In John 10:30: 'I and My Father are one,' and in Matthew 28:19: 'Go therefore and make disciples of all nations, baptizing them in the name of the Father, the Son, and the Holy Spirit.' This verse references the one name, God, yet associates it with the three names—Father, Son, and Holy Spirit."

I must have looked confused, because he said, "I'll try to summarize.

"Each person of the Godhead is equally, fully, and eternally God. Each is necessary; each is distinct, yet all are one. These three Persons appear in a distinct order. The Father is the unseen, the omnipresent Source of all being, revealed in and by the Son, experienced in and by the Holy Spirit. The Son proceeds from the Father, and the Spirit from the Son. With reference to God's creation, the Father is the Thought behind it, the Son is the Word calling it forth, and the Spirit is the Deed making it a reality.

"We see God and His great gift of salvation through the Son, the Lord Jesus Christ, and experience their reality by faith, through the indwelling presence of His Holy Spirit that resides in each and every one who has been saved. I admit this is difficult to comprehend, but it is an important truth that must be dealt with if you are to grow in your faith.

"I hope this lays the groundwork that enables you to develop a deeper understanding of this basic doctrine of the Scriptures."

I nodded, but that answer nearly went over my head. Without doubt, it would require a long run accompanied by some deep thought. But everything else hit the mark.

Round Four

"I'm beginning to understand much that was always unclear and somewhat of a mystery," I told him. "I also now see why Mandy wanted you and me to have these discussions. She certainly knew what she was doing. This is probably a good stopping point. Let me absorb this latest round, and we'll meet again tomorrow. I do believe our next round will exhaust my box of questions."

Chapter Twenty

Round Five

David and Mary called early Friday morning to tell us they would arrive on Sunday afternoon. Mandy told them the wedding was less than two weeks away. When her mother casually asked what our plans were after the wedding, Mandy took the question in stride. I leaned forward to hear her reply myself.

We were still working on a number of issues, she replied blithely, but when things became clear, Mary would be the first to know. What a polite way of saying we did not have a clue! We both sensed we were guided, though, and that when the time came, the answer would be waiting.

After we talked to her parents, I asked Mandy about the Stones River National Battlefield. She asked if I would like to visit the monument. I thought that was a great idea. So Brenda packed us a lunch, and we set out for a grand tour.

It was a beautiful, sunny day and unusually warm for winter. We spent hours walking over the site of the bloodiest battle of the Civil War. We talked, held hands, removed our shoes, and dangled our feet in the river. On a plateau that sloped toward the river stood a giant

Round Five

oak tree that must have witnessed the entire battle. We ate our picnic lunch under this old tree and then leaned against its massive trunk to gaze out over the thousands of grave markers for the men who'd given their lives in the battle.

Surely there'd been no winners that day, only losers. Young men lost their lives; mothers lost their sons; wives lost their husbands. Those grave markers represented hopes and dreams never realized. Our country pulled back together and became a great nation, but these men were not part of it. Their lives ended as our nation moved forward. Those grave markers reminded those who came after of the price these men paid so that our country could mend.

Thinking back to all the events that had occurred so rapidly over the past few days, I realized there was something important that I'd neglected to tell Mandy. As I'd left McLaren Hospital, Kim and Janice each shared something from their past that had escaped Mandy's prying for months.

So I said, "Remember when I left McLaren to drive here?"

"Certainly," she replied. "And I remember being one scared girl."

"Well," I said smugly, "how would you like to know what caused Kim and Janice to join the missionary training program?"

Mandy's eyes lit up. "You know! How? When?" she shouted.

I was relieved that she didn't ask why I'd waited so long to tell her. "As I was leaving McLaren, I stopped by the waiting room to say good-bye to Kim and Janice. But before I could speak, Kim said that she had something she needed to say. Our tragedy made her want to face a tragedy from her past.

"Seven years ago, when Kim was fifteen, both of her parents worked for the Sandia Casino. Kim had an older brother, Carlos. On her brother's eighteenth birthday, Kim rushed home from school to prepare for his surprise party. She found a note on her bed from her brother that said, 'Tell Mom and Dad I am sorry. I have gone to find peace on the mountain – Love Carlos.' Carlos had jumped to his death from a cliff on the Sandia Mountain.

"The tragic death of her brother turned Kim's life upside down. That's the reason her parents quit their jobs at the casino, opened the shop, joined the mission, and became involved in the mission's social services for the reservation."

Mandy interjected, "Why did Carlos take his life?"

I was prepared for this question. During the drive through the snowstorm, her brother's tragic death occupied my mind for hours. "I couldn't bring myself to ask, but I think I know. The youth on reservations struggle with their native traditions, customs, and values in relation to today's society. They have difficulty establishing their identity. I think Kim's parents realized this and, after their son's death, turned to Christ to save Kim—and it worked."

Mandy nodded in agreement. "That's the reason Kim joined the missionary training program."

"Yes. She plans to return to the reservation to work with the youth there. She wants to prevent what happened to her brother from happening to other kids. But, that's not all. After hearing Kim, Janice told us about her tour of the Netherlands. That trip opened the doors to a world beyond the limits of her hometown. On the streets of downtown Amsterdam, Janice witnessed kids

Round Five

getting high on drugs and saw pretty girls her own age sitting half-clothed in shop windows, attempting to attract their next customer. The loud music, the flowing liquor, the next high, the free love—nothing could banish that lost look from their eyes. First from shock and then from compassion, Janice searched for a way to offer comfort and hope to the youth of this city of sin. On the flight home, she decided to complete her degree in nursing, but put her career on hold and do missionary work in Amsterdam."

"Wow," Mandy exclaimed, "you did good!"

"Actually," I said, "they volunteered and I just listened. But, that brings up a question for you. Why did you join the missionary training program?"

Mandy pushed her long, silky black hair away from her face, looked out across the battlefield, and said, "That's a good question, especially since Kim and Janice have confided in you. But, as for me, I'm not really sure. Yes, I want to do missionary work, but not like Mom and Dad. Do you remember me telling you about that lost look in the kids' eyes? I don't want to work with adults. I want to reach the kids and keep them from going through that period of hopelessness. Does that make sense?"

"Sure," I replied. "It makes plenty of sense. You have a heart for the kids and I have a heart for orphans. We're on the same page."

As I said page, I glanced down at the book in our picnic basket. We'd brought *Evangelizing India through God's Orphan Army* with us. Now we lifted the book from the basket and took turns reading the chapters aloud. It was a short book, with no more than six chapters and forty pages altogether.

India is a country with more than one billion people, representing close to one-fourth the world population. According to the Indian government, 98 percent are Hindu, Muslim, and other religions. Less than 2 percent of the population is Christian.

Now, picture orphanages designed first to love and care for orphan children. Inside these orphanages are schools that not only educate the children but expose them to the powerful Word of God, teaching them God's love and instilling within them God's burden for a lost and dying world. Then add to this a Bible institute, where these children, as they become adults, are trained to go out and start churches in some of the 600,000 cities and villages that have no Christian witness.

Dr. Thomas not only wanted to provide a haven for the orphans living in the streets of every city, he wanted to offer them salvation, and then send them out to the cities all over India, where they could spread the Good News about the Gospel of Jesus Christ. There were currently more than twenty Emmanuel Orphanages scattered across India. Their *Christ for India* program needed donations from churches and Christians in this country so they could continue to expand. More important, though, they needed missionary volunteers to establish and manage new Emmanuel Orphanages. It would take a long-term commitment and much effort, but the reward would be beyond all expectations.

As we read those last few pages, we both knew why Dr. Thomas made the special trip to the hospital to hand deliver this book. Neither of us said a word. We leaned up against the tree, both holding onto the book, and looked into each other's eyes, each knowing exactly what the other was thinking. As we headed back to meet with

Round Five

Gary, we said nothing, but we both knew that our answer was just around the corner and closing fast.

As we went into the study, I tried to put the book and the battlefield behind me and focus on the task at hand. I felt sure this would be our last round of questions.

I began with, "This is not something I've questioned; rather, it's a matter of not understanding. In the New Testament, Jesus makes many references to His Church, not churches. So why do we have so many denominations?"

Gary leaned forward in his chair, laughed out loud, and said, "Boy, have you hit on a sore spot for me. Let me attempt to respond out of wisdom and understanding instead of being swayed by my feelings and emotions. First, we founded Christ Followers Church over twenty years ago in response to that very issue. CFC is a gathering place for a group of interdenominational Christians. We meet and worship in our building, but those Christians worshipping in the building are actually the Church.

"The first point I want to make is that 'His Church' is not about buildings or denominations. It's that group of Christians who believe and practice the Gospel of Salvation through Jesus Christ our Lord. One important point—the doctrine of the denomination's beliefs must line up with those we established the other day as far as being Christian. Those who believe Jesus was just a good man or a prophet and not the living Son of our almighty God are not part of His Church, since they can't be considered Christians.

"With that said, here's my opinion, not necessarily shared by all. Christ established only one Church, His Church, and there is still only one Church today. All Christians are part of the body of Christ and are therefore members of His Church. Being a Christian is what qualifies you to be a member of the body of Christ, not being of a certain denomination. Don't you agree?"

"Sure," I replied. "So why all the denominations?"

"For centuries, groups of Christians have established denominations based on a specific doctrine that was unique and fulfilled the requirements for their belief. Since even Christians are far from perfect, many denominations believe their doctrine is so correct that all others must be wrong. But, since both believe the basic truth of salvation through the cross and the blood of Jesus Christ, can't both be members of His Church?

"Surely they can, but both groups contain their share of selfishness, hypocrisy, and other flaws. This can be discouraging to the unbeliever and to some Christian believers, but selfishness and hypocrisy should not drive believers away from church involvement. It should make us aware of how much we need to be members of His Church. All denominations are made up of imperfect people, but as we mature, we grow in discovering how much we owe to God's grace and how little we earn through our own efforts.

"This is why it's so important for us to move from being Christ believers to Christ followers. In Luke 6:41 it says, 'And why do you look at the speck in your brother's eye, but do not perceive the plank in your own eye?' Yes, there is sometimes hypocrisy in the church, no matter the denomination, but our awareness of these imperfections makes it easier to see how God is able to use His Church to mature us toward being more Christ-like.

"One should not judge Christianity based on these imperfections. Christ followers constantly seek to be more like Jesus and thus, hopefully, become less of a

Round Five

deterrent to those unbelievers looking from the outside at those members of His Church. Sure, the quality of an authentic Christian life, no matter the denomination, will fluctuate, but over time, the Christ follower will mature and become a beacon to light the way for not only the unbeliever but also the Christ believer."

"I understand," I said. "Is baptism a good example of how doctrines differ between denominations? When I was very young, I attended the Baptist church with my mother. They baptized by submerging. When I went to the Methodist church with my father, they baptized by sprinkling."

"Yes," Gary replied, "that's an excellent example. In fact, not only do denominations differ in their methods of baptizing, some question whether baptism is necessary for salvation. At CFC we submerge, but if having enough water became an issue, we wouldn't have a problem with sprinkling.

"While baptism is an important act of obedience, is it necessary for salvation? There are many passages in the New Testament that make it clear that God's grace through faith alone brings salvation. At CFC we believe the only requirement for salvation is faith in the Lord Jesus Christ but, in reality, we are asking the wrong question. The real question should be: Why should you not want to be baptized? It's a new believer's first opportunity to demonstrate obedience to Christ's teachings.

"Many verses in the Scriptures clearly affirm salvation by grace through faith alone. The dying thief on the cross who repented was promised companionship with Jesus in Paradise —salvation—even though he died without baptism.

"Some denominations select the few passages that seem to make baptism a requirement for salvation and ignore the many that declare salvation is by faith alone. Is our doctrine at CFC wrong and theirs correct? Let each believer decide. Aren't we members of His Church, no matter whether baptism is an act of obedience or necessary for salvation? Why do we argue among ourselves over the correctness of our doctrine? Instead, shouldn't we be pulling together to find the lost and bring them into His Church?

"His Church in each generation has a responsibility to carry out His work, no matter the denomination. It is our watch. We have a world full of responsibility. Are we not accountable for this generation? Is Christ's interest not better served if we go about his work of offering salvation to the lost and weary instead of bickering among ourselves over the correctness of our doctrine?

Gary sighed and sat back. "I hope my response was not too negative. I tend to let my emotions and feelings interfere on this issue."

"Your responses have been enlightening," I replied, then paused for a long moment. "There is one—well, I've been thinking about Travis. Has he contacted his family to let them know he's all right? I figured that maybe he was visiting them earlier this week, when he was out of town."

The expression on Gary's face made me wonder if my question was inappropriate. But, before I could speak, Gary replied, "No, he wasn't visiting his family. Travis went to Atlanta for the Southeastern Building Supply Auction. He drove a rented U-haul to the auction and returned with windows, doors, plumbing supplies, and lighting fixtures for his house. All in all, the whole lot cost less than one-third their retail value."

Round Five

"Wow, what a bargain," I said self-consciously. "Oh, well, I hope I wasn't out of line, asking about his family."

"Not at all," said Gary. "Heaven knows, the two of you have much in common. From infant to eighteen, Travis lived in an orphanage outside of Austin, Texas."

Gary's words took me completely by surprise. Instantly, I could relate to this brave man. We were two of a kind, except for size. What did Brenda see in those eyes that caused her to circle the block? Was it the same thing Mandy had seen in my eyes?

"At eighteen, Travis joined the Marines," Gary continued. "The Vietnam War broke out toward the end of his first term of enlistment; he reenlisted and went to Vietnam. When every member of his squad died in the ambush, he lost more than comrades; they were his only family. His squad was all he had and their loss was—"

"It was more than he could accept," I blurted. "Like when I lost my mother."

"Yes. I knew you would understand."

I nodded. That God reached a little further for both Travis and me was not mere coincidence. Without doubt, we were now brothers in Christ. If I had my way, we would become a close family. With these thoughts in my mind, I turned to Gary and said, "I can't express in words the impact these last five days have had on my life. Only time will reveal how your wisdom and knowledge have strengthened my faith, opened my eyes to truth, and pointed me in the direction of God's will. I want to meet one more time; not for questions, but so that I may respond."

Chapter Twenty-One

Victory Round

Since it was Saturday, I approached Gary about meeting earlier than our normal time. Gary suggested 3:00 p.m.

These last five days had been an awakening, but they followed that time when I knew in my heart and soul that Jesus had become real in my life. That moment occurred when I was driving from Flint to Nashville through the snowstorm. While praying to God, I'd said, *I surrender to you, Lord.* When I yielded, my eyes became open.

I tried to tell Mandy that first day at Vanderbilt Hospital, but she interrupted. She suggested the rounds of questions so that every issue that created doubt in my mind could be resolved. Mandy knew what she was doing. Gary settled issue after issue. Because of his constant pursuit of truth through the Bible, the Holy Spirit unveiled knowledge of the ways of God to which few are privileged.

Why would this wonderful girl and her God-fearing family accept me without really knowing whether I could change? There was only one reason: faith. Mandy had

Victory Round

so much faith, she told Babu not to worry about me, told him to go back to India; we would be married before he returned.

Where does faith like that come from? My mother said God gives everyone who believes a measure of faith the size of an acorn. Each must plant it in fertile soil, feed it the living Word of God, and water it from the living streams of the Holy Spirit. In time it will burst forth, reaching for the heavens, and mature like a giant oak tree. My mother had such faith; Mandy had it; her whole family had it; and now I could have such faith. This was not only an answered prayer; it was another miracle.

As we entered the room, I recalled how I'd waited patiently for five days for this moment. Really, ever since the sixth grade, I'd wanted to reach this point, but it was always beyond my grasp. Now I just had to express what I already felt in my heart and soul.

I leaned forward eagerly as we sat down. "I don't profess to understand why I have been singled out and given this miraculous opportunity for salvation. Mandy's ability to see the light from a person's spirit is totally beyond my understanding. But, I don't question it. The fact that my spirit is hidden from her sight confirms I've been singled out.

"It is humbling to admit you are lost. Pride must be swallowed, which is a painful but essential first step. Wrong turns and bad choices have kept me going in the wrong direction. I questioned why God extended his reach for me. There are many who are lost, but they may miss out. I want all to have the same opportunity.

"Maybe the reason I was singled out goes back to my mother. She had mountain-moving faith and prayed with full confidence that God would respond. As I look back, I think her continuous prayers on my behalf brought me to this point. She loved the Bible just as Mandy does. She carried her Bible from room to room, even when she wasn't reading from it. She said it is impossible to live your life to the fullest without an adequate grasp of the Bible. She would quote Scripture after Scripture to enforce her point. When I was a small boy, much went over my head, but I saw her character and its Source.

"In the front of her Bible she penned a quote from Daniel Webster and a poem by Sir Walter Scott. I have read that page a thousand times. Daniel Webster said, 'If we abide by the principles taught in the Bible, our country will go on prospering, but if we and our posterity neglect its instructions and authority, no man can tell how sudden a catastrophe may overwhelm us and bury all our glory in profound obscurity.' "Sir Walter Scott's poem titled 'The Bible' said:

> *Within this wondrous volume lies*
> *The mystery of mysteries;*
> *Happiest they of human race*
> *To whom their God has given grace*
> *To read, to fear, to hope, to pray,*
> *To lift the latch, to find the way;*
> *And better had they ne'er been born*
> *Who read to doubt, or read to scorn.*

"If my mother is looking down on us now, this is my answer to all those prayers on my behalf. Lord Jesus, I believe You are the one and only Son of our Almighty God, that You were born of the virgin Mary, died on the cross, and rose from the dead and ascended into heaven to sit at the right hand of God. Thank You for dying on the cross for my sins. I know I am a sinner. Please forgive

Victory Round

me. I now place all my trust in You alone for my salvation. Please come into my life. I accept Your gift of eternal life. In your name, Amen."

With tears of joy streaming down her face, Mandy said, "I am so proud, so very proud. And now I'll admit why I've been staring at you for the whole week. I tried to be inconspicuous, but with little success. Do you remember at Vanderbilt Hospital when you attempted to tell me you were ready to accept Jesus as your Savior?"

"Sure," I replied, "and you stopped me."

"I know, but I wanted Gary to resolve all your questions." She leaned forward. "At the exact moment when you said, 'I accept Jesus,' I saw the light flowing from your face."

"Why didn't you tell me?"

After a long pause, Mandy said, "I didn't feel it was the right time. Then each day as you met with Gary, the light grew brighter and brighter. I was amazed at how it increased in intensity each day, but just now, as you verbally accepted Christ as your Savior, my ability to see the light faded away. Now both you and Gary look—well, you both look normal."

Amazingly, this made sense. In fact, now I understood. God allowed us this brief glimpse into His character. Sure, both Travis and I exercised our free will, went our own way, and wandered from His chosen path. But, unknown to either, we had ties to family and ancestors whom God had blessed. And like His curses, His blessings will find you. No matter how far you wander, they will seek you out.

It was now so clear! I replied confidently, "I truly understand. Our spirit's light is still there. But, through Mandy, God accomplished His plan; therefore she no longer needs to see what He sees. Sure, God used Mandy's faith to reach out to me, but in turn He used Brenda's to reach out to Travis.

"There is one more thing I want to do. It's the reason I asked to meet early. I want to go to the Stones River National Battlefield and be baptized in the river at the place where all those men gave their lives for this country."

"I would be honored to baptize you there," Gary said, then warned me, "Even though it's unseasonably warm for this time of year, the water is going to be very cold. I'll only have to wade; you will be submerged."

"I know it will be cold," I said. "Mandy and I dangled our feet in the river yesterday. It *was* very cold, but now I have a fire in my heart that will see me through."

Gary rose. "Let's go—but I'm bringing my waders."

Yes, the river was cold to the point of taking away my breath. But as I rose from the water, I felt washed and clean. For the first time in my life, I felt obedient to God's Word and Will. This was a special crossroads; I marked it in my mind so that it could be revisited at any time.

Chapter Twenty-Two

CJC

Time is supposed to heal, but in this case it would take more than time to right this ship. I got off course and sailed beyond the reefs into dark waters. Lost, without a compass, and with little hope, I ran full speed ahead toward the straits that led right up to the banks of hell.

I ignored the angels battling to keep me afloat. Fueled by pride and blinded by darkness, I forged ahead. When even a lifeline of hope seemed out of reach for this wayward vessel, a whirlwind came down to spin my ship around. With it came a lifeboat that had been specifically sent to rescue me from the sinking ship, and save it did. This lifeboat claimed its castaway and followed the guiding beam from the lighthouse to the safety of the shore.

With so many lost at sea, why was this one spared? Maybe it's not for us to reason why. Instead we must find our course and set sail, looking to the heavens for our compass.

I thought these things as I prepared for my first church service since my mother's death. Carl had asked me to go, but I declined. He continued to ask; I continued to decline. Finally, he quit asking. That seemed so long ago. Looking back, I remembered the emptiness in the pit of my stomach and the feeling of abandonment, but mainly the lost hope.

I thought it would feel strange, walking into a church after so long. Instead it felt as if I was coming back home. But Christ Followers Church was unlike the churches I remembered. Those in the congregation seemed so real and genuine. I could feel the compassion and joy of these people. This church had a vision, a purpose beyond gathering to hold a service together. If Mandy could still see the spirit's light, the building would be overflowing with brilliance.

Mandy introduced me to one person after another. I tried to put names with faces, but there were too many. Mr. Wilson approached and asked Mandy about the wedding, and she added him to her growing guest list. She also introduced me to the nurse from Vanderbilt Hospital. True to her word, the woman had come. She sat down in the front row.

Instead of singing the old, familiar religious songs, we sang songs of praise and worship. During the singing, some lifted their hands in praise. This was not as I remembered either, but it seemed right for this place.

Gary paused while reading from the church bulletin and said there were two special guests he wanted to introduce. Then he looked our way and said, "I want to ask my granddaughter Mandy and her fiancé Mark to stand. Through the grace and mercy of God and thanks to your many prayers, she was healed."

The whole congregation rose to their feet in thunderous applause. I was ill prepared for this sudden attention, but as I looked around the room and saw hundreds of people crying tears of joy, I felt their very spirits reaching out to us. I felt a surge of emotion unlike any I'd ever experienced.

When Gary finished, Adam began the morning message. His sermon was from the book of Esther.

The story of Esther takes place during that time when God's chosen people were in captivity in Medea-Persia. Esther, whose Jewish heritage has been kept secret, is chosen by King Xerxes to replace Vashti as queen.

Haman, an evil advisor to the king, has risen in the king's favor. The king has even commanded that every knee shall bow to Haman, but while others bow the knee, there is one who refuses: *Mordecai the Jew*. Mordecai will not display to any man the reverence that belongs only to the one true God in Whom he believes. Infuriated by Mordecai's refusal, Haman instigates a decree that all the Jewish people in the Persian Empire will be slaughtered on the thirteenth day of the twelfth month.

Mordecai appeals to Esther and urges her to go to the king to beg for mercy and plead for her people. Esther responds that if she approaches the king without being summoned, she could be put to death unless the king extends his golden scepter to spare her life.

At this point in the story, the implicit recognition of God's direct involvement is unmistakable. In Esther 4:12–14, "When Esther's words were reported back to Mordecai, he sent back this answer: 'Do not think that because you are in the king's house you alone of all the Jews will escape. For if you remain silent at this time, relief and deliverance for the Jews will arise from another place, but you and your father's family will perish, and who knows but that you have come to royal position for such a time as this?' "

Mordecai's words reveal his unshakable faith in God and in the indestructibility of His chosen people, but they also reveal the theme of the story. God may have a bigger plan for our lives than we have for ourselves. God may place us in positions of leadership and influence so we can more thoroughly accomplish His purposes. God uses ordinary people to accomplish the extraordinary. We may be born on this earth at just the right time and be at just the right place to accomplish a specific task God has planned for and anticipated. If we fail to accept God's will and ignore His call, God will foresee and provide an answer, but it will be at our expense.

This was the key point to Adam's message, but he finished the story of Esther.

She appeals to Mordecai to have the Jewish people fast and pray for three days. On the third day, Esther enters the inner court and stands before the king. He immediately extends his golden scepter, assuring her that any breach of etiquette is excused.

The king, realizing that only some grave concern could have brought Esther thus, generously reassures her with the following words from Esther 5:3: "Then the king asked, 'What is it, Queen Esther? What is your request? Even up to half the kingdom, it will be given to you.'"

With this sudden turn of events, the crisis that had been anticipated is now amazingly overruled. With consummate skill, Almighty God in heaven turns the tables on the wicked and delivers His chosen people. A few master strokes, and the whole situation is reversed. Instead of the slaughter of the Jewish people planned by Haman, he is sent to his doom. Before another sunrise sheds its light over the city, the corpse of Haman dangles aloft on the very gallows that he himself had built for Mordecai.

CFC

As Adam asked the congregation to rise for a final song, I appreciated his selection of this specific sermon on this particular Sunday. When the song ended, without even thinking or discussing our actions, Mandy and I left our seats and headed down the aisle to talk to Adam.

The nurse from Vanderbilt Hospital also headed from the front row to talk to Adam. We heard her words as we approached. She didn't feel that she was saved. She wanted to accept Jesus Christ as her savior, join Christ Followers Church, be baptized, and live a new life.

Mandy looked at the nurse, looked at me, and said, "We did good."

Adam's sermon only confirmed what Mandy and I felt after reading Dr. Thomas's book at Stones River National Battlefield. We told Adam about meeting Dr. Thomas at the hospital, about the book, about *Christ for India* and the Emmanuel Orphanages. Yes, Mandy and I both had a vision, and we knew our part in the grand scheme.

Adam listened intently without saying a word, only nodding every so often to indicate he understood. As we concluded, he rose and gave both of us a bear hug and said, "Kids, you will be undertaking a monumental task that will require commitment, willpower, sacrifice, and much effort. It will take an investment of time, money, and resources, but you have a unique opportunity to answer God's call and take His message to a distant land that is filled with unbelievers. Instead of seeking success, you will be seeking to please God. This will add meaning, fulfillment, and significance to your lives. May God bless you as you trust Him and prepare for this endeavor."

With Adam's approval, our course was set. Mandy and I looked at one another. Dr. Thomas had inserted a card containing his address and phone number in his book. If it was noon in Murfreesboro, what time was it in India? We didn't have a clue.

Back at Gary and Brenda's home, we again described Dr. Thomas, his book, and India. We got another round of hugs from Brenda and Gary and then Gary said, "I have known for some time that the two of you were being prepared for a purpose not yet revealed. I also knew you were both listening and waiting patiently for the gentle whisper that would explain the reason for the divine intervention in your lives. Now that God's vision is clear, I encourage you to answer the call, take a leap of faith, and invest your talents in His work."

Actually, we now wanted to make a call.

Just as we reached for the phone, it rang. Mandy's parents were at the Nashville airport. They'd decided to wait and call when they arrived, so we wouldn't worry if they were delayed. We postponed our call and headed for the airport.

I have to admit, I was a little nervous about meeting Mandy's parents. Talking to them on the phone was one thing, but meeting them face-to-face was another story.

As Mandy ran ahead, jumped into David's arms, and was spun around and around, Mary came forward, grabbed me, and kissed me on my cheek. I immediately relaxed. Everything would be okay.

Wow, Mary was a beautiful lady. But the first words out of her mouth caught me completely off guard. "So this is Mandy's cute, lean, mean running machine."

I had no idea how to respond, or whether she even expected a response.

Mandy came to my rescue and introduced me to her mother and father. She explained that she referred to me as her running machine in her letters. Okay, I was ready to move on to another subject.

But the next subject was the long flight. I wasn't too pleased by this, either. Hours in the air, long delays at their connections, storms, turbulence—these were things that I could do without hearing.

Mandy began telling them every last detail of recent events, starting with seeing Babu off at the airport. This lasted until 6:00 p.m., when we headed out the door to attend the evening worship service. She even covered Dr. Thomas, *Christ for India*, and the Emmanuel Orphanages.

David and Mary already knew about *Christ for India* and the Emmanuel Orphanages. Although they had never met him, they had heard that Dr. Thomas was considered a saint in his country, India. Mandy did fail to mention our plans and impending phone call to Dr. Thomas.

The church was not filled to capacity as it had been for the morning service, but there was still a crowd. Adam introduced Mary and David, then asked them to come forward and bring everyone up to date on their mission activities in Malaysia. I listened in fascination as first Mary, then David described the day-to-day trials and tribulations and the day-to-day miracles of their work.

No wonder Mandy was such a special person; she came from a special family. How long had it been since I had family? And now, with open arms, this family reached out to me and the loneliness I'd felt for so long became a thing of the past.

Once back at Brenda and Gary's home, Mandy told her parents about our plans and the pending call to Dr. Thomas.

Running with Angels

After another round of hugs, Mary said, "Your father and I have spent our whole life together in the mission field. It is a most rewarding life, but it is also a challenging one. Every day brings new hardships, but when you are doing God's work, there is always an answer. Missionary work is surely not profitable in a financial sense, but it is always productive and abundantly fruitful. When we invest our God-given talent in serving others, we receive a personal joy in seeing God's work being carried out.

"I've felt for a long time that you wanted to follow in our footsteps. My biggest fear was that you would strike out alone. It makes all the difference in the world to have someone you love share in your grief and joy. I'm relieved that the Lord has seen fit to bring Mark and you together. My only wish is that the two of you return with us to Malaysia for a while before embarking on your own spiritual journey."

When our conversation with Mandy's parents ended, it was 9:00 p.m. We decided to make another attempt to call Dr. Thomas. As I picked up the phone, I again wondered aloud what time it was in India.

"India is in the Indian Standard Time Zone," David supplied. "That's ten and a half or eleven and a half hours ahead of our Central Time Zone, depending on daylight saving time."

I started to ask David where the one-half came from, but instead dialed the number. Someone picked up after just two rings. I recognized Dr. Thomas's voice but did not understand a word he said.

"Dr. Thomas," I interrupted, "this is Mark Matthews and Mandy Martin from Murfreesboro."

To this he replied in English, "This is wonderful! I've been preparing for your call."

Confused, I said, "You've been preparing for our call? How did you know we were going to call?"

"Oh, the Lord told me to busy myself and plan the opening of another orphanage. It would not be long before I'd hear from the two of you," he replied immediately. "There is much to be done, but we have narrowed our list of sites to three. Each is in an area of India that is without an orphanage and has little Christian activity. Our first choice is Nagpur, in East Central India in the Maharashtra State. Our second choice is—"

I cut him off. "Dr. Thomas, we want your first choice. I have a good friend who is going back home to Nagpur."

Dr. Thomas chuckled. "There are 600,000 towns and cities in India, and our first choice is your first choice. How can this be, unless we consider the spiritual factor? Are we to stand in the way of the hand of Almighty God? Nagpur it will be."

Mandy had gone to the other phone. Now I heard, "Dr. Thomas, this is Mandy. My mother wants us to visit with her in Malaysia before coming to India."

"Yes, that's perfect," Dr. Thomas said. "We have much to do prior to your arrival. The orphanage won't be ready to open for six months. Now, phones are so expensive; I will write you much detail and keep you well informed of our progress. Please send me a picture of the wedding and include your parents' address in Malaysia. I look forward to working with the two of you. Go be with your family, and prepare yourself for a wonderful undertaking. By ourselves we are nothing, but with God we have no limit. Bless both of you for hearing His call and coming forth to meet the challenge. Good-bye."

As we hung up, I realized we had just agreed to manage a new Emmanuel Orphanage in—of all places—Babu's hometown! This was unbelievable, but I guess no more than the events of the past two weeks.

Wait until I talk to Babu, I thought. Do we have a surprise for him!

And as I thought this, Mandy looked at me and said, "Boy, is Babu going to be surprised, or what?"

Chapter Twenty-Three

Full Circle

So there I was on the Interstate with Flint, Michigan, the next exit. Well, it looked like the Interstate, but to me it felt like Cloud Nine.

Babu had returned from India and was eagerly awaiting my arrival.

Okay, so I skipped a chapter. How can anyone, with mere words, express the feelings and emotions associated with his wedding? It may be possible for some of our great authors, but such expression reaches beyond my natural ability. How do I explain to someone who has never experienced being without family what it means to have a mother-in-law, father-in-law, grandmother, or grandfather?

Many people put down their in-laws. Carl surely did not, and I came to fully understand why. When family is found only in one's dreams, a mother-in-law like Mary and a father-in-law like David are a Godsend.

Since I do not want to leave a void in my story, I will back up and touch on the wedding.

From a small group of close relatives, the list grew out of control to more than one hundred guests. Every person Mandy encountered became another entry on her list.

One week before the wedding, she casually mentioned my passport.

"What passport?"

The procurement of my passport became the number-one issue, even relegating the wedding plans to the back burner. A passport is not like a driver's license, with a one-day turnaround.

On Thursday afternoon, two days before the wedding, Mandy and I drove to the Nashville airport to pick up Carl and Rebecca. John and Beth wouldn't arrive until the next afternoon. All Thursday evening, Mandy asked Carl and Rebecca question after question. I will confess that much of this conversation was at my expense.

At times, Carl's responses concerning a certain hardheaded runner were so funny, Mandy nearly fell out of her chair with laughter. I repeatedly tried to change the subject, but to no avail. Even Rebecca jumped on board and explained to Mandy that I was the most stubborn individual on this planet. On and on they continued, talking and laughing. One thing was for sure—they were instant friends.

I'd just decided that this would continue through the night when Brenda announced supper. During the meal, Gary and Carl carried the conversation. But afterward, when we'd settled in the study, Mandy asked Carl a more serious question. She wanted to know about the two weeks John and Beth spent with them after John injured his knee.

"What did you say to reach John?" Mandy asked.

Full Circle

Now, that was a good question. I leaned forward in anticipation of Carl's reply.

Carl hesitated, then said, "To tell the truth, I really don't know. First we got to know each other. Since John had family, I thought he had it made growing up. But the more we talked, the more I realized his childhood was far from what I imagined. His perfect family turned out to be a mother, stepfather, younger stepsister and stepbrother. John's stepfather was very strict and demanded much more of John than of the other children. Nothing John accomplished was ever good enough.

"John spent his childhood trying to prove himself and trying to measure up. Football was his salvation. Play tough and be the best, he thought, then surely the stepfather would be pleased. But no matter how well he preformed on the field, it was never good enough. This was the John we grew up with but never got to know, because of his tough guy attitude.

"Since he couldn't please his stepfather, he assumed God the Father was not pleased, either. This was our starting point. We talked for hours, separating our heavenly Father from the stepfather. Ever so slowly, he began to understand. Once we overcame this hurdle, we covered issue after issue. But when we reached forgiveness, John could not even comprehend the idea. Forgive his stepfather? Never. I backed away and instead we discussed the exchange that took place on the cross:

Christ exchanged our rejection for His acceptance.

Christ exchanged our sickness for His healing.

Christ exchanged our anxieties for His peace.

Christ exchanged our fear for His trust.

Christ exchanged our sin for His righteousness.

Christ exchanged our suffering for His freedom.

Christ exchanged our grief for His joy.

"We looked up verses associated with each exchange, read them aloud, and discussed their meaning.

"John said he needed some time to think about all we had discussed. So, I waited. Three days later, John said he was ready to accept Christ as his savior. He was also ready to get back to this unfinished business of forgiveness. He was ready to forgive his stepfather, but how?

"We spent hours discussing forgiveness, the fact that it didn't undo or justify the wrong or wipe out the memories; It just released them from the debt. We forgive so that we may be forgiven, I told him. And with that, John jumped to his feet and said that it finally made sense.

"But, there was still one insurmountable problem. How on earth could he expect Beth to forgive him for all the years of his verbal abuse? Now, this wasn't going to be easy. It would take far more than a casual reply. I said that I would pray about it and give him an answer in the morning.

"The next day, the two of us went for a long walk before breakfast. I told John that I had the answer, but he must listen closely and do everything exactly as I described. 'As soon as you get back home, go buy the following items: a porcelain bowl that will hold half a gallon of water, the most expensive royal blue towel and dark purple washcloth you can find, a bottle of Beth's favorite perfume, and half a gallon of distilled water. Have Beth sit in a chair while you pour the water and perfume into the bowl. Take Beth's right foot and wash it with the washcloth and dry it with the towel. Then, do the same for the other foot. While you are on your knees washing her feet, pray for the words to ask for her forgiveness. Then, speak from your heart.'

"John didn't say a word, but one week after they returned home we received a letter from Beth. Words cannot describe the joy contained in that letter. John did everything I described and Beth showered him with forgiveness. That was great news, but there was more. After a lot of prayer by both John and Beth, John was going to seminary school to become an evangelist."

His response left Mandy and I speechless. I felt honored to have Carl and Rebecca—and John and Beth—as friends.

* * *

So, just what is a wedding about? This one was about a bride in her beautiful white gown who held more than a hundred friends and relatives spellbound as she walked down the aisle on the arm of a father beaming with pride.

It was about family, as two joined to become one. It was about love as Adam took us through the wedding vows, establishing the framework for our lifelong commitment to one another. And finally, it was about a kiss that sealed our commitment and left me light-headed.

The reception, a multitude of pictures, and then a limousine ride from Murfreesboro to the Opryland Hotel, where we checked in still in full wedding attire and spent two days in the honeymoon suite on the top floor. These were memories not to be forgotten but too private to be shared.

After much discussion, we realized we needed a game plan for tying up all loose ends before leaving for Malaysia. David and Mary were scheduled to return the Saturday after the wedding.

I had promised to return to GMI for a couple of weeks to help them with the transition. I wanted to spend some time with Babu while I was there, and I wanted to say good-bye to each of my Chinese students. Also, I had to deal with the apartment and all my stuff. I planned to rent a small U-Haul and bring everything back to Murfreesboro, where Gary would store most of it and sell the car after I left for Malaysia.

Although I hated the idea of being separated after only one week of marriage, the drive to and from Michigan would be long and difficult. Finally, Mandy agreed to go with her parents, and I would follow a couple of weeks later.

How long does it take to reach Saturday when, as newlyweds, we were about to head in opposite directions? The time quickly arrived when we stood at the Nashville Airport again, saying good-bye. As I watched them take off, I reminded myself that these plans made good sense. But carrying them out was difficult.

The following morning I was on the road by 5:00 a.m., headed for Flint. After driving for more than twelve hours, I spied the Flint exit. I had come full circle.

I spent the two weeks in Michigan with Babu, telling him about everything that happened after he left for India. One thing happened during those two weeks that had a tremendous impact on Babu's life and the life of every member of his family. I decided to ask Babu to read my mother's Bible. I handed it to him as we waited at

Full Circle

the Detroit Airport for his return flight to India. "Will you read the entire book, including all my mother's handwritten notes?"

Not only did Babu read the book; his wife, sister, mother, and father all read her Bible.

More than six months passed before we saw each other again. Then we spent the next six months working to start up the orphanage.

First Babu became a Christian and accepted Jesus as his Savior; his wife, then his sister, then his mother, and finally his father all followed suit. Every member of his family became a part of the ministry of our Emmanuel Orphanage and contributed greatly to its success.

While Mandy and I were in Malaysia, Mandy received a letter from Rachel that described her and Travis's wedding. This was great news, but there was more. Travis and Rachel were attending missionary school. They had contacted Dr. Thomas; within a year, they would come to India to open another Emmanuel Orphanage.

And me? I had become very adept at seeing people arrive and depart at the airport, but now it was my turn. This story pivots around a miracle on an airplane when Mandy was healed at 30,000 feet. Another miracle occurred on an airplane. Maybe it was not nearly as dramatic, but it sure meant a lot to me.

I boarded a plane at the Nashville Airport, flew for sixteen hours, and landed in Malaysia in one piece.

Although this story starts and ends with my return to Michigan, it was not written while driving down the Interstate. It was started during our six months in Malaysia and completed after our first year in India. At the end of that first year, another blessed event occurred. Mandy and I had an addition to our family. We named him Carl Matthews, but we called him "Little Carl."

Further Reading

Although this story is mostly fiction, my genuine hope is that you as a reader recognized the truth contained within these pages. We live in a nation that has been the recipient of wealth and power as no nation has before us. We have enjoyed peace and prosperity, but have we forgotten God? Has His gracious hand preserved, enriched, and strengthened us based on our Godly heritage? Have we vainly imagined that the blessings our great nation has enjoyed were produced by our superior intellect and virtue? Has our success made us too proud to pray and gratefully acknowledge the Almighty God that made us?

Lest we forget, I will quote Daniel Webster again. 'If we abide by the principles taught in the Bible, our country will go on prospering, but if we and our posterity neglect its instructions and authority, no man can tell how sudden a catastrophe may overwhelm us and bury all our glory in profound obscurity.'

If you read this story, I pray it will make you pause and reflect on the truth woven within its pages. Find yourself below and consider just where you are today. Then, I invite you to set yourself apart and move closer to the Father of creation, our Lord.

Further Reading

If you are ambivalent or unsure about a belief in God and Christ, then pick up a Bible and read the four Gospels—Mathew, Mark, Luke, and John. And pray that the Holy Spirit will reveal their truth to you. Then respond with the same prayer as Mark:

"Lord Jesus, I believe You are the one and only Son of our Almighty God, that You were born of the virgin Mary, died on the cross, and rose from the dead and ascended into heaven to sit at the right hand of God. Thank You for dying on the cross for my sins. I know I am a sinner. Please forgive me. I now place all my trust in You alone for my salvation. Please come into my life. I accept Your gift of eternal life. In your name, Amen."

Now join a church. But don't look for a perfect one. Just find a group that worships a real God. And one whose members are the ones you would want praying for you, if you're ever in need of real prayer.

If you are a believer, put feet on that belief and follow Christ. Salvation is more than fire insurance; it is the doorway to not only eternal life, but also to His kingdom on earth. As a believer, you have entered that narrow door. God has a plan for your life. Find it, step beyond the door, and explore His kingdom. As you travel, there will still be peaks and valleys, but blessings await at the top of each hill. Climb and allow God to bless you.

If you are a Christ follower, continue your journey. But, take time to help others find the door and the path into His kingdom. And don't forget to share your blessings.

Here are the passages that John and Carl referred to in their discussions of the exchange that took place on the cross:

Christ exchanged our rejection for His acceptance
(Acts 15:8).

Christ exchanged our sickness for His healing
(I Peter 2:24).

Christ exchanged our anxieties for His peace
(Philippians 1:2).

Christ exchanged our fear for His trust
(Luke 12:32).

Christ exchanged our sin for His righteousness
(2 Corinthians 2:16).

Christ exchanged our suffering for His freedom
(John 8:36).

Christ exchanged our grief for His joy
(Romans 14:17).

I hope you find the courage to make a heartfelt choice about Who and What will be an Authority in your life. You will never live free of authority. Either the world will own you as it surely owned me, or you submit to the authority of our Lord and accept Christ as your Savior.

If I can be reached, so can you. Maybe He reached out a little farther for me. Maybe this book is His way of extending that reach and making it available for YOU.

Further Reading

This day I call heaven and earth

as witnesses against you

that I have set before you

life and death, blessings and curses.

Now choose life,

so that you and your children may live.

— Deuteronomy 30:19–20